**Praise for the first novel in the spectacular Dark Desires series**

*Break Out*

"The blend of action, treachery, romance, and startling revelations will leave the reader anxious for the next entertaining adventure."
—*Publishers Weekly*

"The dialogue is fun, the action fierce, the love scenes sizzling." —Joyce Lamb, *USA Today*

"An exciting roller-coaster ride . . . Loads of fun!"
—Julia Rachel Barrett,
award-winning author of *Captured*

"Absolutely hysterical! Rico—you had me at 'bring me my goddamn spaceship.'"
—Dawn McClure, author of *Heaven Sent*

## Titles by Nina Croft

### *The Dark Desires series*

*Break Out*
*Deadly Pursuit*
*Death Defying*

### *Babysitting a Billionaire series*

*Losing Control*
*Out of Control*

### *The Order series*

*Bittersweet Blood*
*Bittersweet Magic*
*Bittersweet Darkness*

### *Stand-alone Titles*

*Blackmailed by the Italian Billionaire*
*The Descartes Legacy*
*Operation Saving Daniel*
*Betting on Julia*

# DEATH
# DEFYING

## NINA CROFT

St. Martin's Paperbacks

This is a work of fiction. All of the characters, organizations, and events portrayed in this novel are either products of the author's imagination or are used fictitiously.

DEATH DEFYING

Copyright © 2014 by Nicola Cleasby.
"Crash Landing" copyright © 2014 by Nicola Cleasby.

For information address St. Martin's Press, 175 Fifth Avenue, New York, NY 10010.

ISBN: 978-1-250-05811-9

Printed in the United States of America

Entangled edition / February 2014
St. Martin's Paperbacks edition / December 2014

St. Martin's Paperbacks are published by St. Martin's Press, 175 Fifth Avenue, New York, NY 10010.

10  9  8  7  6  5  4  3  2  1

*To Rob—who I'd be quite happy to spend eternity with!*

# PROLOGUE

*Fifteen years ago . . .*

Tannis lay in the darkness on her narrow cot, every muscle locked rigid as she waited for the guard to pass. Instead, he halted outside her door. Her heart stuttered to a standstill and then started a rapid beat that threatened to explode from her chest.

*Oh, God, oh, God.*

She pressed her fist to her mouth so hard she tasted the metallic sweetness of her own blood.

No one had been near her in a week. She'd known what that meant. However much she hated the experiments, the alternative was far worse.

The harsh rasp of her breath sounded loud in her ears. She wanted desperately to hide. But there was nowhere to go. The cell she had lived in for the last fourteen years was a mere ten feet by ten feet, with bare white walls and only a small cot for furniture.

She had two choices. Submit or fight. Not really choices at all.

Sliding her hand beneath the thin mattress, she fumbled

for the makeshift knife and then wrapped her trembling fingers around the rough hilt.

The hulking figure of Grady, one of her guards, stood silhouetted in the doorway. He flicked the switch on his belt and light flooded the small room. Tannis's grip tightened around the knife, and she swung her legs off the cot and sat up. Maybe she was wrong. Maybe he hadn't come to tell her . . .

But he wouldn't meet her gaze as he stepped inside and shut the door behind him. "Get your things together. You ship out in the morning."

Nausea rose hot and acrid in the back of her throat. She must have made a noise because he shifted uncomfortably, guilt flickering across his face. She hated all the guards. Some were pure evil, but to her mind, Grady's sort were the worst—they knew they did wrong but still continued.

"I . . ." He shrugged. "I can't help—It's more than my job's worth."

In a flash, a tidal wave of black rage drowned out her fear.

*His job. Her life. No competition.*

She gritted her teeth against the need to leap at him, tear him with her nails, sink her teeth into his flesh. But he'd just put her in restraints if she did, and tonight she needed to be free. At least one good thing had come of this hell . . . The long years had taught her to hide her feelings, to keep the rage and terror locked tight inside.

He turned to go, and she pushed herself off the bed and took a step toward him, hiding the hand with the knife at her side. She couldn't let him leave.

"Wait!"

He turned back, a question in his eyes, and she stretched her lips in what she hoped was the semblance of a smile. "Don't go."

Grady wanted her. She had seen him watching with his

pale, protuberant eyes. She had to use that, however repugnant.

One chance, that's all she would have.

Tomorrow, they would send her to the Meridian mines, and a slow and agonizing death. It seemed like all her life she'd lived with that fear hanging over her. She'd known that once her usefulness was over, once they learned what they could from her particular genetic mix, they would dispose of her like so much trash. And at eighteen, she wasn't ready to die. She wanted to live so badly, the need was like a blade piercing her heart.

Along with the knife, perhaps she had another weapon. They regularly drained the venom from the glands at the base of her incisors, but nobody had been near her in days. All she had to do was get close enough.

She would do this or die trying. As she accepted that, her fears calmed, her mind cleared, and she went to a peaceful place where the world seemed to slow down.

Taking the few steps toward him, she came to a halt only inches away, and gazed up into his fat, ugly face. "Please, Grady. Don't leave me. I don't want to be alone tonight."

Shock flared in his eyes, but he was definitely listening.

"Just hold me," she whispered. "Tomorrow, it's over. I'm going to die, and I've never even kissed a man."

Jesus, would he actual believe this crap? Hysterical laughter rose in her throat as his face softened. The stupid oaf was probably deluding himself into believing he was doing her a favor. For a minute, he appeared undecided, and Tannis held her breath. Then he gave a slight nod.

Relief made her limp.

She took the last step, which brought her flush against him. So close that the hot, sour sweat of his body flooded her nostrils. Swallowing her revulsion, she lifted her hand to curl around his neck. He was a good six inches taller, and she had to tug him down in order to reach his throat.

She pressed her lips to his skin, and his hands closed around her. Panic clawed at her insides, and every cell of her being fought the urge to tear free.

Parting her lips, she tasted the saltiness of his skin and almost gagged. Instead, she bit down hard. Her incisors pierced his flesh and his hot blood flooded her mouth. He tried to shove her away, but she wrapped her arm tight around his neck and clung while the venom pumped into his system.

As the first spasm hit his body, she brought up the knife, her hand slippery with sweat, and stabbed him in the neck. She hit the jugular and blood spurted from the wound, blinding her for a moment.

Blinking, she stepped back as he fell to his knees, then crashed to the floor. She stood, staring down as a final spasm shook his body, and finally, he lay still.

Tannis edged away, snatched the sheet from the bed, and scrubbed her face while she waited to feel some sort of exhilaration. Instead all she felt was numb.

The thick, cloying scent of blood was heavy on the air, and suddenly she doubled over, retching. After a minute, she swiped her hand across her mouth and sat while she considered her next move. Killing Grady was the easy part. Now, she had to get out of her cell and off the research station, but she had no clue how. Maybe stow away on a ship. In the back of her mind, she knew she was kidding herself. She would never get off this place alive. They would kill her first. But better that than the mines.

After pushing herself to her feet, she crossed the room to study the body. The knife was still lodged deep in his throat. She reached down and tugged it free, wiped the blade on his shirt, and slipped it into her pocket.

The doors were controlled by handprints. Though Grady was big, she was strong, and she managed to drag the body across the room. He was a deadweight. She almost smiled at the thought as she maneuvered him into position and leaned him against the wall as she pressed his palm to the panel. For a moment nothing happened, then the door slid open with a hiss, and she allowed Grady to slump to the tiled floor.

Out in the corridor, all was quiet. Despair threatened to swamp her as she stood, glancing both ways. She needed to get to the docking bay, but she had no clue which direction to take.

"Over here!"

Tannis jumped at the sound of the low voice. Had she been discovered already? She could see no one, but then he spoke again.

"Here."

The voice came from another of the cells that lined the corridor. She edged forward and peered through the grill in the center of the door. A man stood on the other side, and she gasped. He was the most beautiful thing she had ever seen, with high cheekbones, dark eyes, and midnight-black hair that hung loose to his shoulders. But lines of exhaustion etched his face, and his long, lean body propped against the wall as though the effort to stand was too much.

He stared at her through the grill. "Hey, snake-girl, you've killed the guard?"

She frowned. "How did you know?"

He breathed in deeply, then licked his lips. "I can smell the blood."

A shudder ran through her at the hunger in his eyes, and she made to turn away.

"Wait."

She hesitated, and he spoke quickly. "You'll never get off this place on your own. They'll kill you if you try. But I can help you. Trust me."

"I don't think so. And how? How can you help me?"

"I have a ship. I can get us both away. Get me out of this cell, and I promise I'll get you out of this shithole."

Itching to run, she glanced down the corridor. What choice did she have? On her own, she would fail. But could she put her trust in a stranger? There was a darkness and hunger in his eyes, something not quite human, but despite that, she sensed no evil. Then he smiled and the darkness vanished. She bit her lip and nodded.

His cell looked the same as hers, presumably with the same security. She hoped Grady had access. "Don't go anywhere."

Back in her own cell, she looked down at Grady. His open eyes returned her stare, bulging with shock.

No way could she drag his body all that way; he was too big. She took the knife from her pocket and crouched beside him. The blade slid easily through the flesh but stuck at the bone, and she gritted her teeth and sawed. Finally, she wrenched the hand free and lifted it gingerly.

Something caught her eye: Grady's shirt bore the company's insignia. She ripped it off and shoved the scrap of material in her pocket to serve as a reminder. One day, if she got away, she was going to make them pay for what they'd done to her. To her sister.

She hurried back to the stranger's cell and peered inside. Relief flared in his eyes—he'd probably thought her gone. She showed him the severed hand, then pressed it palm down to the panel. The door slid open and she let out a breath. Maybe there was a small chance she would get out of here after all, and a first flicker of hope awoke inside her.

The man stood just inside the door. She was tall, but he was far taller. His nostrils flared, and at the last moment, her mind screamed at her to run. Too late.

He reached for her, his fingers biting into her shoulders.

She had no time to struggle, just the impression of vast, inhuman strength as he hauled her into the cell.

"I'm sorry," he murmured. Then he turned her in his arms and dragged her against him with an arm wrapped around her below her breasts. His cool breath shivered across her skin as his teeth sank into her throat.

No pain, just a rhythmic tug that pulled at places deep inside her. The life drained from her body as he fed voraciously, his hunger an almost palpable thing. Darkness grew behind her eyes, the light faded to a pinprick, then nothing.

When she came to, she was moving. It took her a second to realize she was clasped in muscular arms, held against a rock-hard body. Blinking open her heavy lids, she looked straight into the handsome face of the bloodsucking monster. Instinctively, she struggled—she hated being held—but his arms tightened around her, holding her easily, and she forced herself to relax. She wasn't dead, which was a surprise. She'd thought it was over.

"You bit me."

He glanced down. His eyes were no longer dark, but tinged with crimson. "Hey, I said I was sorry. I had to eat, or we weren't going anywhere." He studied her through narrowed eyes. "*Dios*, I hope you're not the type to hold a grudge."

"What are you?"

"I'm your worst nightmare, darling." He grinned. "Actually, I'm a vampire, but I'm also the vampire who's going to get you off this crap place."

A vampire? She'd thought they were the stuff of legends.

"Where are we going?"

"To my ship—if she's still here. If not, we'll find another."

He carried her in silence for a while and she closed her

eyes. The night had taken on a surreal quality, and she was filled with a sense of fatalism, as though what would happen was now out of her hands. When he came to a halt, she opened her lids reluctantly.

"*El Cazador*'s still here."

She heard the satisfaction in his voice and peered over his shoulder. Through the doorway, she could see a large open area that must be the docking bay. A space cruiser stood at the far side of the room, sleek and black, with a name written in silver along the side. "*El Cazador de la Sangre*," she murmured. "What does that mean?"

"The Blood Hunter."

Her gaze flew to his face. "Oh."

He flashed her a smile that revealed the tips of his razor-sharp fangs, and she shuddered, her hand darting to the small wound at her neck.

Two guards came into view, patrolling the area in front of the ship. Her heart sank. How could they take on heavily armed guards? They'd be cut down before they got close to the ship.

The vampire lowered her gently. For a second, her legs refused to hold her, and she gripped his shirt while the room swam around her. "I feel woozy."

"Blood loss. I took a little too much, but you'll be fine."

He studied the ship and the guards, then turned to her. "Can you walk?"

She tested her legs and nodded.

"Okay. I want you to approach the guard on the left, distract him, and hopefully draw the other one closer."

"What if he shoots me?"

"He won't—well probably not." He reached across and ripped the shoulder of her dress, baring the curve of her breast. "Just to increase the odds. Now off you go."

Tannis glared at him for a second, then nodded. She limped onto the docking bay, doing her best to look pathetic. It wasn't hard. Both guards swung around to face her. She didn't recognize either man, so hopefully they wouldn't recognize her. At least they made no move for their weapons.

"Help," she whispered, then crumpled gracelessly to the floor. The guards hurried over. One crouched next to her, and the other hovered behind. There was a blur of movement and the standing guard vanished from her sight. Blood sprayed over her as the body was hurled across the docking bay.

The second guard fumbled for his weapon but was yanked away before he could draw the pistol. Tannis rolled onto her feet and rubbed the blood from her face. The vampire had the man in a death grip, his fangs buried in the guard's throat. Fascinated, she watched him swallow convulsively, his face a rigid mask, all signs of humanity obliterated.

He finally released his grip, and the body collapsed to the floor. Wiping his hand across his mouth, he grinned. "Let's get out of here."

She shivered. Was she right to put her life in the hands of such a creature? But she hadn't fared too well with humans up to now, so why not trust the monsters instead. Could they be any worse?

She nodded and stepped toward him as more guards appeared in the open doorway.

"Shit," he said, but he was still grinning. He was enjoying himself.

Was he totally crazy?

He tugged the laser pistol from the holster at the dead guard's waist and tossed it to her. Then he lunged for the second body, grabbed the weapon, and was shooting as he straightened.

Someone got off a shot. It flashed by and, behind her, the vampire cursed. Then the men were down.

Tannis stared at the weapon in her hand, absolutely no clue what to do with it. The monster grabbed her hand and rearranged her finger to rest on what she presumed was the trigger.

"Just press that. Now let's get out of here.

A wave of weakness washed over her when she took a step. She swayed and the vampire swept her into his arms and headed for the ship.

He grinned down at her. "What's your name, sweetheart?"

"Well it's not 'sweetheart.' I'm Tannis."

"Tannis—it's a good name for a snake-girl. So, Tannis"—he nodded toward his ship—"you want to be captain?"

She almost smiled at the idea. "Aren't you the captain?"

"*Dios*, no—I'm the pilot—the captain has way too much responsibility."

"So what happened to your last captain?"

"I guess he didn't make it." His grip tightened on her. "Crap. More incoming." He leaped for the cover of a pillar and whirled around so his shoulders pressed the metal.

"Where will we go?" she asked.

"That depends on what you want to do. What do you want, Tannis?"

She didn't have to think. "I want to be one of the Collective—I want to be immortal, and then I want to come back and I want to destroy this place and everyone in it."

"Sounds like a plan."

The first shot rang out. He swore and the scent of scorched flesh filled her nostrils.

"You shoot. I'll run." Still holding her, he raced toward the ship.

Tannis peered over his shoulder. The doorway was crammed full of guards all drawing their weapons. Stretching out her arm, she screwed up her eyes, then pressed her finger to the trigger. And kept it pressed.

"Good shooting," the vampire said. "But you can stop now."

She peeked through her lashes. Bodies littered the ground.

He was running up the ramp.

Almost there.

They came to a halt at the top, where he shifted her in his arms and pressed his palm to the panel. The double doors slid open just as a movement behind her caught her gaze.

"More coming."

"How the hell many more are there?" He almost hurled her into the ship so she crashed to the floor, then he dove in after her as a blast of laser shots slammed into the ramp where they'd been seconds ago. Her heart thundering, Tannis lay on her side as he crawled across the floor, shooting with one hand. The guards were close, already running onto the ramp.

They were going to die, and she'd never felt more alive in her entire life.

Then the vampire slammed his fist on the panel and the doors closed with a hiss.

Beneath her, the floor rumbled and the engines fired up. Swiping the blood from his face, he caught her gaze and cast her a wicked grin.

"Welcome to *El Cazador,* Captain."

At his words, a burst of laughter escaped her. The sound was strange, and she realized she couldn't remember the last time she had laughed. But she was alive, and she was a captain. For a second she lay on her back and giggled, probably hysterics, but she didn't care.

Finally, she rolled to her side and watched the vampire pull himself to his feet and brush himself down.

She took a deep breath. "So, who are you?"

"Ricardo Sanchez—Rico to my friends."

"And what do you want, Rico?"

"Hell, I just want to have fun." His lips curled into a smile. "You ready to have some fun with me, snake-girl?"

He was certainly beautiful, but she'd had her first kiss that day and as far as she was concerned, it was her last. "Hell, no," she said. "But you keep your fangs and your hands to yourself and I'll be your captain and maybe I'll even be your friend."

Head cocked to one side, he considered her for a moment, then gave a brisk nod. "Friends it is then."

# CHAPTER 1

*El Cazador, year: 3049*

"You do know that this is probably a huge mistake?"

Tannis slammed her spoon down and glared at the crew seated around the dining table, her gaze finally settling on Skylar. "Yeah, I know. And you know how I know, because you've told me like a gazillion times."

Skylar, as usual, didn't seem in the least intimidated by the fierce look. Her inhuman violet eyes studied Tannis for a moment, and then she shrugged. "Well, even you have to admit that there's something extremely odd about the most powerful man in the known universe asking for *our* help."

"Maybe he's heard that we're the best," Rico drawled from beside her.

Skylar grinned. "Yeah, but the best at what? And why would he hear that?"

"Because we are?" He leaned in and kissed the side of her neck where Tannis could see the faint fang marks. As a member of the Collective, Skylar was tough, almost impossible to kill, but still it might be best to get the ship stocked with iron supplements if she planned to play around with Rico for any length of time.

And amazingly, it looked like that was the case. Tannis couldn't get her head around it—Rico in love. It was as though she'd slipped into some weird alternate dimension where nothing made sense.

But even Tannis had to admit that however much Skylar irritated *her*, she was perfect for Rico. Skylar stood her ground, didn't take any shit, and they looked good together. Rico's long, lean figure was dressed all in black with black knee-high boots, his shoulder-length hair pulled into a ponytail that showed off his perfect bone structure. Skylar matched him in a black jumpsuit, a laser pistol holstered at her waist, her blond hair cut military short, her violet eyes glowing. They sat close together, almost touching. It wasn't only a physical closeness, but a mental bond as well, and a small prick of some unrecognizable emotion stabbed Tannis in the middle.

She didn't want that sort of intimacy with anyone—it was the last thing she wanted—she hated to be touched. Many nights, she still woke up in a cold sweat as her subconscious relived those years in the research station. All the same, something ached inside her chest when she saw them together. She'd never imagined Rico would fall in love.

He was her friend, and she was glad for him, really, she was. That didn't mean she had to put up with watching them over the supper table.

"Yuk." The bloody ship was turning into some sort of love nest, and she wasn't sure she liked it. Actually, she knew she didn't like it. Everywhere she went, she tripped over some canoodling couple. Though at least Jon and Alex—the newlyweds—were out of the way. They'd been dropped off on Trakis Two to ensure the place was safe for *The Blood Hunter's* arrival.

Tannis pushed her plate away, reclined in her chair, and studied the pair opposite, allowing her upper lip to curl up in disdain.

Rico grinned at her expression. "I reckon the captain has a crush on our new client, and it's making her snarky."

"More snarky than usual you mean?" Skylar asked.

Tannis gritted her teeth. "Ha-ha."

"Why shouldn't she have a crush?" Daisy glanced up from her food. "After all, Callum Meridian is the most powerful man in the universe. And he has wings. How cool is that?"

Across the table, Skylar twitched as if she could feel the appendages sprouting from her own shoulders.

"I'd love wings," Daisy said dreamily, tucking a strand of dark green hair behind her ear.

Tannis picked up her spoon and played with her food. Of course, she didn't have a freaking crush on Callum Meridian. She might be a little intrigued, but that was only because she'd always had a fascination for the Collective, and he was the oldest and most powerful of their kind.

A shiver ran through her as an image of those glowing violet eyes flashed in her mind. They'd had a brief meeting just over a month ago where she'd acted like a tongue-tied moron and hardly said a word. Though there hadn't been much to say. He'd been in the process of attempting to kill them all, and she'd gazed at him like a starstruck teenager. But he'd been beautiful, so beautiful he'd made her ache.

But she didn't have a crush.

She was just restless, unable to shake the feeling that everything was changing. For fifteen years, she'd worked side by side with Rico. They'd watched each other's backs, even saved each other's lives on occasion. Other crew had come and gone, but they'd stayed together. He was her best friend, and now he had someone more important in his life.

She took a mouthful of food, but tasted nothing.

In her time as captain of *El Cazador*, she'd amassed a small fortune. This last job would give her enough to apply for the Meridian treatment and finally become one of the exalted Collective, immortal, never having to fear death.

And that would change things again. Her dream was finally within her grasp, and she couldn't understand why she felt so unsettled.

She'd put aside her plans for revenge, partly because getting the Meridian treatment was her priority. Once she achieved that, she would have time enough for everything else. But also because she'd realized, with Rico's help, that she couldn't allow hatred to control her life. That wasn't the person she wanted to be. Rico was old, he'd lived over fifteen hundred years, and while he wasn't always wise, he'd learned a lot about survival in that time, both mental as well as physical. He'd told her there was no point in living forever if you didn't enjoy it. He'd warned her about centering her whole life on revenge, because once you'd obtained it, you were left with nothing.

Janey strolled into the galley. Perfectly groomed as always, long red hair artfully styled, Janey would have made Tannis feel totally inept as a woman if she hadn't known that the ship's beautiful and brilliant tech expert actually had more issues with men than Tannis. The good looks were a mask she hid behind. She pulled out a chair, sank down, and then leaned toward Tannis.

"You know, Captain, I've been thinking."

"You have?" Why did she get the impression that whatever it was Janey had been thinking, she wasn't going to like it?

"Yes. I've been going over the intel, and I reckon this is probably a really bad idea."

This time, Tannis put her spoon down very slowly and

looked around the table. Skylar's face held no expression. Rico was grinning.

"Okay," she said, keeping her tone even. "Time for a reality check. Who the hell is captain here?"

Janey answered. "You're the captain, Tannis."

Tannis would have felt better if the flicker of a smile hadn't accompanied her words.

"Yes, I'm captain, and we've already agreed to do the job. My honor is at stake."

Someone sniggered, but she ignored the sound.

"It's just . . ." Janey obviously didn't know when to shut up, but the glare Tannis shot her way did the trick. Her mouth snapped closed.

"I don't get it," Tannis said. "This job is going to pay good money. Hell, more than good—brilliant money."

"I didn't like him," Rico said. "Except the wings—I liked them a lot."

"He was trying to kill us—what was there to like?" Tannis ran a hand through her short hair. "And since when have we needed to 'like' our clients—as long as their money is good, who gives a fuck what they're like?"

"I don't trust him," Janey added.

"You weren't even there."

"I've been doing some research and something's not right. The whole thing is giving off bad vibes."

"*Holy freaking Meridian.* Give me a break."

Rico studied her for a moment, and then he nodded. "Okay. It's your call, but let's just be careful on this one."

Tannis frowned. Rico was never careful. Hell, he was totally reckless; the more dangerous a job, the more he was eager to jump right in. Maybe he was scared for Skylar. Maybe that's what being in love did for you, made you worried for the one you loved. Still, the strangeness of his behavior added to her unease as though there was something not quite right with her world.

"So have we heard from him?" Daisy asked. "Do we know where the rendezvous point is?"

"Not yet. He said someone would contact us nearer the time."

They were in orbit over Trakis Five, which in itself was enough to make everybody twitchy. Trakis Five was where the headquarters of the Collective was based, along with their own personal army—the Corps. Nobody wanted to mess with the Corps, and it was hard to forget that only weeks ago *El Cazador* had been on the run, with the Collective in deadly pursuit. Their differences had been resolved—sort of—but all the same, she guessed they'd all rather be a long way from this particular planet.

"Nearer what time?" Janey asked.

At their first and only meeting, Callum had indicated he was soon to make an announcement to the world about the nature of the Collective. Very few people were aware of the wing thing, or that the supposedly indestructible Collective could be destroyed. When the crew of *El Cazador* had threatened to expose their vulnerability, Callum reluctantly called off the Corps poised to kill them.

"Okay, we wait then," Rico said. "In the meantime, *we* have important things to do . . . alone." He stood up and held out his hand to Skylar, who slid her palm into his and rose to her feet.

Sweet Jesus, Tannis had honestly never thought she'd see Rico holding hands. Yup, the world as she knew it was gone forever. She needed a drink.

At that moment, Skylar gave a small cry of pain, put her hand to head, and swayed. Rico caught her as her knees gave out.

Tannis jumped to her feet. "What's the matter?"

"How the hell should I know?" Rico sank down in his chair with Skylar in his arms. Her eyes were closed, as if she'd fainted, but behind the lids, they moved rapidly. Rico shifted her so she lay across his lap, and stroked his hand over her head, down her cheek.

"Sweetheart, wake up."

For a minute, it looked like she wouldn't respond, and then she blinked. Her violet eyes were dazed, but they cleared rapidly.

"That was Callum Meridian." Her voice filled with awe.

"Couldn't he have commed, like any normal person?" Janey asked.

But then Callum Meridian was hardly normal—and why comm when you shared a telepathic link with all the members of the Collective, including Skylar?

Tannis frowned. "I thought you had to let them in—that anyone who wanted to make contact had to ask first."

"Usually, that's true." She pinched the bridge of her nose, then shook her head. "He was *so* powerful. It was like being hit with a blaster shot at close range."

"Fucking bastard," Rico snarled. "What the hell would have happened if he'd pulled that stunt while you were doing something dangerous? He could have killed you."

"You know we're not that easy to kill."

"That's beside the fucking point."

"So what did he say?" Tannis tried to keep the excitement from her voice, but knew she'd failed when Rico shot her a dirty look.

"He wants us there now," Skylar replied.

"Where?"

"Down on the planet. He's transmitting a code to the ship to guide us in, and he wants us to be ready to take off fast."

"And did he say why?"

She shook her head.

"Why doesn't that surprise me?" Rico muttered. "Arrogant bastard."

Janey jumped up from her place at the table. "Let's have

a look at what's going on." She strolled across the room in her high heels and switched on one of the viewing screens. The monitor showed a large stadium filled with milling people. An empty podium stood at the front.

"Apparently, the Collective are about to make an announcement—"

"About bloody time."

"—and the whole world's listening."

A wave of excitement built inside her. This was it. "Let's get to the bridge," she ordered. "Make sure we're ready for that fast getaway." Her mind was already turning over the possibilities. Would he come on board? Why did they need to leave fast? What was he actually going to reveal to the world?

"Tannis—"

She paused in the doorway as Rico spoke her name. "Yes?"

"Be careful."

It came to her then. Rico wasn't worried about Skylar. He was worried about *her*.

"We think you're making a big mistake."

Callum broke off the contact with Skylar and opened his eyes. After looking around the room, he had an urge to crawl under the table and sleep away the rest of this meeting. He'd long ago reached the conclusion that being the most powerful man in the whole universe was not all it was cracked up to be.

In fact, the job was a pile of shit.

Some days, he thought he might scream from the constant, petty-minded bureaucracy that was his life. But even in a never-ending string of boring, meeting-filled days, this one was pretty high up on his list of "times that make me wish I'd never encountered Meridian."

Yeah, he knew the Council thought it a mistake to

go public with the changes the Collective were going through—they'd told him constantly for a month now.

He shoved back his chair, jumped to his feet, and paced the chamber, only turning to face his Council when he reached the far wall. He flexed his wings and every single one of them winced. Well, everyone except the colonel, who stood at the rear, leaning against the wall, arms folded across his chest, a slight smile on his face.

*What do you think? Is it a mistake?* Callum spoke in his mind on a level that wouldn't be picked up by the others.

*Probably.* The colonel gave a small shrug. *You're fighting a losing battle. They're afraid.*

*What about you?* Callum asked. *Are you afraid?*

*Nah.*

*You ever been afraid?*

*Nah.*

The colonel wore the uniform of the Collective's private army, the Corps, a black jumpsuit with the violet insignia at his chest. He was the best soldier Callum had ever encountered, but he looked like a boy dressed up. He'd been eighteen when he'd taken the Meridian treatment, and while some people changed, the colonel hadn't aged at all in the years since. But while he hadn't been a boy in over three hundred years, he was still two hundred years younger than the rest of the Council. This small group was the first to have encountered Meridian over five hundred years ago when they'd crash-landed on Trakis Seven.

"I wish you wouldn't do that," Tyler mumbled.

It took Callum a moment to realize he meant the wing thing, and he flexed them again.

Tyler leaned back in his chair and winced again, this time from pain, because he'd amputated his own wings—an operation that needed to be repeated every few weeks as they simply regrew.

But Callum liked his wings and had no wish to cut them off. He'd practiced in private and now could fly short distances—how cool was that? Now that the one month he'd given the Council to decide how to go about revealing the changes to the world had passed, he couldn't wait to go outside for a real fly.

He flexed them again just to piss the Council off a little more and caught a grin on the colonel's face. Then he sighed. He wanted their cooperation, and this probably wasn't the way to go about getting it.

But hell, the wings were great. He gave them one last little flap, bit back his smile at their sour expressions, and folded them neatly.

"We still believe it's in all our best interests to keep this under wraps," Tyler said.

"How long can we do that?" Callum stalked up to the table, placed his palms down on the smooth metal, and searched each face for some sign that they were breaking, but they were resolute as ever. Stubborn bloody bastards. "I'm done with skulking away."

"Well, do what we've done, and then you wouldn't need to skulk."

Callum's eyes narrowed. "No thank you. I'm not into self-mutilation."

They'd been locked in argument all day. Callum wanted to go public—let the world see what was happening. Whatever that was.

He was eager to find out.

Until they announced their changes, any research had to be clandestine, and he wanted a major push—put a shitload of money and every resource they could get their hands on to find out exactly what they were becoming. That meant research into Trakis Seven, as that was the only planet where Meridian had ever been found. But no one spent time on Trakis Seven unless they had to. The planet was lethal to anyone who hadn't had the Meridian treatment—those sentenced to the mines lasted anywhere between two weeks and two years, but eventually, they all died, and not a good death. And even those who had taken the treatment found the planet uncomfortable.

Unfortunately, it appeared he was the only one who wanted to know the truth. The rest of them would rather pretend the changes weren't happening.

They'd been shaken by Aiden's suicide. Hell, Callum had been shaken—despite the fact that Aiden had always been an asshole, and he was hardly going to miss the man.

But while the suicide had shocked them, that a motley bunch of misfit space pirates knew the truth terrified them. They'd gone all out to silence the crew of *El Cazador* and been furious that Callum had them in his grasp a month ago, but let them go free.

They claimed the Collective's wealth was based on the sale of Meridian and no one would be willing to pay the exorbitant prices if they knew they'd turn into something other than human. Personally, Callum thought they'd pay, but that was beside the point. Their financial security was no longer dependent on Meridian. They had expanded until they controlled half the known universe—the profitable half.

He'd told the Council that he'd had no choice but to let the *El Cazador* go after that final showdown. But the truth was, an idea had been forming in his mind for a long time. *El Cazador* had been the catalyst that crystallized the idea into something tangible.

And if he was honest, there was something else. As he closed his eyes, an image formed in his mind. A woman with a long, sinuous body and yellow snake eyes who hadn't left him for the entire time they'd been together.

His body tightened at the memory, and amazingly, his cock hardened in his pants. He frowned at the unexpected feeling. How long was it since any woman had affected him that way? He'd presumed his low sexual libido was another long-term response to Meridian. Now he wasn't so sure. Maybe he'd just been as bored with sex as he was with everything else these days.

For the first time in years, he was looking forward to something. He pictured her again and savored the heat that coiled low in his belly.

"So?" Tyler asked. "Are we all in agreement? You'll go along with the majority vote of the Council and give out the publicity statement we prepared."

Callum nodded.

"And you'll cover those up?" Tyler nodded at the wings.

"Of course," he said smoothly and watched the relief blossom on the faces around the table.

*Your new friends are coming in to land.* The colonel's words sounded in his mind.

*Good. Let's do this.*

He picked up his cloak and flung it around his shoulders, covering, if not hiding, the wings. After a quick nod to the colonel, he strode toward the big set of double doors that led to the stadium.

Outside, he could hear the murmur of a thousand voices. He'd invited the entire worlds' presses here, and now the Council wanted him to keep quiet. He was fed up with the lot of them. They'd had a month to come to terms with this and still they cowered in fear.

He hesitated in the doorway, and the colonel came up beside him.

*You're sure about this? You won't wait and take* The Endeavor *when she's done.*

*The Endeavor* was Callum's new superstar cruiser. She was a beauty, the most advanced ship ever built, but there had been some problems with the initial test flights, and he didn't want to wait until the modifications were completed.

*I'm sure.*

*You still plan to go to Trakis Two?*

Callum glanced at his friend, but the colonel's face was expressionless. *If you still want me to.*

The colonel reached into his pocket and pulled out a small package. *Would you give Rosalie this from me?*

Callum stared at the package for a second, then up at the colonel's face. *Why don't you come? Give it to her yourself?*

*She doesn't want to see me. She made that perfectly clear. But she'll see you, and I need to know she's all right.*

Fifty years ago, the colonel had fallen in love with a mortal. Rosalie had stayed with him for over thirty years until she'd started to age, while the colonel had stayed exactly the same.

Callum had offered her the Meridian treatment, but she'd refused. Some people couldn't face the idea of eternity. Nor could she face growing older while the colonel stayed forever young. She'd left and nearly broken his friend's heart. Now she ran a bar on Trakis Two, and Callum had offered to visit her, check that she was doing okay—it was as good a place as any to meet up with Venna, his science officer.

*Then come along for the ride—it might be fun.*

*Fun? I've forgotten what that is.* The colonel gave him a wry smile and pressed the package into his hand. *I can't. If I was so close, then I'd need to see her. I couldn't do that to her. Besides, I need to stay with my men. I have a feeling you might be in need of an army in the not too distant future.*

Callum glanced at him sharply. *What have you heard?*

*You know the Church has been in chaos since their High Priest disappeared.*

The old High Priest, Hezrai Fischer, had vanished over a month ago. The timing was suspect, and Callum had the idea that the disappearance was somehow tied in with Aiden's death, but if anybody within the Church knew anything, they weren't talking.

*Well it looks like they've picked a new leader. I just got word Temperance Hatcher was appointed High Priest a week ago.*

*Great. Why the hell wasn't I told before?*

*We didn't know. Fischer was our main source of information within the Church and now we have to build our network from nothing.*

Hezrai Fischer had been another asshole, but he'd outwardly supported the Collective, and Aiden had made some sort of deal with the man before going completely off his rocker. Temperance Hatcher was a total fanatic who loathed the Collective.

*Are you monitoring them?*

*We have people in there. Apparently, his first order was to mobilize the Church's army.*

*Why didn't you tell me before?*

*There was nothing to tell. Until Hatcher was given the job, it was all speculation. Besides, I never actually thought you'd go through with this.*

*This?*

*This carnival. Do you really plan on leaving?*

*Hell, yeah.* He cast the other man a speculative look. *You think they're right? You think we should just hide this away?* He waved a hand at the wings folded neatly under the cloak, but still very obvious. *Pretend it's not happening?*

*No. But you've been building up to this for a long time.*

*I reckon you need to blow off some steam, then maybe you can come back and make some sensible decisions.*

*Sensible?* He shuddered.

*We need leadership now more than ever. This isn't just going to affect the Council but every member of the Collective.*

*I've left you in charge.*

*What?* The colonel sounded shocked.

*I've left a document stating you have my full powers within the Council.*

*Shit, I don't want that, Callum.*

*Hard luck. Now, let's do this.*

He strode through the open doors and the crowd roared as he came into sight. Glancing across the vast stadium, he spotted the Mark Three space cruiser touching down lightly on the landing pad. Black and sleek, with the words, *El Cazador de la Sangre,* in silver script on the side. It looked like his ride was here. He stepped up to the podium and raised a hand to quiet the crowd.

"Welcome, people of the worlds."

The masses quieted, until an expectant silence filled the stadium.

"Over a thousand years ago, we fled our dying world in search of a place we could call home. And for over five hundred years, we roamed the vast emptiness of space until we finally came to rest in the Trakis system. And here we found suns that would warm us, air we could breathe, and food we could eat."

So far so good. He could sense the waves of complacency wafting off the Council behind him. Time to shake them up a little—or a lot.

"We also discovered something else, something beyond our wildest dreams and the secret to man's greatest fear. We found the gift of immortality. But every gift comes with a price. I have come to believe it is a price worth paying. I hope the rest of the world will see it as the same."

He fingered the edges of the cloak. "So, with that in mind, I have brought you together today to show you the new, improved Collective."

# CHAPTER 2

They'd touched down smoothly on a raised landing platform that looked out over a vast, packed stadium. Tannis pressed her palm to the panel, and the doors of the docking bay slid open.

Rico and Skylar were at her back, though Rico stayed in the shadows of the docking bay—he didn't do sunlight, and the midafternoon sun was hot and bright. Skylar followed her out. They stood side by side and stared down at the mass of writhing humanity ringed with the black uniforms of the Corps.

All attention focused on the podium at the front of the stadium and the man who stood alone. He made an imposing figure. Even from a distance, she could see his eyes glowing violet in his lean, handsome face as he stared out over the crowds. For a second, he looked straight at her, and a frisson of sensation skittered down her spine. He was tall, and the dark cloak he wore gave him a bulky appearance. Tannis had seen what was beneath that covering. Was he about to reveal himself to the world?

A movement to the side of them distracted her, and she swung around as four men in Corps uniforms stepped onto the landing pad. She cast a brief glance at Skylar, who gave a casual shrug.

"Can we help you?" Tannis asked.

"We're the private bodyguard of the Leader."

"So?"

"We were ordered to wait with you."

"Are these guys for real?" she asked Skylar.

"Yes, look at the insignia."

Tannis peered at the chest of the first guy. The usual violet insignia of the Corps was there, but circled with a gold C. "Freaking cool. Just don't get in the way."

"Something's happening," Skylar murmured.

Tannis turned her gaze from the soldiers to the podium, where Callum leaned forward and spoke, his voice rolling around the stadium. He had the most amazing presence and his words—despite being nothing new—sent little shivers running through her. She'd never been one for speeches, but she could have listened to that voice all day. Quite happily just stood here and stared at him. She sighed.

"You have got him bad, haven't you?" Skylar sounded amused. Tannis ignored the comment, mainly because at that moment, Callum paused.

Was this it?

"So, with that in mind, I have brought you here today to show you the new, improved Collective." His voice boomed.

Taking a step back, he loosened the cloak at his throat and it slipped from his shoulders, revealing the wings folded neatly behind him. Then they spread, almost six feet in span, black and leathery. They flexed slowly, beating the air with an audible whoosh. The crowd gasped.

He looked up toward where Tannis stood and nodded once. Then he flexed the wings again and rose into the air.

"Holy freaking moly."

She'd known what to expect but all the same, her mouth

dropped open. For a few seconds, he hovered over the podium, then the wings flapped and he headed toward them. Sort of. He didn't appear to have much control and wavered almost as if he'd taken too many pinkies—the popular recreational drugs found in every bar on the planet. Finally, he straightened and hurtled their way fast. Too fast.

"Shit, he's going to crash."

Close up and spread wide, the wings were enormous, shadowing out the sun. Tannis poised, ready to dive out of the way, but at the last minute, when it seemed impossible that he wouldn't smash straight into them, the wings folded and he dropped to the ground with a *thud*.

He rolled onto his feet in moments—she got the distinct impression he'd had a lot of practice at falling—then brushed himself off and looked around.

"Bloody exhibitionist," Rico muttered from the doorway behind her.

Too right, but who wouldn't be if you were five hundred years old and The Leader of the Universe and you had wings . . . All the same, she'd rather put off a confrontation with Rico until they were safely in the air. She turned to him briefly. "Go get us ready for takeoff."

His eyes narrowed, but he spun on his heel and stalked away.

"Are we ready to go?" Callum asked.

Tannis opened her mouth to answer and then realized he wasn't speaking to her, but to the guard beside him. A flicker of irritation poked her in the gut. She was captain; it was up to her to say whether they were ready to go or not. And what the hell did he mean by "we?" No way was she having a load of hard-assed, heavily armed bodyguards on her ship. "We?"

He turned to look at her, and she was caught in that violet stare. He seemed to look straight into her mind, then he frowned.

"Captain?"

"Yeah, that would be me."

"I thought I made my instructions clear. You were to be ready to take off immediately."

"Yeah, but just who exactly is taking off?"

He'd half turned away, and then swung back around and stared as though he didn't quite understand the question. She was beginning to think he might not be too bright, which was a pity. Maybe he was some sort of figurehead, not in charge at all. Just somebody who acted as a front because he was stunningly gorgeous, which took people's minds of the fact that he was spouting garbage—like all politicians.

"None of your concern. I've hired this ship. Now get us in the air."

"I don't think so. You'll tell them"—Tannis nodded toward his guard—"to stand down, or you won't be in the air unless you flap those pretty wings again."

He appeared puzzled. Yeah, he obviously wasn't all there. That was maybe another side effect of the Meridian treatment: killed off the brain cells. A mixture of emotions washed over her, mainly regret mingled with relief—she really hadn't wanted to have a crush on him. She'd turned to go when she caught a slight movement of his head and heard the rasp of a weapon as the guard beside her drew his laser pistol.

Bastard. Did he think she was an idiot?

Blasters drawn, Skylar and Daisy emerged from the ship side by side.

Tannis glanced from the guard with the laser pistol—the other three hadn't drawn their weapons yet—to Skylar and Daisy. She smirked. "I think my guns are bigger than yours."

Callum frowned. "What's the problem? I've employed you. Are you incapable of taking simple orders?"

Someone sniggered behind her. She guessed it was Daisy. She'd had enough. They were out of here.

"Keep them covered," she said and stepped back. She kept moving backward, not taking her eyes off Callum until she reached the ramp of the ship. He was still frowning. Obviously, it hadn't occurred to him that not everyone was willing to blindly follow his every command. This would be a good learning process.

"I don't go anywhere without my bodyguards."

Tannis paused as he spoke, but no way was she letting four heavily armed men on board *El Cazador*. She'd seen Skylar in action, so she knew what the soldiers trained by the Corps were capable of, and four of them might be able to take the ship. She wouldn't risk it. "Then I guess we'll see you around. Or not."

She made herself turn and walk away, but it was hard. She wanted to do this job so much each step was a torment, but something told her if she showed any weakness, he would walk all over her. Too used to getting his own way, he had to realize that everybody on board *El Cazador* put themselves under her command.

"Wait."

She'd reached the top of the ramp and was about to step between Skylar and Daisy when he spoke again. She turned slowly.

"For some strange, godforsaken reason I trust you."

"That's sweet of you. So?"

He said nothing out loud, but the guard holstered his weapon.

"Sir, the colonel said—"

Again, Callum didn't speak, but the guard shut up abruptly and stepped back.

"Would you reassure my guard and tell them you're not going to shoot me? You're not, are you, Captain?"

"Well, *I'm* not, but then I'm not the one with a blaster

aimed at your chest. Then again, I suppose they can always patch you up."

He gave a smile that creased the corners of his eyes. "I'd prefer it not to come to that. And if we're going, I suggest we leave. I made sure there was a window, but any minute now, I'm guessing the space around this planet will be locked down so tight a fly won't get through."

He was giving in. Tannis kept her expression deliberately deadpan, but inside she buzzed with excitement.

"Let's go."

Well, that hadn't gone as planned. The thought flickered through his mind as he stepped between the pair who still held their blasters pointed in his direction. He gave them a quick sideways glance. Skylar he knew, and he could have blasted her with brainpower, but that would have still left the other. Though on closer inspection, she didn't look much of a threat despite the weapon in her hand. What she did look was . . . green. He'd never seen anyone quite that green before. Skin, hair, eyes. Shades of green from palest grass to deep emerald. She wasn't tall, but she held the huge blaster with an easy confidence and her finger rested on the trigger.

It occurred to him, not for the first time, that perhaps he was actually making a huge mistake.

*Goddamn right, you're making a mistake.* The colonel's words echoed in his mind, and he grinned. Mistake or not, it felt good.

Of course, once they had him on board, they could murder him—the only person to successfully destroy one of the Collective was actually a member of this crew—or, more likely, hold him for ransom. But he didn't think they would—while the majority of the jobs they took on skirted the boundaries of "legal" they had a reputation for honesty and integrity.

*I'm closing down all links,* he told the colonel. *I'll be in touch if I need you.*

*Good luck.*

He stepped into the docking bay and looked around. He'd never been on a pirate ship before and a shiver of anticipation prickled down his spine. It wasn't what he'd expected—the place was immaculate, gleaming black and silver, and the air smelled fresh and clean.

Behind him, the door slid shut. He turned to see the three of them lined up, staring at him. None of them looked happy. The captain stood in the center, her hands shoved into the pockets of her tight black pants. She wore a scarlet shirt, knee-high boots, and a weapon's belt strapped to her thigh. Her dark hair was cut short, her narrow face dominated by yellow eyes, the irises almost slits. This close, he could see the faint luminosity of her skin—she wasn't beautiful but again he felt that stab of lust.

He wanted her, and soon. But she hadn't been the pushover he'd expected, and when he'd tried to probe her mind, he'd hit a brick wall. That was another skill he'd developed over the past few years—another sign he was changing. He'd always been able to communicate with the Collective members, but now he could also read non-Collectives—not their actual thoughts, but their emotions, so he could tell whether they were lying or telling the truth—which had come in handy. But with this woman, nothing.

He raised an eyebrow, as they all remained unmoving. "Are we waiting for something?"

The captain shrugged, then pressed the comm unit strapped to her wrist. "We're ready to go."

She listened to something said in reply. "I don't know." She glanced at Callum. "Are we still heading to Trakis Two?"

"Yes, but for the moment, just get us away from here." When she remained silent, studying him out of those cold yellow eyes, he continued, "Did I mention there might be a lockdown? Could we leave? Now?"

She shrugged again and then spoke into the comm unit. "Head into deep space."

His ultimate goal was Trakis Seven, but it was probably best not to mention that just yet. Most people had no wish to go anywhere near the planet and usually had to be transported there in cryo—it was a one-way trip. But if he was going to find any answers about the nature of Meridian, he reckoned that was where they'd be.

Beneath his feet, the ship rumbled as the main thrusters were engaged, and then they were off. A wave of exhilaration washed over him. They were on their way. For a while, he could forget the weight of responsibility. Forget the rest of the world. Wasn't it about time he had something for himself after all the years he'd devoted to running this rotten universe?

"Could someone show me to my room?" he asked.

"I'll take you," the captain said. "By the way—we haven't been properly introduced. I think you were too busy trying to kill us last time we met."

Callum ignored the comment.

"Skylar, you know. I'm Tannis, and this is Daisy." She waved at the green girl who now stood with a wide smile on her face and her weapon holstered. "I'll introduce you to the rest of the crew later. Except Jon and Alex, they're meeting us on Trakis Two. So, what do we call you?"

"Your Great Holy Leadership," Daisy suggested with a grin.

Callum was getting the distinct impression that the crew didn't like him. He supposed he couldn't blame them—he had tried to have them all killed.

He smiled. "Call me Callum."

Besides, he wasn't interested in the rest of the crew. He

was interested in Tannis. This was a chance to get her alone, see how she really felt about him.

"Let's go," Tannis said and then paused. "Shit. Where the hell are we going to put you?"

The ship was almost full. It could support a crew of eight comfortably, and that was what they had right now. Luckily that included two couples who were more than happy to share. Skylar had moved in with Rico, and Jon and Alex had moved into Skylar's guest suite, which was empty at the moment, but full of their stuff. Tannis had the captain's suite, the best rooms on the ship, but she certainly wasn't giving them up; they had been her home for fifteen years. When she'd first come on board and Rico had shown her the rooms she'd broken down and cried—something she'd sworn she would never do again.

She'd avoided looking at Callum directly. He had a strange effect on her insides, and she didn't know why, so she'd limited herself to oblique glances. Now she allowed herself to study him. He was tall, lean and rangy in build, but the wings made him appear larger. They probably made things awkward—like dressing. He wore dark pants and a purple shirt, likely custom-made, that perfectly matched his eyes. She glanced up to find him watching her. His face was long, with prominent cheekbones and a full, sensual mouth, but dominated by his eyes. The rest of him faded into insignificance when she looked into those inhuman violet orbs—almost. They radiated a sense of power and age that sent a shiver running through her.

She gave herself a mental shake. "Come on."

The ship was built on three levels. The large docking bay took up most of the central level, with the engine rooms situated on the lower, and the bridge and living quarters on the upper level. She headed up the ramp, Callum following close behind.

They didn't speak on the way, but she was intensely conscious of him at her side and it was a relief to reach their destination. She pressed her hand to the panel, and the door slid open.

Lip curled in disdain, he stood and stared into the room. "Don't you have somewhere bigger?"

"No, all the bigger cabins are taken."

"Can't you move someone?"

"Well, I'm sure Rico would be happy to discuss giving up his cabin for you, if you ask him nicely. On the other hand, maybe you won't get the answer you're looking for. So, I'm afraid it's this or the docking bay."

He frowned, but when she gestured at the open doorway, he stepped through. As she was about to leave, he turned and asked, "Would you come in for a moment?"

She didn't want to. The room appeared very small with him inside, but she was going to have to get used to him, and now was as good a time as any. She stepped inside but left the door open.

This close, she could see the tracery of veins in the black, membranous wings. If she got the Meridian treatment, would she have wings like that one day?

"Does everyone get them?" The question was out before she could think about it.

He raised an eyebrow, but answered. "We think so, eventually. So far it's just the oldest of us—the founding members—but they all have them."

"Wow."

"My feelings exactly. Unfortunately, it's a sentiment not shared by the rest of my Council. Would you like to touch them?"

Shock hit her in the gut, but her feet moved her forward until she was near enough to breathe in the warm, masculine scent of him. It was closer than she had been to a man in a long time, and a little alarm buzzed in her head. But if she really wanted the Meridian treatment, she had a duty to find out as much as she could—this was research. Ignoring the buzz, she reached out and traced the tip of one black wing. The skin was silky soft under her fingertips, and a quiver ran through him.

Before she realized what he meant to do, his arms had clasped her shoulders and he dragged her to him, closing the small space between them.

"I've wanted to do this since the first time I saw you," he murmured.

The words hardly registered. Tannis had gone rigid with shock. Her mind screamed at her to run, but her muscles locked solid.

As his head lowered toward her, she swallowed the whimper that rose in her throat. She was transported to that earlier time, that other life. She tried to tell herself that this was different. Here she had a choice, just pull free and go, but she froze in place, her mind numb. His body was hard against her, and when his lips touched hers, she opened her mouth to scream, and his hot, wet tongue thrust inside.

Then she did struggle. Biting down hard, her teeth sank into flesh, and she tasted blood. Her venom was poised for release, but he pulled away, and she wrenched out of his grasp and backed into the wall behind her.

Eyes narrowed, he raised one hand and wiped the blood from his lips.

"What the hell was that for?" He sounded more puzzled than angry. Maybe he was used to women falling over themselves for his kisses. He probably hadn't been rejected since he'd become Leader of the Universe. Well, he'd better get used to it on this ship.

Like she'd always done in the research station, she blanked her face of all expression. But he must have seen something, because a small frown played across his face.

She licked her lips. "I just like to keep business and pleasure separate—you're strictly business. And I don't like being pawed by clients. From now on keep your hands, and any other appendages, to yourself."

She whirled around and was through the door when he called out, "Could you get someone to bring me some food?"

Teeth gritted, Tannis answered, "We're not your god-damn servants. You want to eat, you join us in the galley."

Halfway to the bridge, she started to shake. Halting, she leaned a hand against the wall and rested her forehead against the cool metal. She'd forgotten the taste of fear. Now it was bitter on her tongue.

Pushing herself up straight, she forced herself to move and was pretty sure she had herself under control by the time she walked onto the bridge. While he still sat in the pilot's seat, Rico had switched to autopilot and was relaxed, legs stretched out, as he watched something on the monitor.

His eyes narrowed at the sight of her. "What happened?"

"Nothing," she said. "I've put him in Jon's old cabin."

Rico grinned. "I bet that's a comedown."

"Yeah, he wanted yours—I said he should ask you." She was proud of how cool her voice sounded.

Rico patted the chair beside him. "Sit a moment. I want to talk to you."

"What is it?" She crossed the room and sank into the seat.

"I think you're making a mistake. Yeah." He waved a hand to shut her up as she opened her mouth to argue. "I know—it's good money, but I have a bad feeling about taking this job."

"It's too late now."

"No it's not—we can shove the bastard out of the airlock."

"You want to shove the Leader of the Known Universe out of the airlock?"

She studied his face, trying to decide whether he really considered it a viable option. You could never tell with Rico. He could come across as a smooth charmer, but beneath that lurked a darkness. No one managed to survive for over fifteen hundred years by being nice.

"We should consider it."

"And what do you reckon that would do to my chances of getting the Meridian treatment?"

"I've never really understood why you were so set on joining the Collective. You're a loner, and they're about as close a group as you're likely to come across. They're in each other's heads. I'm not sure you'd cope with that."

"Skylar has broken away."

"She's still in contact. I think it's something she'll always need." He didn't sound too happy about the idea. "So why? Why do you want it so badly?"

"I don't know." She studied her fingernails. "Okay, I do know—but it's a bit pathetic."

He raised his eyebrows, and she pushed herself to go on. "I have this one happy memory of my time in the research station. I'd only been there about a year or two, and there was this visit by a member of the Collective—"

"What were the Collective doing there?"

"How the hell should I know? I was only six at the time, and they didn't exactly discuss policy with me. But anyway, she was like an angel, so beautiful and nice—she gave the children chocolate and . . ." She shook her head. "You don't know what it was like in that place."

"I saw some of it, and I can guess the rest," he said softly.

"She just stuck in my mind. I lived with the fear of dying every day—they taunted us with it—how we would end up in the mines and everyone knows that's a death sentence.

So I had this dream that I'd get the Meridian treatment, and I'd be immortal, and I'd never die." She shrugged. "I told you—pathetic."

"There is another way to get immortality."

At last, she knew where this was going.

"After the god-awful mess I made with Bastion, I promised I'd never change anyone again," Rico said. "But I'll do it for you. Just say the word, we'll toss flyboy out of the airlock, and I'll give you immortality."

For long minutes, she stared at the toes of her boots while she considered what to say to him. After that first time, Rico had never bitten her again, never even hinted he wanted to. She knew he was immortal, but she'd also seen what else he was, the hungers that drove him. He'd once told her that sex helped him keep the darkness at bay. She never wanted to be like that. Never!

"I can't, Rico. I appreciate the offer, but really I can't."

"Why? There's no pain, and I've never known anyone not to survive."

"I don't want to be like you." She bit her lip.

"Really," he drawled. "You'd rather be like that arrogant bastard?"

"And Skylar," she said quickly. "Skylar is Collective. So, they're not all bad." But Rico was her friend, and he deserved to know the truth. She took a deep breath. "I don't like being touched, and I can't face sex. Back in that place . . ." A shudder ran through her and she took a deep breath. "In the research station—"

"They raped you?" he interrupted, his tone harsh.

"No. They would have had to see me as human for that, and most of them didn't. But they did experiments on us. Week after week, year after year." She hated this; even talking about it revived the memories. Waking on a table, strapped down, while they—No, she wouldn't think about it. "I thought maybe I was over the fear. But just now, Callum kissed me and—"

"He did what?" Rico's outraged question cut off her flow. Maybe she should have kept that to herself, if only for the sake of shipboard harmony.

"He kissed me."

Rico jumped to his feet. "Where is he? I'll kill the bastard."

For the first time since Callum had kissed her, she smiled. "Goddamn it, Rico, you're not my freaking father."

After a long moment staring at her, he sat back in his chair. "You're right. Finish what you were saying."

"There's not much else—he kissed me, and I was right back in that cell. It was as if the last fifteen years just vanished. I was so full of fear and rage. You told me once that you use sex to keep the darkness at bay—I don't want to live with that choice."

Lips pursed, he looked at her for long moments, then nodded. "Okay."

Janey and Daisy entered and the conversation was over. Janey sat down at her console and immediately her manicured fingers were flying. Daisy took the seat next to Rico. Daisy was genetically modified, a GM like Tannis, though in Daisy's case, her DNA had been mixed with some sort of plant—Tannis had no clue what.

*El Cazador* had picked up her escape pod floating in deep space after her family had been slaughtered three years ago, as part of the Church's purge of GMs. Daisy was now copilot and loved flying, taking the controls whenever Rico would let her. According to Rico, she was a natural, though he never said it where Daisy could hear.

Today, as usual, she was dressed as some sort of mini Rico—whom she had a huge crush on—black shirt and black pants tucked into knee-high black boots. Her green hair was pulled into a ponytail, her pale green skin glow-ing. Her chlorophyll levels were high—she must have been on her sun bed.

"Where is he?" she asked.

"Who?" Tannis replied, although she knew exactly which who she meant.

"Callum Meridian." Daisy almost bounced with excite-ment. With her boundless enthusiasm, she made Tannis feel old. "Those wings were just amazing. Did you know he was a fighter pilot back on Earth? And he was the best."

"*Christos*," Rico muttered.

Tannis almost grinned. It looked like Rico was in for some competition in the hero-worship department, and he obviously didn't like the idea. It wasn't funny, though. This trip was already fraught with potential catastrophes, and they could do without any testosterone-fueled pissing con-tests.

What they did need was a meeting.

"Get everybody together in the conference room in half an hour, including his Leadership—we need to find out just what it is he's paying us to do."

Callum was hungry. It wasn't something he was used to—he had servants to make sure he had everything he de-sired, the second he desired it. He only had to think he wanted something and it would be there.

Obviously, not any more.

He'd go in search of this galley as soon as his other hun-ger was under control.

He stared at the open doorway where Tannis had ex-ited ten minutes ago. Her reaction to his kiss had been unexpected. So had his. At least it confirmed there was nothing wrong with his libido—his dick was rock hard. His disinterest must have merely been boredom. There were too many women all too eager to bed him for reasons he'd not bothered to question, but in the end the charm of having anyone he wanted had faded.

Now, it felt as though his body was coming awake after years of hibernation. Heat pooled in his groin and he shifted. He could still taste her, hot, spicy woman tinged with the exotic, and he wanted to finish what they'd started. Except, *they* hadn't started it. *He* had. And from her expression afterward, he'd been the only one to enjoy their kiss. Before she'd wiped it clean, he'd seen shock and even fear on her face.

She was such a mystery, and that intrigued him.

*Callum.*

The colonel's voice sounded in his head, and a ripple of unease ran down his spine. They'd agreed no contact except in emergencies. *What is it?*

*Trouble. The Council have refused to recognize me as a member.*

*I left specific instructions—*

*Which they're ignoring. But there's more—all hell broke loose after you did your flying stunt. They are not happy. They put out a comm that you've been kidnapped, and they're sending out everything they've got after you. They've also already posted a reward. A big reward.*

Shit. *You can at least stop the Council coming after me. Hell, you're in charge of the Corps, they can't move without your order.*

*Not anymore. They're suggesting I'm complicit in your "kidnapping." I think they're planning on arresting me any moment, so if you don't hear from me again—good luck.* He was silent for a moment. *They're at the door. I'll—*

Callum swore loudly as the colonel was cut off. He must have been knocked unconscious.

*Tyson?*

The man's mind was closed, but Callum shoved his way in—he was the only one of them who could do it, which came in useful if people were ignoring you.

*Callum, you're not very popular around here right now.*

*Like I give a shit. I'm finished with hiding—I told you that. Now reinstate the colonel, recall the Corps, and get rid of that reward.*

*Come back, and we'll call everyone off. We can do some damage control, say it was a stunt.*

*Piss off.*

He broke the contact. It looked like the Council had some balls after all. Pity they had to wait until now to show them. At least his hard-on was gone. He supposed he'd better go and tell the captain that they should expect company, so they could start thinking about how to avoid it.

The crew of *El Cazador* had spent two weeks being pursued by the Collective and had managed to successfully evade them. He hoped they could do it again—one of the reasons he'd employed them. He'd wanted someone with no connections to the Council who could keep him out of sight while he worked out what he was and what he wanted to do with the rest of eternity.

The comm unit beside the bed buzzed. He pressed it to open.

"Meeting in the conference room in half an hour," a brusque voice barked. "Be there."

"Where—" But the comm was cut off abruptly.

Why did he get the impression nobody on this ship liked him?

Clearly, they were the type to hold grudges. He didn't give a toss whether they liked him or not as long as they did what he paid them to do. But he realized that wasn't entirely true. There was one member of the crew he wanted to like him.

An image of the captain flashed in his mind. Though

she'd told him she didn't mix business with pleasure, he would have to persuade her otherwise. From her reaction to his kiss, he had some work to do. For once, he was going to have to exert himself for what he wanted. The idea had a certain novelty value.

"You're late," Tannis snapped.

Callum had wandered around the goddamn ship for what seemed like an age. He hadn't found the galley and was still hungry. He had only found this place because he'd pushed his way into Skylar's mind and asked for directions. He'd guessed she hadn't been pleased by the intrusion. Hard luck. They should have sent somebody to escort him. *And* given him some goddamn food.

The room was big and airy. The decor, like the rest of the ship, black and silver. He quickly counted the people. Five. He reckoned this must be the whole crew on board, except for the ship's engineer who, from the reports he'd read, appeared to be some sort of recluse. The assassin and his little priestess were obviously elsewhere—he'd seen no sign of them.

His gaze was drawn first to Tannis leaning against the far wall, arms folded across her chest, one booted foot tapping the floor. She briefly caught his eye and looked away.

He moved on to the vampire, Ricardo Sanchez, owner and pilot of the ship, with Skylar next to him, one hand resting on his thigh as if to restrain him.

Finally, two women. One he didn't recognize. She was beautiful, well dressed, with dark red hair. The other was the green girl, Daisy. She was the only one who appeared pleased to see him. She had a wide grin on her face and waggled her fingers in his direction.

The vampire shook off Skylar's hand and stood in one fluid move. He stalked toward Callum, moving with the lithe grace of a predator, and suddenly Callum was afraid.

His mouth went dry, and every brain cell screamed at him to run. Rico was dressed all in black, with a pistol at his thigh and an honest-to-God sword at his back. But it wasn't the weapons that caused Callum's heart rate to speed up, it was the fact that the vampire was snarling, one corner of his upper lip curling to reveal a razor-sharp fang.

He came to a halt in front of Callum, drew back his fist, and punched him in the face.

# CHAPTER 3

Callum heard the *crunch* of bone as his nose broke. Pain flooded his face, and his mouth filled with the metallic taste of blood. He swallowed and looked around to see if anyone was going to help him. Only the green girl appeared alarmed—well the grin was gone at least. Skylar looked resigned and shrugged when she caught his gaze. The redhead was studying her nails. Tannis hadn't moved—she certainly wasn't rushing to his rescue. He was on his own. Something told him that he couldn't back down now. If he showed just a little of the fear he was feeling, his credibility would be lost forever, but no way could he win this fight. He would be lucky to survive it.

He forced his gaze to the vampire and decided he wanted a gun, a big fucking gun.

"That's for messing with Skylar's head," Rico growled. "And this is for kissing Tannis."

The fist flew again. This time it landed on his chest, and he went down under the force of the blow. He lay unmoving for a minute. God, that hurt as though his chest had caved in. Bloody vampire—he had an urge to sack the whole lot of them right now. Except if he did that, they might just dump him out of the airlock without a space-suit.

He pushed himself onto one elbow and stared the vampire in the eyes. "Finished?" he snarled and called up the power from deep inside him, allowed it to glow from his eyes.

A flash of surprise crossed Rico's face.

Tannis moved at last to stand in front of the vampire, hands on her hips. She looked annoyed. Maybe she did like him, after all. "Great, just great, Rico. Why don't you tell the whole freaking ship that he kissed me?"

And maybe she didn't. She was just annoyed the vampire had told everyone he'd kissed her. But why had she told the vampire?

Rico didn't answer. He looked down at where Callum lay. "Yeah, I've finished. For now."

Callum staggered to his feet and shook his head, spraying blood from his broken nose around the room.

Rico's eyes narrowed and his nostrils flared. "Will somebody stop him from bleeding all over my ship? He's making a mess. And he's making me hungry."

"I'll go get something." Daisy jumped to her feet and hurried from the room. Nobody said a word. Rico strolled to his chair and threw himself down. Callum's legs trembled, but he waited until the vampire was seated before he sank into the nearest chair, perching on the front to accommodate his wings.

Daisy returned a minute later, her expression sympathetic as she handed him a damp towel. He pressed it to his face and realized his hand shook as well.

Callum couldn't remember the last time someone had hit him. He reckoned it must have been back on Earth over a thousand years ago. Shit, his nose hurt.

But one thing was for sure—he wasn't bored any longer. The corners of his mouth twitched in the beginnings of a smile. Tannis glanced at him sharply, and he blanked his expression.

"Right," she said. "If everyone has finished playing, perhaps we could we get on with the meeting now?"

Rico grinned. "Aye, aye, Captain."

She ignored him and turned her attention to Callum. "So you're paying us a lot of money—what do you want in return?"

The blunt question surprised him; he'd prefer to keep his plans to as few people as possible. "Can we discuss this in private?"

"No." She waved a hand around the room. "They're going to be there and they have a right to know. Besides, I don't keep secrets from my crew. So talk."

Wincing, he sat back and prodded his nose. It was definitely broken, and he'd gotten blood all over his shirt. And he had no more clothes. Why hadn't he thought to bring luggage? The problem was he'd had people to do everything for him, until he'd just about lost the ability to think for himself. He was almost embarrassed.

What to tell them, when he hadn't expected to have to explain anything? He'd planned to have his bodyguards deal with any awkward questions and keep the crew in line.

"I need to lay low for a while."

"Why?"

Annoyance flicked at his nerve endings. He was also unused to having to justify himself. Why couldn't she accept what he said and just do what she was told? When he remained silent, she raised one arched brow, and he pushed down his irritation and organized his thoughts. "The Council was against us revealing the changes." He gestured at his wings. "They wanted to keep them hidden, pretend they weren't happening."

"A little hard to hide," Rico murmured.

Callum ignored the interruption. "I decided my people had a right to the truth. They should know what was going on with their leaders—"

"*My people?*" Rico scoffed. "Has anyone ever told you you're a pompous git? And are you really expecting us to believe you're doing this out of pure altruism? I mean—do we look like idiots?"

Someone tittered.

Callum gritted his teeth and took a deep breath. "Okay, *I* want to know the truth. I want to find out what we're becoming, and I'm fed up with hiding."

"That sounds more like it."

"So I needed somewhere to lay low until they cool down and are willing to listen."

"Is anyone buying this crap?" Rico said. "You know this is a load of bollocks. I say we take a vote and shove him out the airlock. Get rid of the problem."

They *really* didn't like him. But he wasn't too worried. He'd only handed over half of the fee so far—the rest they would get when the job was over. If they were still alive.

Tannis must have realized that her money was at risk, and she shrugged almost apologetically. "Rico has a little problem with the fact that you messed with Skylar's head. And you did spend a lot of effort recently trying to kill us."

"You assassinated one of us first," Callum countered.

"Yeah, but he paid for the job himself—it was actually suicide," Rico pointed out. "Besides, Aiden Ross was an asshole. We were doing you a favor."

"Jesus, it's like kindergarten in here." Tannis pressed her fingers into her short hair.

It was damp, slicked back from her face. She must have showered since he'd come on board. Had she needed cooling down after he'd kissed her? Though remembering her reaction, he doubted that had been the reason—more likely wanted to scrub herself clean. The idea intrigued him.

"So, you want to lie low," she said. "What else?"

"I've arranged to meet with my head of research. In two days' time on Trakis Two. Then we'll make a plan. I might or might not need you after that. But if I do, I'll pay you more. The fee I've offered so far is for keeping me out of the way for two days and then getting me to Trakis Two. Easy money."

"Sounds too easy."

"Well, there is something else you need to know."

She gave an exaggerated sigh. "And that is?"

"I just got a report that the Council has sent the Corps after me."

"What? And that didn't occur to you before you arranged this stunt?"

"No, I didn't think it would be an issue—the colonel is a good friend, but it appears they've arrested him and put their own person in charge."

"They've arrested the colonel?" Skylar said. "The Corps won't be happy about that." Skylar was herself an officer in the intelligence section of the Corps, or she had been until she'd gone AWOL.

"Maybe not, but in my absence, and the absence of the colonel, they'll take their orders from the Council. There's more."

"Really?" Tannis asked. "Why aren't I surprised?"

"They've reported me as kidnapped. By you. They're offering a huge reward for my return." He had a thought. "You didn't actually send a ransom demand, did you?"

"No, but I'm thinking about it. Jesus, we'll have every bounty hunter in the known universe on our tail." She paced the room. "Great, just great. Janey, can you start a scan for anything that might be heading in our direction?"

"I'm already on it."

She turned back to him, studying him as though he was something rather unpleasant. "Anything else?"

"Yes, I'll need some clothes and some food and—"

She waved a hand. "Anything else important." But she gave him no chance to answer. "No—good. Right. If this meeting is over, I have things to do."

She was leaving, and he didn't want her to go. Not without him. He stood up, stepped toward her, and lowered his voice. "About the kiss . . ."

"Forget it. I have." With a final shrug, she whirled around and strode from the room.

Callum watched her go. She had a great ass. And he was pretty certain she hadn't forgotten the kiss—*he* had no intention of doing so.

As she disappeared from sight, he glanced across to find Rico watching him. His hand went to his nose without conscious thought. One of the advantages to the Meridian treatment was they healed incredibly fast, but right now it felt sore and swollen. He winced, but at least the bleeding had stopped.

The vampire's gaze was speculative. He strolled over, and Callum made himself stand his ground. Just for good measure, he spread his wings until the tips touched the walls on either side of him. The idea occurred to him, that perhaps he wouldn't survive his sojourn aboard *El Cazador,* that he'd been a fool to trust these people. He'd started to believe himself indestructible, and that wasn't the truth. He could be destroyed. And that the only person to ever kill one of their kind was a member of this crew—if not actually on board right now—didn't bode well.

But Rico merely smiled, though the expression didn't reach his dark eyes. Callum tried a quick mind probe. The vampire's eyes narrowed, and Callum hit a wall. Another one he couldn't read—it was bloody inconvenient.

Rico reached out a finger and poked him in the chest.

"Keep out of everybody's minds, and keep your dick in your pants, and we'll all be fine."

Callum was hungry, his nose hurt, his chest hurt, his only clean shirt was covered in blood. In fact, he was pissed off, and these bloody peasants seemed not to appreciate just how important he actually was. He twitched his wings and opened his mouth to tell Rico to mind his own sodding business—he'd do what he liked with his goddamn dick—when the whole ship lurched to the side and he was thrown to the floor. Something hit him in the chest and everything went black.

When the lights flickered on, he found he was lying on the floor with the vampire on top of him. Thankfully, not for long—his ribs were killing him. Rico rolled to his feet and strode across to where the redhead was sitting. How had she managed to stay in her seat looking totally unruffled?

"I thought you were checking if anyone was after us?" Rico said.

"I was. Whoever it is, they didn't show up on the monitors."

"Well, are they showing up now?"

Janey flicked a few switches. "Nope."

Callum knew instantly who was out there. "It's the Corps."

"So why can't we see them?"

"New stealth technology." He strode across and leaned over her shoulder. "Here, let me try something." He pressed a few buttons, changed the frequency, and the monitor filled with a huge ship. He recognized her immediately—his ship, *The Endeavor*. They must have pulled her from her trials, the fucking idiots.

She was flanked by three smaller ships that hugged close to take advantage of the stealth technology of the newer, more advanced star cruiser.

Skylar came to stand beside him and peered at the monitor. "That's the new Corps flagship. I'd heard she'd been commissioned—wow."

"She's a beauty," Rico said, a faint tinge of jealousy in his voice.

"What's going on?"

Callum turned from the screen as Tannis spoke from the doorway. She sounded irked. "You've been on this ship one hour and already we're under attack. How come they caught up so soon?" Her eyes narrowed on him. "Have you been in contact with anyone? Perhaps you've decided you don't want this trip after all."

"No."

"So how have they homed in on us so quickly? There's a lot of space out here—this can't be just good luck on their part."

"Do you think we've got a bug on board?" Janey swiveled in her seat and eyed him curiously. "Like Jon had?"

"You bugged?" Tannis asked him.

"Not that I know of. They wouldn't dare without my knowledge."

"Yeah, right, of course they wouldn't, because you're so big, bad, and important. Get the scanner, Janey."

Callum stood still as Janey ran the machine down over his body. Nothing happened, and he slowly relaxed. Then she moved around behind him.

*Beep, beep, beep.*

"They always put it in the ass," Janey murmured. "Lend me your knife," she said to Skylar.

Skylar drew a wicked-looking blade from the weapons belt at her waist and handed it to the redhead.

His mind reeled. They'd bugged him without his knowledge. When the hell had they done that? And why hadn't they told him? The Council had suggested it years ago as a security precaution and he'd refused. It looked like they'd gone ahead anyway, must have been during one of the medicals. Bastards. And what the hell was that woman brandishing a knife at him for? No way was she cutting into him with that blade.

"Spread the wings and drop your pants."

"What?" He peered over his shoulder as she crouched behind him, the scanner in one hand, the knife in the other. She grinned with relish as though she could sense his discomfort.

"I need to get the bug out, or we'll never get away from . . ." She waved a scarlet-tipped hand at the monitor, where the Corps ships still hovered. He couldn't see how they were going to get away anyway. *The Endeavor* was a Mark Five cruiser. He'd commissioned her himself. She was the fastest ship in space, with more than fifty times the firepower of *El Cazador*.

"Well . . ." Janey prompted.

He shrugged. Everyone backed away as he spread his wings. His hand went to the fastener at his waist, and he hesitated. Five sets of eyes watched him avidly. He glanced at Tannis, and she raised an eyebrow as though daring him. He couldn't remember feeling this uncomfortable. Ever. This was no big deal. He turned to face the console, and Janey shuffled around so she was behind him.

He flicked open the fastener and pushed his pants down. Someone whistled, and he cringed inwardly but didn't react.

"Do you all realize we're looking at the most powerful butt in the known universe?" Janey said.

"Wow—I feel honored," Tannis replied. "Now get on with it."

Callum ignored them. Leaning one arm against the curved silver wall, he willed this whole humiliating experience over. Fingers ran lightly over the curve of his buttocks. "Got it," she murmured. "This might sting a little."

Was that anticipation he could hear in her voice?

*Bitch.*

He peered over his shoulders and caught Tannis with her gaze glued on his ass. She looked up and straight into his eyes as the knife probed his flesh. Shit, that hurt. It must have shown on his face, because she grinned. "Don't be a baby."

He gritted his teeth as the blade dug deeper. Was she deliberately taking her time? Finally, something popped free from his skin and fell to the floor.

"Okay, done," Janey said. "You can put your pants back on."

A slow trickle of blood ran down his left buttock, but he couldn't think what to do about that, and he wanted his pants back on sooner rather than later. He pulled them up, folded his wings, and turned around just as Tannis smashed her booted foot on the small silver bug. She ground down, so he heard the splinter of metal.

Now his ass hurt as well. He tried the at-least-I'm-not-bored argument again, but it was losing its potency. He wanted to go home, to his palace, where people at least pretended to like him. A smile tugged at his lips at the pathetic thought.

"Okay, so that's one problem solved. All we need to do now is get away from that ship and stay away, and we're all good. Any ideas?" Tannis looked around the room. No one answered.

"They're trying to comm us," Janey said. "You want to hear what they have to say?"

"Not particularly, but I suppose we should."

"This is Captain Harris of *The Endeavor*. Please lock your weapons and get ready to be boarded."

Callum knew Captain Harris—he was Tyler's man. Fuck. He stepped closer to the comm unit and spoke.

"Captain, this is Callum Meridian. I'm ordering you to stand down and return to Trakis Five."

"Sir, we have orders to ignore your orders. We're here to take you home."

Tannis reached past him and slammed her palm on the comm unit, closing off the sound.

"I didn't like the sound of his voice," she said to the room in general. "Rico, can we outrun them?"

"Not a chance in hell."

"Shoot it out?"

"I reckon we'd last about thirty seconds."

The ship lurched sideways as another blast hit them. This time Callum managed to keep his feet until Tannis knocked into him, and they both went down. He landed on his back—an uncomfortable position when you had wings and a hole in your butt—with Tannis on top of him. His arms went around her automatically, and for a second he held her close. Her body was slender and firm, though he could feel the softness of her breasts against his chest. As he pulled her tighter, she stiffened, pushed her hands between them, and shoved hard. He loosened his grip, and she got to her feet, wiped her hands down the side of her pants, and glared at him.

Sighing, he pushed himself to his feet. "Don't look so pissed at me," he said. "You must have known this was a possibility—I was hardly going to pay you that exorbitant sum just to go on a joyride. The reason I chose this fucking crappy ship and its fucking misfit crew was because you'd successfully managed to evade our forces. So whatever it is you did last time, do it again."

"Rico?"

"Won't work. That was one ship. We try and do the same, the smaller ships would spot us."

"What did you do?" Callum asked. He'd read the

account. The captain had reported that *El Cazador* had simply vanished from the monitors.

"We landed on the ship. It took us out of range of the scanners."

"Clever." It was, but he could see it wouldn't work in this situation.

Rico crossed the room and sank into the pilot's chair, running his hand through his hair, which had come loose from its ponytail. Skylar moved to stand beside him, resting a hand possessively on his shoulder. It was obvious the two were a couple, which explained why Skylar had parted ways from the Collective. No one had ever left before, and he wasn't even sure it was possible to leave. Maybe physically, but not mentally. Whatever else Meridian did, it tied them together until at times it felt as if they were one consciousness.

They were a gestalt and gained power from being united, though they'd never understood how it worked and how they could make the most of that power. It was another of the things he wanted to investigate. Another of the things the Council didn't want to look at too closely. They shied away from scrutinizing anything that might suggest they were somehow no longer human. As though by ignoring it, they would take away its potency.

Fools.

But it was another reason he'd chosen *El Cazador*. The colonel had reported Skylar's defection and hadn't understood the reason, though he said Skylar's recent psych reports had stated she was bored and restless. That sounded familiar, and Callum had been interested to meet her. She didn't look bored and restless now. She appeared vibrant, unconcerned about the possible attack.

As he watched, the vampire dragged her down onto his lap. "For inspiration," he murmured, and she laughed.

"Get used to it," Tannis said from beside him. "Bloody

ship's like a love nest these days. Rico, we're under attack here."

"Oh yeah, but I reckon they're not going to completely obliterate us, not with his Leadership on board."

"Another incoming," Janey said. This time everyone was prepared and managed to stay on their feet or in their seats.

"What we actually need now," Rico said, "is a miracle. Like divine intervention."

"Like God coming in to save us, you mean?" Janey asked.

"Just like that. Where the hell is Alex when we need a few prayers?"

"Well, I don't know about God, but how about the next best thing?" Janey tapped a few keys to reset the viewer. *The Endeavor* vanished, to be replaced by a whole fleet of smaller ships. She focused on the leader, getting a close up. The ship was a Mark Three cruiser, white with a huge black cross on the side.

"The Church of Everlasting Life," Rico murmured. "How nice of them to join the party. Have I mentioned how much I hate the Church?"

"Frequently," Tannis said drily. "Are they after us, do you think? Could they still want Alex back?"

"I have no clue. Maybe they're not happy that we killed their High Priest."

"You killed Hezrai Fischer?" Callum asked.

"Rico did."

"Yeah, he was an asshole. But all the same, they might not see it that way."

"Or maybe they're not after us at all," Janey said.

"Why do you say that?" Tannis asked.

"I just plotted their course. They're heading for the Corp's ship. I don't think they've even noticed us. And they're battle ready—looks like they're about to attack."

"Why would they do that? The Church has always been allies with the Collective."

"Not anymore," Callum said.

"Why? What's changed?"

"We got intel just before I left—they finally got around to appointing a new High Priest. A guy called Temperance Hatcher."

Tannis shook her head. "Never heard of him."

"Unsurprising, as he's kept a low profile, which the Church were more than happy to allow him to do—he's hardly the caring face of God. The man's a fanatic—makes Fischer look like a real sweetheart in comparison. And he hates the Collective."

"Can they take on that space cruiser?" Tannis asked.

"Probably not," Rico answered. "But they might keep them distracted while we slip away."

Callum sank into a chair where he could still view the monitor. He got up almost straightaway, as his butt hurt like hell, and caught a grin on Tannis's face. He leaned one shoulder against the wall instead and studied them.

They were all so calm. They must have known *The Endeavor* could utterly destroy them, but no one had panicked.

Long ago, he'd been a fighter pilot in the British Royal Air Force, before the Earth had become unstable, and he'd left on board the *Trakis Seven*. He remembered the sensation of going into battle, the calmness that had taken over, the sense that he was immortal and nothing could harm him. Now he really was just about immortal, very nearly impossible to kill, and he'd all but forgotten the feeling.

When they had finally accepted that the Earth was dying, they'd put a plan in motion to try and save humanity. It had taken twenty years to bring to fruition, every resource directed toward developing the technology they would need to survive. Wars had broken out as it became clear that not everyone would be saved, and he'd seen a lot of action toward the last days. He'd loved the adrenaline rush; facing death every day made him appreciate life.

In the end, twenty-four ships had left the Earth, named *Trakis One* to *Twenty-Four*, each carrying ten thousand people. Most were kept in cryo, with just a small crew awake to monitor the ship's systems. There had been other crews, ten in all for each ship, and when the crew became too old to function the next was awakened—enough, they reckoned, to last five hundred years. Callum had been the tenth and last captain on *Trakis Seven*, and he'd been ten years into his captaincy when they'd finally come upon what was to be known as the Trakis system.

In the previous five hundred years, they'd encountered no planets that would maintain human life. They'd lost contact with twelve of the ships early on, after they'd separated. Three others had been destroyed by unexplained explosions. And *Trakis One* had been lost in the black hole that guarded the system. The others had all landed safely—except for his—on whatever planets were deemed habitable, the planets taking the name of the ship that landed. He'd been allocated to what was now known as Trakis Seven. Coming in, he'd realized something wasn't right and tried to abort the landing, but the planet had sucked them in and they'd crashed.

And the rest was history.

"They're within range," Janey said. "I think they're communicating, but I can't pick up the frequency."

"Looks like that Corps ship is still focused on us—we try and leave now and they're going to shoot us down. Come on," Rico urged. "Shoot each other."

As if they were listening to him, a series of volleys blasted from the Church's lead ship. They hit *The Endeavor* on the rear end, with no visible effect. For a moment, it looked like they would ignore the offensive, but shots came again in a longer blast and finally, *The Endeavor* swung around and laser fire flashed from her guns. The smaller ship dodged, then came back straightaway, firing a continuous round of blasts, most of which hit their target but bounced harmlessly off the surface. Still it must have riled Captain Harris, because he returned fire, his attention diverted from *The Cazador,* at least for the moment.

"Hey, that Church guy's good," Rico said. "Beautiful. Let's get out of here—nice and slowly—and hope no one notices us."

Skylar stood to give him room, and he punched in a new course. They peeled away and headed slowly in the opposite direction. Callum narrowly resisted the urge to tell them to hurry up.

Finally, as the ships grew smaller in the monitors, Rico punched *El Cazador's* main thrusters and she shot forward. After a few minutes, he glanced up. "So we still heading to Trakis Two?"

"I have no clue." Tannis turned to Callum. "Well?"

He nodded. "I have a rendezvous there in a couple of days."

"We're eight hours out from the planet," Rico said. "We can hole up at Bastian's old place if Jon and Alex give us the all clear. It will keep us out of sight until your meeting."

Callum liked the idea. He didn't know who Bastian was, but he could visit with the colonel's old love and do a little sightseeing. In five hundred years, he'd never been to Trakis Two—the planet that never sleeps. He'd heard it was a wild place. "Sounds like a plan to me."

Tannis studied their faces. Callum appeared eager. His nose was clearly broken, his shirt stained with blood, and he obviously had trouble sitting. She almost grinned—she bet it was a long time since he'd felt like this.

She didn't have happy memories of Trakis Two, but

since most of the unhappy ones were because of Bastian, she reckoned she could overcome her misgivings. Bastian was dead, staked by Rico, after he'd nearly raped and drained Alex.

And Bastian did have a huge hideaway where *El Cazador* could lay up undetected. Alex and Jon were there now making sure nothing else moved in. There were rumored to be strange things living on the dark side of Trakis Two. Still, it was better than wandering aimlessly in space, and no one would be tempted to toss their client out of the airlock.

"Okay, Trakis Two it is."

"Excellent, we can go clubbing," Daisy said.

"You cannot go clubbing. We're laying low."

Daisy's green eyes took on a mutinous expression. "We never got to go clubbing last time, either."

Tannis pursed her lips. But maybe they all needed a bit of downtime. "I'll check things out—if it looks safe, you can go. But only if it looks safe."

# CHAPTER 4

Directly below them, a great, hulking structure appeared to grow out of the darkness itself. Closer inspection revealed that it was man-made, but hewn out of the black rock that made up the surrounding landscape. Callum stared at the monitor and tried to ignore the feeling of misgiving the view gave him.

There were rumored to be all sorts of sinister things living in the murky lands surrounding Pleasure City. The place was a big tourist draw, but visitors were cautioned against traveling beyond the city limits. Those that ignored the warnings were seldom seen again.

The planet came up frequently in Council meetings. Some wanted to go in and clean up the city. Others believed that a place like Trakis Two was needed—at least all the lowlifes were concentrated in one area. So far, they had done nothing.

Rico hovered *El Cazador* above the structure. He was a great pilot, but Callum itched to get his hands on the controls.

"You heard from Alex or Jon?" Tannis asked.

"They're not answering at the moment," Janey said. "But

they called in last night and said everything was clear. And the heat sensors are picking up just the two life-forms." Janey frowned. "Hey, do vampires show up on heat sensors? Aren't they, well, sort of dead?"

Rico grinned. "Are you suggesting I'm a coldhearted bastard?"

"We're going to see a vampire?" Callum asked. He looked to Tannis, but she was doing her best to ignore him. And had been since their kiss yesterday.

Janey answered his question. "Nah, the vampire's dead. Rico killed him last visit. We're just making sure the place hasn't been taken over by something equally unfriendly."

"Or more so," Rico added darkly. "Let's see if the systems are still online. Otherwise, we're going to have to find another way in. Where the hell are Jon and Alex? They'd better not be off somewhere boinking again. Wait, there's something happening."

As Callum watched, a fissure formed in the black rooftop.

"Welcome to vampire city." A voice came over the comm unit. Jon, the assassin, Callum presumed.

"We're in," Tannis said.

The two sides of rock parted, revealing a cavern inside with a landing pad directly below them. Rico took them down and landed light as stardust.

"Right." Tannis rubbed her hands together. She looked pleased. "I'll go see what the newlyweds have to say."

Tannis headed for the door and Callum followed. She paused and a flicker of annoyance passed over her deadpan features when she caught sight of him, then it was gone.

Callum trailed behind her to the docking bay and waited as she pressed her palm to the outer doors. They glided open. The place was in darkness, but as he watched, lights flickered on and illuminated a huge black-walled cavern with black sand floors and several tunnels leading off into stygian darkness. A shiver ran through him—the place gave him the creeps, and he couldn't work out why.

Two figures appeared from a tunnel opposite and headed toward the ship. The assassin and the priestess—an incongruous coupling. Jonathon Decker was huge, broad as well as tall. Next to him, Alexia appeared tiny in her bright pink jumpsuit.

He studied her as they came to a halt at the bottom of the ramp. There was something different; he just couldn't pinpoint what. Last time he'd seen her she'd been dying. Now, she looked vibrantly alive, her huge gray eyes sparkling, her skin glowing. A low growl sounded to the side of her; the assassin wasn't happy that he was looking at the girl. Or maybe he just wasn't happy that Callum was on board.

"Everything okay?" Tannis asked.

"Yeah. We'll tell you over dinner. We're starving."

They hurried past into the ship, and Callum turned to watch them go. There was something not quite right about the two of them, something not quite human, but he couldn't work out what.

"Werewolves," Tannis said.

"What?"

"I don't need any of your fancy mind-reading tricks to guess what you were thinking. You were wondering what was odd about them. With Jon on his own, you could overlook it, but the two of them together . . ."

"Werewolves? Do werewolves even exist?"

"Oh yeah, and other things, apparently. Rico's promised to tell us about them one day."

"The priestess—was she always—"

"A werewolf? No. But your people nearly killed her, and it was the only way to help her live."

"I never even knew they were real," he murmured.

"Me neither, until we broke Jon out. Rico recognized what he was straightaway."

"He would. I presume they came with us from Earth. But how?"

"Ask Rico. Come on, let's go get some food as well."

He realized she was leaving. He wanted to reach out and take her arm, but something in her demeanor stopped him. She was giving off don't-touch vibes in waves. But still he didn't want her to go.

"Wait."

She turned back, her face expressionless. "What?"

"I think we need to talk about what happened yesterday."

"Nothing happened. Or at least nothing important."

He opened his mouth to argue, but she held up a hand. "Look, let's just get the job out of the way. I meant it when I said I don't mix business with pleasure."

"How about if I fire you?"

She smiled, though it didn't reach her eyes. "Then we dump you here and we're off."

He took a deep breath. "Okay. Let's go get that food."

The others were all in the galley when they got there. Even the elusive Trog, the ship's engineer, was sitting beside Janey, silently eating. He raised his shaggy, blond head briefly when they entered, then returned his attention to his food.

Jon and Alex were already seated with food in front of them.

"So?" Tannis asked.

"Nothing," Jon said. "The place is clear." He went back to wolfing down the food. He glanced up after a few seconds. "What? We're hungry. Takes a lot of energy— shifting."

"So does boinking," Tannis said sourly.

They ignored the comment and cleared their dishes. Tannis stood leaning against the counter, foot tapping. Only when his bowl was scraped clean, did Jon look up again. "I told you, nothing to worry about. The place is cleared out. Found a few dead people but nothing alive."

"Good," Tannis said.

She sank into a chair. For the first time since Callum had met her, she appeared tired. He went to the food dispenser, got a bowl of stew, and placed it on the table in front of her.

She looked up, surprise flashing across her features, and then she picked up a spoon and started to eat. After collecting his own food, Callum took the chair opposite, where he could watch her. He realized he liked to watch her. He liked the clean lines of her face—not really beautiful—but exotic. The yellow eyes with their thick fringe of dark, spiky lashes, the lustrous, black hair, usually standing on end, from where she'd run her fingers through it. This close, he could see the faint luminosity of her skin, with its fine sheen of scales. He knew her skin was soft. He'd run his fingers over it yesterday. And felt that long, lean sinuous body pressed against his. He shifted in his chair as his body reacted to the memory, and she glanced up to find him watching her. For a minute, she returned his gaze then she broke the contact and continued eating.

The conversation had started around him, and he allowed himself to relax. A casual camaraderie existed between these people that he hadn't experienced in many years. Again, he realized how empty his life was, how cold and sterile his existence had been for centuries. While he ate, he allowed the atmosphere to loosen the tenseness in his muscles. Tension that had become part of him. Finally, he put down his spoon and looked around.

Rico caught his eye, one eyebrow raised in query. And Callum remembered what Tannis had said at the docking bay.

"Where do werewolves come from?" he asked. "For that matter, where do vampires come from?"

Rico relaxed in his seat and pursed his lips as if considering whether he should answer. Then he shrugged. "From Earth."

"But how did they get here? The places on the ships leaving Earth were limited."

"I know. Twenty-four ships each carrying ten thousand Chosen Ones—the hope of the human race—each person selected by a totally rigged lottery system."

"So?"

"Well there were a few of us excluded from the lottery, and we didn't think that was fair. So we took matters into our own hands."

"Wait a minute. Are you telling me you were actually on Earth? You're that old?"

"One thousand five hundred and ninety-six to be precise."

Callum did the math. "You must have been born in the Middle Ages." His mind reeled, and he forced himself back to the topic, but one day he'd love a long chat with the vampire. What had the Earth been like all those years ago?

"When you say 'we' do you mean more vampires?"

"Vampires, werewolves, a few other things you might hope never to meet."

"Nice friends you have," Skylar commented.

Rico cast her a grin. "They weren't exactly friends— you could say we came together for a common cause. Anyhow, we needed a ship, so we approached one of the captains and made him an offer."

"An offer?"

"In exchange for dumping half his load of Chosen Ones and replacing them with our little group, I would give him immortality."

Shock hit Callum in the gut. "You turned the captain of one of the Trakis ships into a vampire?"

"I did, and it was one of the worst mistakes I ever made. Not that we had much choice—we did our research and Bastian was the only one who came up a possibility. You flyboys were such a load of goddamn heroes."

"Fucking hell. You're talking about Sebastian Faulk. Captain Faulk of the . . ." He trailed off as the implications filtered through his mind.

"Captain Faulk of *Trakis Two*," Rico finished for him. "Yup, that was Bastian. I take it you knew him."

Callum found this hard to believe. He'd known Sebastian, though they'd never been friends, just coworkers—the guy had been a complete dick. "We trained together. All the crews did in the years before we left. What happened to him? I take it he was alive until recently."

"Yeah. Rico staked him a few weeks ago."

Callum frowned. "Why? I mean—why now—after all this time?"

Rico gave him a slow smile that curled his lips, revealing the tips of his sharp white fangs. "Because he pissed me off."

A shiver of primordial fear trickled down Callum's spine. Occasionally, it was possible to forget what Rico was. Now wasn't one of those times. Despite the relaxed outward appearance, there was a darkness in the vampire, kept under rigid control, but there nevertheless. Callum refused to be intimidated. Again.

He returned the smile. "I'll have to make sure there are no stakes around next time I annoy you."

Because he was pretty sure if they spent time together, he was going to piss Rico off.

Rico grinned. "Good idea. Waste of time with you anyway."

"We should be safe here for a couple of days," Tannis said. "We just need to keep a low profile until your person turns up."

"I need to go into the city," Callum said.

"Not a chance. This isn't a freaking holiday. I'm going into Pleasure City with Janey and Skylar. We need some supplies, and we can check how hot things are. If there's nothing happening, the rest of you can go in later. But not you," she said to Callum.

"Why not me?"

She gave him a look as though he was mad and waved at his wings. "Because there's a reward out for your return and you're hardly inconspicuous."

Though she was right, he still needed to go. He'd made a promise to the colonel. He would keep a low profile, slip into the city, and out again before anyone noticed he was there.

Folding his arms across his chest, he sat back but didn't say anything further.

Tannis actually liked Pleasure City—she wouldn't have wanted to live there, but the occasional visit was fun. The place was vibrant, full of color and noise. She'd even done some shopping. Janey had appeared slightly perplexed when she'd told her she wanted help picking new clothes—well, it was a first.

But she had bad news for the rest of the crew. Unfortunately, when they arrived back, there was no one around to give it to. The ship appeared curiously quiet as she strolled onto the bridge.

Alex and Jon had shifted and gone out to do whatever werewolves did in the dark—she wasn't sure she wanted to know. Rico had warned them to be careful. Jon had just grinned and they'd headed off into the perpetual night.

Tannis had left everyone else with instructions not to leave the ship until she returned. Only the promise that they could have a trip into the city if all was clear had kept the crew from mutiny.

So where the hell was everybody?

Because all was not clear. There were comms about the kidnapping and reward all over the city, and she was just about to give out the "good" news that everyone was confined to ship. Except just about "everyone" was conspicuous by their absence. Only Daisy was present, and she looked decidedly shifty.

At that moment, Alex strolled onto the bridge, hands shoved in the pockets of her hot-pink jumpsuit. She appeared relaxed. "Have you told her yet?"

Daisy shook her head, her ponytail swinging. "No."

"Told me what?" Tannis said.

"Where is everyone?" Janey asked, as she and Skylar stepped onto the bridge.

"I was just about to find out."

"They've gone," Alex said.

"Gone? Who's gone and where?"

"Callum, Rico, and Jon."

"Jesus," Tannis muttered. "Is no one capable of taking orders on this ship? Did I not say, 'do not leave the ship'? Is that so hard to understand?"

"So where have they gone?" Skylar sounded way too reasonable.

"We're not sure," Daisy said. "It was Callum's fault."

Irritation pricked at her nerve endings. He was turning out to be more trouble than he was worth. "Why doesn't that surprise me?"

"It was just after Alex and Jon turned up. Callum came and told them he wanted to go into the city. Said he had something important to do and apparently he's never been to Pleasure City—fancy that—living all that time and never—"

"Will you get on with it?" Tannis ground out.

Daisy pursed her lips but continued. "Well, Rico told him no. That you'd said none of us were to leave the ship. There was a bit of an argument. You know, I really don't think Callum is good at taking orders. He seemed to back down and stalked off in a sulk. Next thing we know, he's pinched a speeder and set out on his own." She giggled. "Rico wasn't happy. In fact, he was livid. He took Jon and they set off after Callum, but that was an hour ago."

"Have they called in?"

"No. But I'm sure they'll be all right. They'll catch up with Callum. Rico might punch him again—or Jon might—I don't think Jon likes him very much—then they'll bring him back."

Tannis tried to ignore the worry gnawing at her insides. Janey was right; chances were they would all get home without any problems. But bloody Callum was hardly likely to blend into the crowd with those wings. "Try and get hold of them. If you can, stop them before they get into the city. There are pictures of Callum blazoned over every building in Pleasure City."

She paced the bridge and choked back the urge to rant. Why the hell couldn't he have stayed put? And what the hell did he want in Pleasure City?

Stupid question.

He'd been trying to get it on with her since he'd come on board. No doubt, when he'd failed, he'd decided to go somewhere he could guarantee a more certain result. There were more pleasure providers on Trakis Two than the rest of the known universe put together. The idea of Callum screwing one of them filled her with rage.

She tried to tell herself that her anger was because she'd

ordered him not to leave, but she knew there was more to it than that. The thought of him with another woman made her blood boil. Maybe she didn't want him, but that didn't mean anyone else was going to get him.

"Wait," Janey said. "It looks like they're back. They're pulling up outside right now."

Tannis hurried from the bridge and down to the docking bay. Through the open double doors, she could see Jon and Callum exiting the speeder. They both appeared okay, and some of the tension left her. Though she was still going to give him a bollocking.

She waited until they had entered the docking bay then strode up to stand in front of Callum, hands on her hips. His expression was closed, but irritation flickered in his eyes as he looked at her.

"Just which part of 'do not leave the ship' did you not understand?"

Callum shrugged. "I wanted to see the city. I—"

"Wanted to get himself a blow job more like," Jon interrupted.

Callum ignored the comment. "I was going to keep a low profile. If these assholes hadn't come along, I'd have been in and out without anyone noticing."

"You had half the bloody city on your tail by the time we caught up with you."

Callum opened his mouth, closed it, hugged his cloak tighter around himself, and stalked away. Tannis watched until he'd disappeared then turned to Jon.

"Where's Rico?"

"They got him."

"Who got him?"

"One of the many groups who decided to go for that reward. Rico covered us while we got away, but I'm pretty sure he was overpowered."

"Shit."

"Yeah, that about covers it. I was just bringing His Leadership back, and then I'm heading out there. We'll find him."

"I'm coming with you," Skylar said from behind them.

Tannis turned to see Skylar and Alex loitering in the open doorway.

"The three of us will go," Tannis said. "Alex, you stay here, get yourself a blaster, point it at His Majesty, and make sure he doesn't even breathe without permission."

"Will do."

"You two, come with me."

They took the speeder into Pleasure City. She wasn't too concerned. Rico hadn't lasted this long without being able to look after himself, but something or someone must have stopped him from returning to the ship. He had an unfortunate habit of pissing people off—especially if he didn't like them.

Tannis drove, Jon giving her directions, and soon they were into the clamor of the city. Her hands gripped the controls as she willed the vehicles in front to shift faster. After five minutes stuck unmoving in the traffic, she pulled the speeder into a parking space. The atmosphere hit her as soon as she climbed down. Music spilled out from the bars that edged the street, clashing with the sound of speeders and the raucous cries of the street vendors. The stench of fumes hung heavy on the air, mixed with the nauseating scent of every sort of food available to man.

"Look at that," Skylar said.

Tannis was looking. The whole side of a building was taken up by an enormous picture of Callum. It must have been taken as he did his flying stunt on Trakis Five because it showed him with black wings outspread. Then his picture vanished and was replaced by a collage of the crew of *El Cazador*. Rico, Tannis, Jon, Skylar, Alex. Why did she suddenly have the overwhelming feeling that everyone was staring at her? Maybe because they were.

"Hey, I always wanted to be famous," she muttered.

"Come on," Jon said. "Let's keep moving." His hand rested lightly on the laser pistol strapped to his thigh. Skylar also looked ready to draw, and it occurred to Tannis that coming into the city might not have been a good move, but then she hadn't realized there were pictures of them as well as Callum.

"Shit. So how do we find Rico?"

"I was thinking of going to the spot we last saw him and following the trail of bodies. This way."

"Sounds like a plan." It sounded like a shit plan actually, but there wasn't a lot of choice. Rico still hadn't answered his comm unit.

Jon led them down the main thoroughfare of the city. Bright, flashing lights and loud music bombarded them from every side. "Down there," he said, waving at one of the many side streets.

A knot of people had formed at the end of the alley, milling around what looked to be two dead bodies. When they got closer, she saw one of them had been decapitated, his head sliced cleanly from his body. It lay about a foot away, the eyes open and distinctly surprised.

"Looks like Rico's been here."

Rico had a sword, and he liked to use it.

The group were looking their way now and muttering among themselves. Tannis glanced over her shoulder and realized more people had entered the alley behind them, effectively cutting them off. "Shit. Anyone got any ideas."

"Shoot our way out before any more of them get here."

"Too late."

A whole speeder full of them had arrived dressed in the uniform of Pleasure City's militia. They'd parked their vehicle across the entrance to the alley and jumped out.

Their attention was on the dead bodies right now, but who knew how long that would last.

Not long at all.

One man separated from the crowd and took a step toward them. He looked from her to Skylar to Jon, recognition dawning on his heavy features.

"Hey, it's them," he shouted. "The ones who kidnapped Callum Meridian."

# CHAPTER 5

"Great, just great," Tannis growled. Everyone had turned their way now, including the local militia. Their pistols were still holstered, but it looked as if that was about to change. "Let's get the hell out of here."

"Good idea," Skylar said.

They all drew their weapons and Tannis searched for the best target. The militia looked a good bet, as they blocked the entrance to the alley, but they also appeared the best armed.

"Let's do this."

She flicked her laser to stun—no point annoying the local force more than necessary—and aimed at the leader of the small group. Then she spun around and shot the fat man still pointing a pudgy finger at them. He went down with a squeal of pain and chaos erupted. The militia returned fire. Tannis deflected the shots with ease, but they weren't making any headway, and things could only get worse if reinforcements arrived. Why hadn't she thought to bring a blaster or a few stun grenades?

A second speeder had stopped at the end of the alley and disgorged its crew. For the first time, it occurred to her that they were in real trouble, that they might not manage to fight their way out of this. Maybe they should give themselves up. Callum could explain they hadn't really kidnapped him, and they intended to return him . . . eventually.

At the thought of Callum, her temper rose. This was his fault. Arrogant bastard. If she got out of this, she was going back there and she was going to—

One shot got through, singeing the skin of her arm, and she swore loudly. "Crap, that hurts."

It looked like these guys weren't going to give them a chance to explain anything. They meant business, and their weapons weren't set to stun. The stench of burning flesh filled her nostrils. Her burning flesh.

"Any ideas?" she yelled over the noise of the laser blasts.

When she got no answer, she glanced sideways. Legs braced, Jon fired off continuous shots, his eyes gleaming with excitement. She shook her head. Next time she took on a new crew member, she was going to get someone nice and levelheaded. Skylar was no better, though at least she looked her way when Tannis yelled again.

"I'll stay," Skylar shouted. "Hold them off while you two get away."

Tannis didn't like that idea. She didn't leave anyone behind.

"You know it makes sense," Skylar continued. "They can't kill me. You can work out how to get me out later. Callum will do something."

It did make sense, but Tannis still didn't like it.

A huge scarlet-and-black speeder hurtled down the center of street. It collided with the speeder still disgorging its crew, and men flew in all directions. The shooting eased as the militia turned to look.

The new vehicle had stopped momentarily, but now turned and headed down the alley, straight for them. They leaped out of the way, only just escaping. The speeder pulled up beside Tannis and the door was flung open from the inside.

"Come with me if you want to live." Rico grinned down at them. "Sorry—I've always wanted to say that. All the same, I suggest you get in now."

Whoever was in the back of the vehicle was shooting a continuous stream of laser shots around the alley, completely random, but very effective. Everyone had dived for cover.

Tannis scrambled up into the front of the hovering speeder. Jon and Skylar climbed in behind and the door slammed shut. She glanced over her shoulder at the other person, still blasting shots out the window at the cowering crowds.

"Hey, Sardi, you can stop shooting now," Rico drawled as he spun the speeder around and headed out of the alley. He rose high above the other traffic and soon they were whizzing away from the scene of the fight.

They traveled for about five minutes, then mingled in traffic with the other vehicles. Though it was hard to mingle in something as ostentatious as this scarlet-and-black monster of a speeder.

"I don't think anyone is following," Rico said and pulled over into a parking space. He turned to her. "Having a few problems back there?"

"We came to rescue you."

"Sweet, but it's just as well. I didn't need rescuing."

"So where have you been?"

Rico gestured behind him at the stranger who sat behind him. "This is Sardi. He's an old . . . friend of mine."

"Shit, Rico, not another of your old friends. We nearly didn't survive the last one."

Rico ignored the comment. "Sardi was going for the reward, then he realized it was me, and we went for a drink instead."

"You've been drinking while we were out trying to rescue you?" She leaned in close and caught a whiff of alcohol fumes. "Are you drunk?"

"I may be a little inebriated. We haven't seen each other in a while—we've been reminiscing about old times."

Tannis looked at the other man closely. He appeared to be human, though the air around him rippled with a strange energy. And even sitting he was exceptionally tall, and he wore a hat that made him appear even taller.

"Is he human?" she asked Rico.

"He's . . . never mind."

"What an insult," Sardi said. He doffed his hat and bowed low to her. In the thick dark hair just above his forehead nestled a pair of horns. Either, he was some sort of GM with goat DNA, or he was a . . .

"I am a demon and proud of it." He grinned and grabbed her hand where it rested on the back of the seat. He raised it to his mouth and kissed the palm. "Charmed."

A shiver of something like magic ran through her from the point of contact, and Tannis pulled her hand free and rubbed it against her pants leg. Sardi grinned, not seeming at all put out.

"We need to get out of here," Tannis said.

"Tell me where you parked the speeder, and we can let Sardi have his vehicle back." She gave him directions and rested her head against the seat. It took only minutes.

Sardi got out with them, towering over Rico and Jon, who were both big men. He gave them all a little bow, then turned to Rico. "Sure you won't join me? We made a good team once."

"Nah, I'll pass, thanks, Sard. Maybe next time."

"No problem. You never did like to stay in one place." He handed a flask to Rico. "For the journey home—your little captain looks like she needs a drink."

Rico turned to her, his brows drawing together. "You

okay?" His gaze ran down over her, snagging on her arm. "You've been hit?"

"It's nothing. I'll see to it on the ship."

"Okay, let's go then."

Tannis could feel her anger rising as they sped through the darkness. Her arm hurt where she'd caught the laser blast, and her head throbbed.

No one put her crew at risk.

She was an idiot, and this whole thing had been a huge mistake. Just like everyone had told her. Why couldn't she have listened to them and never picked the bastard up? He probably didn't think it mattered if her crew were hurt. He probably thought of them as expendable. Hell, he probably thought of *her* as expendable.

Or why couldn't she have listened to Rico and tossed him out the airlock?

"Stop grinding your teeth. There are people trying to sleep back here." Rico was in the rear with Skylar, while Jon was beside Tannis, swigging from the flask. She occasionally felt his eyes on her.

"He wasn't going for a blow job."

"What?"

"You know I said at the ship that Callum was going for sex. Well he wasn't."

Tannis glanced sideways at him. "Why would I care?"

"You do care, and I still think this whole job is a mistake, and I still hate his guts, and I still think he's an arrogant asshole, but he wasn't going for sex."

"Christ, the last thing I need is relationship advice from Mr. I-Want-To-Be-Alone."

"I've changed," Jon said virtuously. "I've found the love of a good woman, and I am a changed man."

"Jesus." She cast him an incredulous glare. "What is that you're drinking?"

"Excellent stuff," Rico said. "Sardi might be a complete bastard, but he knows where to get good liquor."

But Jon was right. He had changed. It was hard to believe this was the same person they'd broken out of the high-security prison on Trakis One only six weeks ago. He'd been a hard and embittered man who made his living killing people, until he'd been caught up in the machinations of the Collective. He'd been a loner, the last person she would ever have expected to fall in love, and especially not with someone like Alex. But if Jon could change, maybe she could as well. Wasn't there hope for everyone?

But even if she were to overcome her fears, there could never be any future for her and Callum Meridian. One day, he would presumably return to his job as Leader of the Universe, at which point their worlds were unlikely to cross again, even if she succeeded in getting the Meridian treatment. The best she could hope for was maybe he'd send her one of those mind messages every once in a while, for old time's sake.

He could have any woman he wanted. Why would he want her?

Shit. She couldn't believe she was thinking like this. She must be imbibing fumes from that flask. Still, she couldn't resist the question.

"What was he going for then?"

Jon shrugged. "Who knows?"

Did it really matter? He was a liability, a selfish bastard who thought of nothing but himself. He'd put Rico and Jon at risk and then the rest of the crew. No amount of money was worth risking the lives of her crew for an outsider.

"It doesn't matter." Suddenly, she felt tired. "It's finished."

She'd find another way to earn the money. Though once she'd pissed off Callum, as she fully intended to do as soon as they got back to *El Cazador,* she could probably kiss her chances of being accepted into the Collective good-bye. She sighed.

"Here." Jon handed her the flask. "You sound like you need this."

She unscrewed the top and took a sip of the smoky liquid. It burned her throat, settled in her belly like fire. She took another swallow.

As the alcohol went through her system, the anger started to rise again. She liked the anger much better than the self-pity. By the time the speeder came to a halt beside *El Cazador,* she'd emptied the flask and managed to build herself up into a fine rage.

She stalked up the ramp, through the docking bay, up the next ramp, and found them in the conference room. Their heads close together, Alex and Janey were talking, Alex with a blaster resting across her lap. Callum sat across the room. He looked relaxed, unworried, and her fury ratcheted a notch.

He rose slowly as Tannis strode into the room. Closing the distance between them, she eyed him and tried to tell herself she shouldn't do this. And failed.

Coming to a halt in front of him, she drew back her fist and punched him on the nose. He collapsed into the chair behind him, more from shock probably than the strength of her blow.

She stared down at him. He returned her gaze with those glowing eyes, and she had to force herself not to be sucked into their depths.

"I want you off the ship," she said. "In five minutes. You're free to call for someone to pick you up as soon as we're gone."

She whirled around and left the room. And almost ran smack into Rico. He put up a hand to stop her headlong flight. "Are you all right?"

"Of course I'm all right. Why the freaking hell shouldn't I be all right?"

His brows drew together, and he turned to Skylar. "Go check that everything's okay, sweetheart. I want to talk to the captain."

"No problem."

"What do you want to talk about?" Now she sounded sullen. She shook her head. "Sorry."

He put a hand on her arm and steered her toward her cabin.

Once inside, she threw herself on the scarlet couch and stared at the ceiling. Her room was one place where the black-and-silver decor didn't prevail. When she'd come on board, the whole ship had been that way, but as she'd started to feel at home, she'd introduced color into her own room. Well red at least, shades of red, scarlet and crimson, deep dark reds. She loved red.

Rico disappeared inside the bathroom, came out a moment later with the small medical kit from her cabinet. He placed it on the table, then sat next to her. "Let me look at your arm."

"It's nothing," she snapped.

He gave her a long look, and the air left her lungs in a huge sigh.

She unbuttoned her shirt and pulled it off one shoulder.

Holding onto her wrist, he turned her arm so he could study the burn. "You're right, it's nothing. I'll just spray it with sealant and painkiller."

She didn't argue as he sprayed the wound, and in fact, she did feel marginally better as the pain receded. Refastening her shirt, she sat back.

Rico settled himself into the seat opposite, long legs stretched out in front of him. "Well?"

"Well, it's done. We're out of here, and he's staying. I suppose the whole Meridian thing was only a dream." She forced a grin. "Who wants to turn out like him anyway? I'm guessing those aliens must be real assholes."

"Maybe. But I reckon it's not the alien part of him that's causing the problems right now."

"It's not?"

"No, I'm guessing it's the human bits."

She frowned. "Why do you say that?"

"You know on Earth he was famous?"

Her gaze flashed to his face in shock. "You knew him?"

"Not personally, but as I said, he was famous. Don't tell Daisy I said this, or she'll be all over him, but he was this daredevil pilot—more kills than the rest of them put together. Nerves of steel and a complete adrenaline junky."

"You sound like you're the one with a crush on him now."

Rico grinned. "Maybe back then—a man crush. I wanted to be a pilot, and he was the best."

Yeah, she'd bet he was. "Your point is?"

"You don't go from that to being a bloody politician. He's been living a life he's not suited to, playing a role for five hundred years, and I'm betting he's bored out of his mind. He might tell himself it's the Meridian, but he's lying. It's not that he's *not* human, he's just forgotten how to act it."

"It doesn't matter," she said. "It's finished. We're out of here and he can comm someone to come and pick him up. You know, I need a drink."

"Well, it just so happens I have some." He pulled a silver flask out of his pocket and placed it on the table, then got to his feet. "Unfortunately, it's mine and not Sardi's good stuff, but it'll do the trick. Take the night off. Give yourself a break. We'll sort this out—just don't give up on that dream yet."

When he was gone, Tannis got up and shuffled across the room to stand in front of the mirror and stare at herself. She wasn't beautiful. She'd never been beautiful. She didn't think she was ugly either, and strangely, the signs of her nonhuman DNA—the yellow eyes with their narrow slits, the faint luminosity to her skin—had never bothered her. Probably because she had grown up hating the humans around her. She was into action, not thinking. Thinking only got you into trouble—she'd leave it to the politicians. Like Callum.

But maybe it was time to give up on the dream. She'd clung to it for so long. How many nights had she fallen asleep in her cell at the research center and dreamed of the beautiful Collective woman. Her angel. The one person who'd been kind to her. How sad was she? But she didn't want to give up. There were whole worlds out there to explore, and one lifetime was never enough.

Besides, she didn't want to die.

After returning to the sofa, she put her feet up on the table and picked up Rico's flask. She unscrewed the top and took a deep swallow. Then she rested her head against the cushion and tried not to think. Closing her eyes, she saw an image of Callum's face and knew she would never see it again.

It was for the best. Really it was.

# CHAPTER 6

Blood trickled down over his lips and chin.

His nose was broken. Again.

Alex had disappeared, probably to check that her man was all right, but Janey was still in her seat watching him, her expression blank. She rose gracefully to her feet, strolled across, and handed him a cloth. He wiped the blood away and glanced at her.

"You want to take a punch at me as well?" he asked.

A grin flashed across her face. "Tannis doesn't let anyone mess with her crew. She's very protective."

"I noticed."

For a brief second, he wondered how it would feel to have Tannis protect him. Never going to happen.

He dabbed at his nose and winced. But the strange thing was, he didn't blame her. He'd been an idiot, and he'd nearly gotten himself taken prisoner and Jon and Rico killed. He'd made a promise and he'd had to go, but maybe he should have explained the situation. They could have gone with him, made sure he stayed out of sight. He just wasn't used to this clandestine stuff. He also wasn't used to explaining himself.

The visit had depressed him as well. Rosalie had been so old. She didn't have much longer, but she'd seemed strangely happy. He'd stayed and talked to her about the colonel. She was clearly still in love with him, but believed she had made the right decision.

Callum didn't know. He'd never been in love . . .

He didn't want to leave *El Cazador*. For all sorts of reasons. Some of which he wasn't willing to examine too closely just yet. He hadn't realized quite how restricted and stultifying his life had been. The first couple of hundred years had been a challenge. Planets to discover, finding out they were telepathic, then realizing they were immortal and almost impossible to kill. Extending the Collective and gaining great wealth in the process.

Gradually, their power had grown. But at what point had he decided he wanted to rule the goddamn universe? It had just happened, like ropes of responsibility, wrapping themselves around him and slowly tightening.

For the past century or so, he might as well have been buried alive. What was the point of immortality if you didn't care whether you lived or died? But to care, you had to have something worth caring about. For him, it had always been things rather than people. Things had long ago lost their meaning, and he had no one he cared enough about to take their place.

He was in danger of getting maudlin.

Since he'd boarded *El Cazador*, he'd felt as though he was waking up. Even the pain in his nose reminded him he was alive.

Rico appeared in the open doorway and every muscle in Callum's body locked solid as tension radiated through him.

Yeah, he might have deserved that punch from Tannis, but no way was he willing to stand still while someone else took a potshot at him. This time he was getting in there first. He spread his wings, his fist clenched at his side, and he came up on the balls of his feet ready to move fast.

Rico strolled into the room. He cast a glance in Janey's direction and waved at the doorway. Her eyes widened slightly as she glanced from Rico to Callum, then left the room.

Rico reached up and pressed the panel by the doors and they slid shut, leaving Callum alone with the vampire. Why? An audience hadn't bothered Rico the last time he'd hit him. What was different now? Had he come to finish the job and didn't want any witnesses?

He was also armed, and Callum still hadn't gotten hold of that gun he wanted.

"Stand down," Rico said. "I'm not here to punch you . . . this time."

So what was he here for? Maybe he was going to do the whole vampire thing and drain Callum dry. His hand moved up to his throat without conscious thought.

Rico must have caught the movement because a grin flashed across his face.

"I'm not here to eat you either." He licked his lips. "Thanks to your stunt earlier, I've had plenty today."

Callum frowned. He was supposed to be the mind reader, and he didn't like the idea of anyone being able to read him so easily.

Rico must have caught that thought as well. "I can't read minds, but I've had plenty of practice reading people, and you're pretty transparent.

"I am?"

"Oh yeah. You're not happy because no one's doing what you say, but at the same time, you don't want to go back. You've had a few hundred years of ruling the universe and you're bored out of your mind. I bet that broken nose is the first thing you've felt in years."

The words so exactly mirrored Callum's earlier thoughts

that he turned away to hide his expression. Shoving his hands in his pockets, he paced the room for a minute, trying to work out what it was the vampire did want. In the end, he decided the easiest thing was to just ask. Even if he had an inkling that he wasn't going to like the answer.

"So what do you want?"

Rico pursed his lips, but a small smile still played across his features, and irritation flicked at Callum's raw nerve endings. So the vamp found him amusing, did he?

Rico's smile broadened. "You know, you shouldn't take yourself so seriously."

"Just get on with it."

"Okay. Ricardo Sanchez, vampire and relationship guidance counselor, at your service."

For a second, Callum was sure he hadn't heard right. "What?"

"I've decided it's not in our best interests for you to leave the ship at this time. I'm willing to give you one more chance to overcome your asshole tendencies."

"You are?" Callum had always thought himself quite bright, but he was finding this conversation hard to follow. "So you're not going to kill me, eat me, or throw me off the ship?"

"Not just yet. On the other hand, I'm not in charge."

"Why?" Callum asked. "Why aren't you in charge? I've read the reports—*El Cazador* belongs to you—why aren't you captain?"

"I like living on the ship, but I don't like responsibility. Tannis, on the other hand, loves telling people what to do— you might remember that—so this setup works well for both of us."

Callum wanted to ask where they'd met, since they seemed an unlikely coupling, but he decided it was a conversation for a later date. Right now, he wanted to know what was going on.

"And Tannis wants you off the ship," Rico continued. "You have about five minutes to change her mind."

"And how do I do that?"

"You're going to have to apologize. Can you remember how to apologize, flyboy?"

Callum tried to recall the last time he'd apologized to somebody. He couldn't bring it to mind. Maybe he'd never apologized in his life. Surely, that couldn't be true. He couldn't really be that much of an asshole. Could he? Maybe he'd never done anything he had to apologize for—he liked that idea better—but he didn't believe it.

Rico let out a short laugh. "If you're thinking that hard, I'm guessing the answer is no. Well a simple, 'Tannis, I'm sorry for being a dickhead and not following your excellent orders,' will suffice."

Callum turned the words over in his mind. They sounded painless enough. "I think I can do that."

"You don't sound too sure."

"No, I'm good."

"Excellent."

"But will it be enough? She seemed pretty pissed off."

"Probably not. So you're going to have to offer her something she wants."

"What does she want?"

Rico seemed to think for a moment, and Callum got the notion he was considering what to say. What did Tannis want? And why wouldn't the vampire come right out and say it? "More money might do it," Rico said at last. "Tannis likes money."

Hmm, Tannis hadn't struck him as the mercenary type.

Rico must have seen his doubts. "She's saving for the Meridian treatment."

Shock hit him in the gut, though he didn't know why. Most of the world's population were saving for the Meridian treatment, so why not Tannis? Another less pleasant thought occurred. Was that why she was fascinated by him? Because she was; he'd sensed her watching him. Was that because she wanted something from him—like everyone else in the goddamn universe? But as quickly as it had come, the idea vanished. If that had been the case, she would have been a little nicer to him. He stroked a finger down his nose where she had punched him only fifteen minutes ago. No, he reckoned Tannis was the type who would say and do what she meant no matter what the consequences.

"So are we good?" Rico asked.

"Yeah. Money is one thing I have plenty of." He studied Rico. "Why are you doing this? I got the distinct impression that you would have preferred it if I'd never come on board."

"That may be true, but it's too late now—you're here." For a moment, Rico was silent and Callum presumed he wasn't going to get an answer, and then the vampire shrugged. "For as long as I've known her, Tannis has had a dream. Now she's giving up on it, and I don't believe she's ready to let go." He took a step closer and poked a finger at Callum's chest. "But you fuck up her dreams, and I will kill you." He smiled with a flash of fang. "That sound like a good deal to you?"

"You could try."

"And I'm betting I'd succeed. You've grown soft, forgotten what it's like to live on the edge."

He was probably right. But from now on, that was changing. Callum was going to toughen up.

"So what are we waiting for?" Rico said. "Go to it, flyboy. And when you apologize, try and look as though you're sorry."

Callum twisted his features into what he hoped was an expression of contrition.

"*Christos*," Rico muttered. "But I suppose that's going to have to do."

Tannis stared into the viewer. Callum stood in the corridor, hands in his pockets, and for the first time, the ingrained arrogance was missing from his features. She couldn't quite work out what had replaced it, and she frowned.

Why hadn't Rico gotten him off the ship, and why weren't they in the air by now?

He pressed the buzzer again, and her hand hovered over the panel as she tried to decide whether to let him in. But she'd downed half of Rico's flask of whiskey, and she was feeling way too mellow to be mean.

In the end, she decided to open the door, tell him to get off her ship—again—and then finish the rest of the flask. With a bit of luck, she'd pass out, and when she woke, this whole thing would be in the past. She could forget about Callum and Meridian and . . .

She slammed her palm down and the door slid open.

"I'm sorry," Callum said.

The words didn't make sense. Not coming out of that particular mouth anyway. "Pardon?"

He took a deep breath. "Tannis, I'm sorry for being a dickhead and not following your excellent orders."

Still no sense. She put her hand back on the panel and the door shut. Leaning against the wall, she closed her eyes and fought the need to lie down—she was obviously hallucinating.

The buzzer sounded again. She straightened, turned to face the door, and placed her palm on the panel.

"Get off my ship."

"Can I come in first? There's something I need to say to you."

When she continued to stand there, unmoving, a small

frown flickered across his face as though he didn't quite know what to do next. "Please?"

Shock made her stand aside. She guessed she might be one of the only people in the civilized universe who had heard Callum Meridian say the word "please."

He stepped past her into the room and looked around. "Hey, this is nice. It suits you. You going to shut the door?"

"No."

Unease shifted inside her. No way was she going to change her mind, but this nice-guy approach made her nervous. She stared at him through her lashes, and he shifted then cleared his throat.

"As I said—I'm sorry."

"As I said—get off my ship."

"I won't do it again. From now on, I follow orders."

Tannis snorted. "Yeah, right."

She moved across to the table and picked up the half-empty flask, took a swallow.

"Can I?" He nodded at the flask.

"Why not?"

He took a sip, coughed, took a gulp. "Jesus, that's good. It's a long time since I tasted whiskey. Where the hell did you get it? I thought this stuff was illegal."

"Rico and the Trog make it. Rico designed some sort of setup, and the Trog built it."

He took another swig. "How about I double the fee?"

She was so tempted, but it wasn't the money tempting her. Or not only the money—he was talking a huge sum. At the thought of him staying, something unraveled inside her, and some of the cold, hard lump of despair in her middle dissolved. And that was dangerous, because however amenable he appeared right now, that wasn't who he was. He was a politician; he'd no doubt been using the art of manipulation since before the Earth had died.

Still, she was tempted.

The wings were folded neatly against his back, and she could see the tips above his broad shoulders and down beside his long, muscular thighs. He wore what looked like a pair of Rico's black leather pants and a sleeveless T-shirt that probably belonged to Jon—Rico never wore T-shirts—that he'd somehow managed to get on over the wings. She'd really have to ask him how he managed that. Or she would if it wasn't for the fact that he was leaving five minutes ago. His shoulders and arms were bare, the skin smooth and golden over the swell of muscle.

The rest of the cold, hard lump melted, then heated up to simmering. She forced her gaze from his chest up to his face and caught a small glimpse of triumph in his purple eyes before the expression was blanked.

"No." His eyes narrowed on her. He took another sip and handed back the flask. Tannis drank automatically and waited while Callum stood with his head tilted to one side as he considered her. She wished she was a mind reader and could tell what he was thinking.

"Look," she said, forcing the words out of her reluctant lips. "There's no amount of money you can offer me. Just go."

"How about I don't offer you money?"

"What?"

"How about I offer you Meridian?"

She licked her lips. His gaze followed the movement. "I don't understand." And she didn't, though her mind raced to come up with ideas.

He strolled across the room and sank down onto the sofa, patted the seat beside him. "Come and sit down, and I'll tell you."

Unable to stop herself, she sidled around and sat in the far corner, but his thigh was still only a foot from her own. She waited to feel the fear and revulsion, but when nothing happened, she sat back and tried to relax. It was important that he didn't realize how much he unnerved her. "So tell me."

"Once I meet up with Venna, my scientific officer, we'll be heading to Trakis Seven. Why don't you come along? There's Meridian on Trakis Seven."

He was the devil tempting her. He even looked like she might imagine the devil looking, with his black wings, his almost inhuman beauty. "I can wait," she said. "I'll soon have enough money."

"Hmm, maybe. But most likely not. Are you aware Meridian has become scarce in the recent years?"

"I know the price went up. I just presumed you were getting greedy."

"No—it appears there's a finite supply. Oh, I'm guessing, given time, the planet would produce more, but not in your lifetime. In the first years, we found the caches easily. There were so many. But for the past fifty years, only two have been found. One has been used. The other is sold, but the buyer hasn't yet taken possession."

"And it's on Trakis Seven?"

"The Meridian doesn't leave Trakis Seven. The buyer goes there for the treatment—it loses its potency away from the planet, turns into so much useless crap. We tried in the early years because Trakis Seven is not a pleasant place to visit, even for us."

She eyed him suspiciously. "Are you telling the truth?"

"Would I lie?"

"Hell, yeah. You're a politician—you probably find it easier than telling the truth."

A smile flickered across his face. "Maybe, but in this instance I'm not. You could always check with Skylar—she can confirm what I've told you—at least about the treatment. Nobody but the Council is aware that it's running out."

Tannis thought for a minute. The flask was still in her

hand and she reached beneath the table, pulled out two glasses, and emptied the last of the whiskey into them. She handed one to Callum and took a sip of her own while she thought through what he had told her. The whole Meridian treatment was shrouded in mystery, so she couldn't know for sure whether he was telling the truth. But as he'd said, she could always check with Skylar.

Anticipation bubbled up inside her. She tamped it down and told herself to be cautious. It wasn't in her nature to be careful, maybe it never had been, but she'd spent too much time around Rico for caution to hold any appeal. This was her dream, to get the Meridian treatment and live forever. Once she had that, she could stick her finger up at the memory of those bastards at the research center who had taunted her with promises of an early death in the Meridian mines.

"Tannis?"

"Give me a minute. I'm thinking."

Once she had the Meridian treatment, she could relax and think about what she wanted to do with the rest of forever. Go after the people who had run that center. Maybe she would get over it, finally put the past behind her once she had found and punished those responsible.

But she also knew that was only part of the reason why her blood thumped in her veins. If she said yes, Callum would stay. Just a little while longer. She sipped her drink and studied him, trying to work out what drew her to him. He was utterly gorgeous, all high cheekbones, arched brows, a full sensual lower lip, those mesmerizing eyes. What was he really doing on her ship?

"I don't understand why," she said. "Why are you here? Why don't you just get your own people to pick you up and take you to Trakis Seven?"

"I don't trust them. They want to shut all the research down and pretend this isn't happening. And they're scared, and scared people make rash, stupid decisions."

"What about this Venna? This scientific officer you're meeting up with—do you trust her?"

"She's been researching what we are since we started to suspect that Meridian wasn't what we thought. She wants to know the truth as much as I do."

"Hmm. There has to be more."

He studied her speculatively for a minute, head cocked on one side as though he didn't know what to make of her.

"What?" Her tone was belligerent.

"You're right, that's not everything." He smiled and his teeth were very white and even. "I want to explore this thing between us."

"There's a 'thing' between us?"

He nodded.

*Holy freaking moly. There was a thing between them.*

"Do you know how long it is since I've been with a woman?" he asked.

"Yeah, of course I do. How the fuck would I know that?" But she was interested, and she had no clue where he was going with this. Well, actually, she did have a clue, but it seemed pretty damn unbelievable.

"Well, it's been a long, long time."

And why did that comment make a little glow start low down in her belly, where she'd never had a little glow before? She shifted in her seat.

"And I'm betting it's been a long time for you as well."

Yeah, that was right.

A frown formed on his face when she didn't answer. "You're not a virgin, are you?"

"No," she scoffed. It was a lie but none of his goddamn business.

"Good."

Good? Did that mean he was looking for an experienced lover? Well, no one fit that description in here.

"You know I noticed you that first meeting?"

She stared at him in disbelief. "No, I didn't know you noticed me then—was this before or after you tried to kill us all?"

"That was politics."

"Well, that makes me feel a whole load better."

Annoyance flashed in his eyes at her sarcasm, but was quickly gone. "I did notice you, and that was something that I wasn't expecting. I haven't wanted a woman in years. I thought it was the Meridian, just another side effect, and then I saw you and—"

"And it was love at first sight. Aw, that's so sweet and a total load of bullshit." She couldn't believe he was trying to get around her like this. Talk about low. Her hand went to the laser pistol at her waist; she fingered the trigger and wondered whether she should shoot him.

"Not love at first sight, no. I'm not even sure I believe in love. Maybe once I did, but not anymore—occupational hazard of living a long time, I guess. No, it was more in the way of lust at first sight, but that was good enough for me." He grinned and for the first time he looked wholly human. "You're the reason I picked this ship. I believed I was no longer a man—you made me think otherwise."

The slimy bastard might not have done it in a while, but he hadn't lost the ability to flirt. Even acknowledging that, and the fact that she knew he was trying to manipulate her, her heartbeat still fluttered. To her complete and utter amazement, she was softening toward him. The sensation was so new that when he reached out and took her hand, tugging it away from where it rested on the butt of her pistol, she didn't attempt to pull away. He held it lightly, turned it palm up, and stroked it with the pad of her thumb. A tingle ran from her hand, up her arm, then down through her body, to settle in the hollow place where her stomach used to be. He lifted the hand to his mouth and placed a soft kiss in the center of her palm. The tip of his tongue touched her skin, moist and incredibly hot, and flames burned along her nerve endings.

Tannis locked her muscles rigid to stop from squirming, but her whole body trembled. And not with fear. Part of her told herself to get up, show him the door, keep this on a strict business footing. The rest of her . . . Well she didn't understand what the rest of her wanted, but whatever it was, she was sure she'd never wanted it before.

"I know you feel the same," he murmured.

"I do?"

Is this how he felt? All hot and heavy. She'd never understood the desires that seemed to drive other people, never known why they went to such lengths for something as messy and unpleasant as sex. Now, for the first time she had an inkling.

"I saw the way you looked at me that day."

"You did?"

Jesus, she must sound like a complete moron, but her brain refused to cooperate—in fact, the traitorous organ had turned to mush.

"Yes, it made me hot and hard." He laughed softly. "And you're doing it again right now."

"I am?" Her voice came out as a squeak. She cleared her throat and tried again. "I am?"

"Oh, yes. Come here." He pulled on her hand, and she almost fell toward him. Her other hand shot out for balance and landed on his chest. She could feel the hard muscle beneath her, the heat of his skin radiating through the soft material. He tugged a little harder and she found herself pressed up against him. She waited for the sense of revulsion to overwhelm her, to give her the strength to back off. But nothing even remotely like revulsion came along to help her.

Breathing in deeply, she caught the scent of warm male, musky and strange to her, and she realized that she hadn't been this close to a man since Rico had carried her on board *El Cazador* all those years ago. The thought pulled her up short, but then Callum's hand slipped under her chin and lifted her face. For a moment she gazed into his eyes, they'd darkened to deep, vibrant purple, and she lost herself in their depths, hardly even noticed his mouth lowering to hers.

His lips were incredibly soft and insistent.

For someone who claimed he hadn't done it in a long time, he was certainly a good kisser. Not that she had much to compare it to—nothing really. Then she forgot about everything, as he parted her lips and his tongue pushed inside.

She stiffened but then relaxed against him with a tiny sigh. Maybe he sensed her incipient fear, because he kept his movements slow, almost languid, as he filled her mouth with the hot, wet thrust of his tongue, and her body melted against him, her insides turning molten.

He shifted her so her back was against the cushions, and his body pressed into her, one of his legs sliding between hers, all without breaking the kiss. She clasped his shoulders, then slid her hands around his neck and into the silky softness of his hair to hold him tight against her.

The kiss was more insistent now and his body was hard, his hip thrusting against her, so she could feel the length of his erection pressing against her. Now was the moment she should start to panic, but it never came, and a sense of wonder filled her.

Tentatively, she stroked her tongue against the velvet of his and he went still, a groan rising up in his throat.

"Hey, flyboy, I told you to apologize. I didn't tell you to stick your tongue down her throat."

Tannis nearly jumped out of her skin at Rico's drawled words. She drew away from Callum, turned quickly, and found Rico leaning against the open door with an amused expression on his face. His words slowly penetrated her brain.

"Shit. *You* told him to apologize. I can't believe this." She ran a hand through her hair. Callum still held her, but loosely, and she pulled away. For a second, his fingers tightened on her arms, but then he let her go.

Her brain was slowly starting to function, but it wasn't making much sense. Rico had told him to apologize? Why the hell would he do that when he'd been so vocal about wanting Callum off the ship? Why would he help him to stay? And what else had he told him? That she wanted the Meridian treatment, no doubt. The one thing she wanted more than anything else.

That was why Callum had known to make the offer.

But what about the other stuff—the wanting her? She needed time to think this through.

In the meantime, if Rico had told him all that, what was he doing here now? "So why are you here?"

He shrugged. "I thought I'd better check up on you."

"Why the hell would you need to check up on me? I can look after myself."

Rico actually looked a little discomforted. "Well, flyboy has already tried his luck once, and it occurred to me that he might try again. And you did say you were scared of sex."

Tannis glanced at Callum, who now stood with one shoulder leaning against the wall, an expression of avid curiosity on his face. He raised an eyebrow when she caught his gaze, but she turned to Rico.

"Jeez, thanks, Rico. I really wanted to share that bit of information!"

"Mind you—you didn't look scared. I was going to tiptoe away, but I thought I'd better be sure. Hard to tell with those wings in the way."

He crossed the room and picked up his flask from the

table, shook it, and pursed his lips when he realized it was empty.

"So I take it the job is back on?" he asked as he shoved it in his pocket.

"Yeah, I guess so." She nodded toward Callum. "Your new best friend over there just made me an offer I couldn't refuse."

Rico grinned. "I thought he might. How much did it take?"

"Not money."

"No?" A frown flickered across his face. "Hey, he's not paying you in kind, is he?"

Tannis ignored the comment. "He's paying me in Meridian."

Shock flashed across Rico's face. He glanced between the two of them. "And you said yes?"

"I hadn't yet. I was just getting round to it."

"Well, I think—"

"If you tell me one more time that I'm making a huge mistake, I swear, I will shoot you."

"I was going to say I think Daisy is readying for take-off. So I suppose I'd better go and let her know there's a change of plans, though it might be an idea to get off this planet anyway. Arrange a new rendezvous."

"Oh." Suddenly, she didn't want to be left alone with Callum. "Maybe I'll go tell Daisy myself." She needed time to decide whether she wanted to take this thing with Callum any further. She'd told him she didn't mix business with pleasure, but the truth was, she'd never been even the tiniest bit tempted to. She cast Callum a quick sideways glance and found his gaze fixed on her. A slow, knowing smile curled his lips, and a wave of heat washed over her. Her breasts ached, and her nipples tightened. He could do that with just a look?

Beside her, Rico coughed, and she swung around to face him.

"You sure you don't want to stay?" he asked.

"Yeah, I'm sure. But we need a meeting, say in half an hour, to decide how we're going to do this. " She strode across the room, but paused in the doorway to peer over her shoulder at Callum. "See yourself out."

# CHAPTER 7

Tannis knew he was behind her, but she didn't turn, just stayed where she was, gazing at the blank screen.

Everyone else was sleeping, or at least she presumed they were. She'd tried to, but sleep had eluded her, and in the end she'd given up and come up to the bridge. It was Daisy's turn on watch, but Tannis had offered to take over and she'd gone to bed.

How had Callum known she would be here? Or maybe he'd been expecting Daisy. But she didn't believe that. She'd avoided him since their kiss. He'd been trying to get her alone, and had even come to her room last night, but she'd ignored the buzzer, and eventually he'd gone away. Afterward though, she couldn't get the memory of his kiss from her mind. Or the rest of her body. She'd never felt this way before. Not even close. And she'd done something she'd never expected to do and touched herself.

Closing her eyes, she'd pictured Callum as he'd looked just before he kissed her, his eyes dark with desire. She'd run her hands over the swell of her small breasts. Touched the nipples lightly with her fingertips. It hadn't been enough, and she'd slid her hand down over her belly and between her thighs and found herself wet with desire. And he wasn't even there. She'd got up, showered, and come up here, but she felt edgy and restless.

The problem was she still didn't know if she wanted to take this thing between them further. She wished she could get to the bottom of why he was the one man who seemed to affect her like this. Maybe she was attracted to the power. He was so different. People usually came on board *El Cazador* because they were hiding, or in trouble. And she'd end up feeling responsible for them.

But despite finding himself on the wrong end of Rico's and her fists, she was quite aware that Callum could look after himself. There was a reason he'd risen to be Leader of the Universe, and it wasn't only the Meridian.

Maybe something inside her liked the idea of someone else taking control, perhaps even looking after her for a change.

After she'd escaped the research center, she'd sworn she would never put herself in anyone's power again. So maybe she should wait until she'd had the Meridian treatment and they could meet on a more even footing. But he would be leaving, returning to his real life ruling the world. And what would she do? She'd never really thought past getting the treatment. What would it be like having other people inside her head, reading her mind? She had problems enough controlling what she said, never mind what she thought. They'd just have to accept her as she was.

Most of the Collective stuck close together. They lived on Trakis Five and found some sort of position within the government. Or they joined the Corps, the Collective's private army. Skylar had been in the Corps, the intelligence section. Maybe Tannis could do that, though she suspected she would make a crap soldier—she hated taking orders—she was much better at giving them. Maybe she could persuade Callum to put her in charge. Or perhaps, she would just stay on *El Cazador*. Why shouldn't she? Skylar had broken from the Collective and nothing terrible had happened. Yet.

Everything had been quiet on the bridge. Janey had all the scanners working constantly, but they showed nothing. No one had followed them from Trakis Two, so it looked as though they were in the clear. They could keep the rendezvous with this Venna woman tomorrow, and then be on their way to Trakis Seven. It could all be over in a week.

Now, she could see Callum's reflection in the polished black screen of the monitor. Should she move? Instead, she held herself very still as he leaned in toward her.

He kissed the side of her neck, and at the soft brush of his lips, a shiver ran all the way through her. His warm breath fluttered against her ear and prickles of awareness quivered down her spine.

"So why are you scared of sex?"

The question whispered against her ear, but didn't make any sense. Was she scared? She was hot, bothered, in danger of melting into a puddle at his feet, but scared?

"Mind your own business," she said, but the words lacked heat.

"Oh, I think it is my business." His voice was dark, rich, and full of promise, and then he kissed the soft place where her neck met her collarbone, and she almost swooned.

She couldn't have moved even if she wanted to, and she wasn't sure she did. Maybe she liked the whole someone-else-taking-control thing after all.

His hands came to rest lightly on her waist, their heat radiating through the thin material of her T-shirt. They slid up over her rib cage, settling on the swell of her breasts. He squeezed gently, as though learning the shape of them, and heat pooled low in her belly. She peered down at his big hands holding her, the skin golden against the bright scarlet of her top. His palms rubbed across her tightening peaks, the friction was delicious, and a funny, little noise left her mouth.

"How scared are you, Tannis?"

She didn't think he expected an answer, which was just as well as she wasn't sure she could speak. Or not make any sense. As she watched, he plucked at the nipples with his long, elegant fingers. Unable to help herself, she leaned back against the hard length of him, her bottom coming up against the rigid proof that she wasn't the only one affected by their encounter. Without conscious thought, she pushed against him, and he growled low in his throat.

One hand left her breasts and stroked over her stomach. She held her breath as he found the gap between her T-shirt and her pants. For a moment, his hand rested on the bare skin, and then he pushed down inside the waistband. His fingers drifted through the curls at the base of her belly. Her insides melted. She could feel herself becoming hot, wet with need.

Every nerve ending yearning for his touch. Screaming for release.

*Beep. Beep. Beep.*

His hand stopped moving. "What was that?"

She wanted to yell at him to ignore it, but he was already withdrawing from her. Closing her eyes, she tried to get herself under some sort of control. She brought up an image of her old guard, Grady, and pictured his hands on her body. It was like liquid nitrogen over her heated skin, and her body was her own again. She stepped away.

When she was sure her voice would sound normal, she spoke. "It's the scanners—looks like we've got company."

"Shit. Bloody good timing."

She turned slowly to find him watching her.

"Are you all right?" he asked.

"Why shouldn't I be?" She sounded terse, but she couldn't help it.

"I just—"

He broke off as Janey appeared in the doorway. For once, she wasn't immaculately turned out but mussed from sleep, her dark red hair loose about her shoulders. If anything, she looked more beautiful without the heavy makeup she normally wore like a mask.

One drunken night, over a flask of Rico's whiskey, Janey had told Tannis of her past. Janey had married young, using her looks to catch the perfect man, rich, powerful, handsome, and a complete bastard. She'd spent five years with him before she'd had the courage to do something about the relationship. She hadn't said exactly what she'd done but from the smile on her face at the time, Tannis guessed it had been terminal. She'd been on the run since—apparently her husband had powerful friends and even after ten years, there was still a reward out for her. She'd said she didn't regret it.

Now, her eyes widened slightly as she took in Tannis and Callum standing close together, and Tannis took another step away. Her brain was slowly clearing from the haze of sexual desire.

"We have company," she said.

Janey yawned. "I know. I set the scanners to alert me if they picked anything up." She crossed the room and sat down at her console, her fingers flicking over the controls. "They're definitely heading this way."

"Coincidence?" Tannis asked, without much hope.

"I doubt it. They're locked right on us."

"Can you get an identification?"

"Give me a minute, and we'll have a visual."

Tannis pressed the comm unit on her wrist. "Rico?" She closed her ears for a moment while he got his moaning done with—Rico was never his best when he first woke up. "Get to the bridge and bring Skylar. We may have a problem."

"Got it," Janey said and Tannis moved closer to get a view of the screen. Callum came to stand beside her.

She frowned, expecting to see the Collective's huge star cruiser, but this was someone else.

"Shit." A smaller Mark Three cruiser filled the screen, similar to *El Cazador*, but white with a black cross on the side.

"The goddamn Church. Again. What the hell do they want?"

Actually, if she gave it any thought, it could be one of many things, but she'd been doing her best not to think too much about the Church. She'd really hoped that with the death of Hezrai Fischer, their Church-related problems had disappeared. Maybe not. They needed their resident Church expert.

She pressed her comm unit and tried to get hold of Alex, but got no reply. She reckoned they must have switched off their comm units, no doubt bloody shagging again, and she called Rico instead.

"Pick up Alex and Jon on your way; they're not answering." She turned back to Janey. "Have they tried to call us yet?"

"No, not yet."

"Well, tell me as soon as they do."

She shoved her hands into her pockets and paced the bridge while she waited for everyone to arrive. She had a bad feeling about this and not just because she hated the Church. Which she did.

When the planets had first been colonized, a great deal of experimentation had gone into genetic modification, mainly using genetic material brought from Earth. The idea had been to make humans more suitable for the conditions on the planets, which weren't always as hospitable as Earth. Later, the experiments had been extended just to make people stronger, faster, whatever they might gain from a particular animal or plant, or what the researchers thought they might gain.

When the Church had risen to power in the aftermath of Meridian, they had called for a purge of the GMs, labeled them abominations, and millions had been slaughtered. That was a couple of hundred years ago, and now any GMs kept out of the Church's way. Mostly they were left alone as long as they maintained a low profile.

But some people still did the research in secret, believing it was the way forward for mankind, and the Church eradicated them wherever they were found. Tannis had always presumed her own family had been scientists killed by the Church, who then sold Tannis and her sister to the research station. But she'd only been four years old, so she couldn't remember much of her family.

"Do you know what they want?" Callum's quietly spoken question broke into her memories. She'd been avoiding looking at him; now she could feel heat steal across her cheeks.

Holy freaking Meridian, she was blushing. At least she presumed she was blushing; it wasn't something she had ever done before. But she couldn't stop remembering that only five minutes ago, the Leader of the Known Universe had had his hand down her pants. Wow. She squirmed at the memory. Her gaze dropped to those hands and her breasts tightened as she remembered how his clever fingers had touched her. She swallowed.

"Tannis?"

Her gaze flew to his face. "Sorry, what did you say?"

He grinned and his own gaze dropped to her chest where her nipples were clearly outlined under her T-shirt, and her face heated even more. Bloody hell, she'd better get herself under control before Rico got there or she'd never live it down. The nipple thing—maybe. The blush—never.

"I asked if you know what the Church want."

She pried her mind away from sex. "Could be one of many things—Alex, Hezrai Fischer . . . Who knows with the Church—they're all mad."

"They're calling us," Janey said.

"Ignore them for a minute. I want the others here."

Rico came in with Skylar beside him. Tannis crossed her arms over her chest. He gave her a quick glance but then crossed to stand beside Janey. "What have we got?" he asked.

"The Church."

"Great. Have I mentioned—"

"Yes, you have," Tannis butted in before he could really get going. Then wished she hadn't as his gaze swung around. His eyes narrowed thoughtfully on her, before moving on to Callum and back to her.

"Are we interrupting anything?"

"Nothing that hadn't already been interrupted. Where are Alex and Jon?"

"On their way."

They appeared in the doorway. "What's happening?" Alex asked with a huge yawn.

"Your old friends have come to play."

"The Church? Why?"

"We have no clue yet. Now, we're all here, so let's find out, shall we? Janey, put him on."

"This is High Priest Temperance Hatcher, leader of the one true Church, seeker of the truth, loyal—"

"For Christ's sake, just get on with it," Tannis snapped. "Say what you want and piss off."

There was a minute's silence, though she could hear his heavy breathing on the other end.

"We want the bloodsucking spawn of Satan who murdered our beloved Hezrai Fischer."

Tannis switched off the comm and turned to look at Rico, one eyebrow raised.

"Does he mean me?" he asked. "Why is it everyone seems to think I'm related to Satan?"

"I wonder," Skylar murmured, and he grinned.

"Beloved Hezrai Fischer?" Alex said. "That's a joke—they hated each other. I bet he did a dance on Hezrai's grave. And we did him a favor. He would never have become High Priest while Hezrai was alive."

Tannis switched the comm back on. "Well, you can't have him. Anything else? Because if not, we have things to do, so good-bye."

"We want our High Priestess returned to us. She is the bride of God."

Alex edged a little closer to Jon, and he wrapped an arm around her shoulder, pulling her tight against him. The Church would have to go through Jon to get to Alex and that wasn't going to happen. He would die first, and that wasn't going to happen either—not on her watch.

She wondered whether they should tell them their priestess was now a werewolf. Would they still want her back? Somehow, she doubted it. Also, there was the little fact that the "Virgin Bride of the Everlasting God" was no longer a virgin—far from it.

"Sorry, that one's a no as well."

"And we want the abomination, Callum Meridian."

"Jesus, you don't want much, do you?" She glanced across at Callum. "You want to go with the nice priest?"

He grinned. "No, thank you."

"You can't have him, either."

"We're giving you five minutes to surrender these three to us. Give us what we ask for and we will let the rest of you go so you can spread the word that the Church is merciful."

"Yeah, right. Like that's going to happen. So let's say we don't—what then?"

"We will obliterate your ship and all your crew."

"Including your priestess."

"We would prefer her returned to us, but her spirit will continue, and a new priestess will be born."

She'd forgotten that bit. Damn—she'd thought Alex would give them some protection. She switched off the comm to give herself a second to think, then turned to Rico. "Can you get us out of here?"

"Probably."

"That's good enough for me." She flipped the comm back on. "Piss off," she said and ended the call. "Right then, get us out of here."

"And quickly would be good," Janey added. "They're locking their blasters on us."

Rico sat in the pilot's seat and flipped off the automatic systems. I suggest you all sit down and strap yourselves in. This might get a little rough."

Tannis flung herself into the nearest seat and fastened the harness. Everyone else did the same. With the exception of Callum, they'd all experienced Rico's evasive maneuvers before and weren't taking any chances.

*El Cazador* turned slowly, shifting beneath them as the main thrusters engaged, and then they were heading straight for the other ship. Fast.

"Aren't we supposed to be going in the opposite direction?" Callum asked.

"Nah," Rico drawled. "They'll just follow us. The ships are about evenly matched, and it will get long and boring and messy. Better to finish them quick. Put them out of the picture."

"Can you do that?"

"He's good, but he's not as good as me. And I'm guessing he doesn't want to die."

"Er, neither do I," Tannis said.

Rico flashed her a grin. "Hold on." And he hit the blasters.

The other ship's shields were up and most of the shots bounced off harmlessly. They countered, and *El Cazador* shook as the blasts took her across the bow. Tannis's fingers tightened on the arms of her chair, but she kept her expression neutral. She wasn't really afraid. In the past fifteen years, Rico had gotten them out of worse situations than this. She glanced sideways at Callum—he was leaning forward in his seat, his eyes gleaming with excitement. He wasn't bored now.

"He's holding his position. He's got balls. I'll give him that," Rico murmured. "Let's see just how big they are." He flicked a switch, and their speed picked up, until Tannis was pressed into her seat with the force.

It looked like they were going to crash. A horrible thought occurred to her—maybe this Temperance guy was as mad as Rico.

"Come on, come on," Rico muttered under his breath.

They were so close now. The ship filled the monitor, the black cross huge and stark on the screen. Was this it? Were they going to crash?

At the last moment, the other ship dodged sideways, but she'd left it too late, and whirled out of control.

"Ha!" Rico punched the air, then swung *El Cazador* around and blasted the spinning ship with shot after shot. Tannis could see that more hits were getting through the shields now. The other ship must have realized it as well because she turned and ran.

Rico took chase, harrying her with their blasters until Janey spoke urgently from her console.

"Rico, I've picked up an outgoing comm from them. They've got backup on the way."

"Shit. I wanted to finish them off."

"Next time."

"Yeah." Rico didn't sound happy, but he fiddled with the controls, and *El Cazador* peeled away and headed off in the opposite direction.

Tannis drummed her fingers on the arm of her chair while she watched the ship get smaller in the monitor. "We clear?" she asked after five minutes.

"Yes, we're clear," Janey replied. "No one on our tail."

Tannis scowled. She would have liked them finished off as well. "What is it about these Church types that is so fucking irritating?" She cast Callum a speculative glance. "And why do they want you? I can understand them wanting Alex and even Rico, but why you?"

He shrugged. "I don't know."

"Have you been in contact with anyone on Trakis Five? Do you know what's happening there?"

"No, I've deliberately kept shut down."

"Well maybe you should try. I don't like this, and I don't like the Church. I have an unpleasant feeling they're up to no good."

"The Council will be able to pinpoint me if I contact them."

"No problem—we're too far out for them to catch us, and we'll be gone by the time they get here."

"Okay." He closed his eyes, though beneath the lids she could see them moving rapidly. After a couple of minutes, he blinked, a frown forming on his features.

"I'm guessing the news isn't good," Tannis said.

"I can't get hold of the colonel—he must be unconscious. I spoke with Tyler. The whole place is in chaos. Shit, you leave them alone for five minutes and—" He broke off and ran a hand through his hair. "Fucking imbeciles."

"So?" Tannis prompted.

"They're under siege—pinned down. The Church has a fleet of ships orbiting Trakis Five, and my council is too fucking scared to take the offensive."

"Sounds like the Church are taking the opportunity to try and get control while you're off playing," Rico said.

Callum tossed him a filthy look. "Thanks for that assessment—very insightful. Apparently, according to the Church, we're all abominations and as such must be eradicated with extreme prejudice. We're all to burn in the Church's fires. Me first."

"Ouch."

"I told them to wake the fucking colonel up and get someone in charge who has a clue what they're doing."

"So we can't expect any help from your people?"

"Once the colonel is back in charge—maybe. Until then, we're on our own. And there's something else."

"Something not good I presume."

"They've received intel that the Church is on their way to Trakis Seven. They plan to destroy the Meridian stocks."

"So we need to get there sooner rather than later."

"Isn't there a garrison on the station orbiting Trakis Seven?" Skylar asked.

"No, we've been pulling people off there. Closing the place down."

"Why?" Tannis asked.

He glanced around the room, then shrugged again. "I told you. The Meridian is finished—there are no stocks. There's no point in anyone else being sent there to die for nothing. We've searched the entire planet—it's over. And by the way, we don't want that information spread around."

"No," Rico said. "I can imagine it would severely deplete your influence if that bit of news got out."

\* \* \*

Callum slumped low in his chair, his gaze fixed on Tannis. She looked so sexy strapped into that harness. Maybe he'd take her like that one day. Or one night, when they had the bridge to themselves. Again. He was definitely making progress with her. She certainly hadn't seemed scared. She'd seemed hot and eager and . . . His cock twitched and his balls ached. Shifting in his chair, he forced himself to look away. Maybe he needed to get his mind on something else. Like the fact that everything was falling apart.

The Collective had ruled for four hundred years. It had taken them nearly a hundred years after the initial discovery to work out what Meridian was doing, to recognize that they weren't aging, and were almost indestructible. After that, they had worked out a plan, how to best utilize their discovery, and they had quickly grown in wealth and power. But the Collective were still only a relatively small number compared with the overall population.

They had maintained control and kept the warring factions at bay by the promise of Meridian—anyone who went up against the Collective could kiss good-bye to any chance of immortality.

But one day, even if the Church didn't succeed in their plan, the news would leak out that Meridian was finished. Or someone would realize there were no new members, and come up with the right answer all on their own. Then their tentative hold on that power would be lost.

He couldn't get worked up about the idea. Mainly because he was fed up with the whole lot of them looking to him to solve their problems. It hadn't taken him long to realize that while great wealth and power weren't all that exciting they were hard to walk away from. Now, he'd made the first move, and it felt good. He couldn't shake the feeling that it was time for him to try something new, and for someone else to take over.

But he didn't want it to be the goddamn Church.

Money was no problem; he had accounts set up all over the place. He could go anywhere, do anything, maybe spend some time trying to understand what he was and what he would one day become. He stroked a finger along the tip of one wing, where it reached up past his shoulder. Was this as far as the changes went? Or would there be more in the future? What would he be in a thousand years' time? If Temperance bloody Hatcher and his cohort of zealous fanatics hadn't cleansed him in their fires by then.

And if Tannis got the treatment, then he'd have someone to share that journey with. He'd told her the truth, he didn't believe in love. But he liked her, and he wanted her, liked the way she stood up to him, the way she melted in his arms, and that was a hell of a lot more than he'd felt in a long time.

So, tomorrow they would meet with Venna and head off to Trakis Seven. Hope they got there before the Church—though how they thought they could destroy the Meridian when it was a death sentence to set foot on the planet, he didn't know.

Even so, their presence could be enough to stop them from getting down to the surface. So they needed to move and fast because Tannis needed her Meridian and he needed answers.

Venna had been a scientist before she was changed, one of those dedicated people hungry for knowledge for the sake of knowledge, and she'd been relentless in her pursuit of the truth. Still, she'd found nothing of any use.

That was why Callum had decided to return to Trakis Seven himself. He'd never been back after that first crash landing, but he had an idea that the answers were there somewhere.

He stretched, suddenly realizing he was tired. Something else he hadn't felt in a long while. Glancing across at Tannis, he found her watching him, and he stretched again and gave her a slow, lazy smile. "I'm going to bed," he murmured.

Her gaze ran over the length of his body, and heat pooled in his belly. Then she looked away. "Good night."

Maybe he hadn't quite won her over. Yet.

# CHAPTER 8

The shuttle landed in the docking bay and the engines went silent. A minute later, the door slid open, and Venna strolled down the ramp. Beside him, Tannis let out a gasp, and he shot her a quick glance. Shock and something else showed on her face, but were quickly gone, her expression blanked out.

He frowned and looked at Venna, but could see nothing to cause the reaction. He was sure the two didn't know each other—he didn't think there was any way they could have met, and he saw no recognition in Venna's eyes.

Venna was beautiful, but he'd always found her cold and rather calculating and so he'd never been interested in making their relationship personal. That had pissed her off; she was used to men falling over her. She was small and curvy, the complete opposite of Tannis, with a mass of blond curls and a rosebud mouth.

She gave Callum her warmest smile, then tossed Tannis a cold glance. "My luggage is in the shuttle. Take it to my room."

She put a hand on Callum's arm, and the smile was back.

"Take it yourself," Tannis snapped.

Venna's violet eyes turned icy. "Who is this . . . person, Callum?"

"Or better yet," Tannis continued, "leave it on board. You can stay on your shuttle. The ship is full."

Callum swiveled and studied her face. His first thought was jealousy, and he liked the idea. Still, he should reassure her, tell her there was nothing between Venna and him. Had never been anything.

But Tannis didn't look jealous. He couldn't define her expression. It was as though a mask had dropped in place. She raised an eyebrow when she caught him watching her.

"What?" she asked. "You want to give her your room—feel free."

He frowned. "No, she can stay in the shuttle."

"But—" Venna began, but he cut her off with a wave of his hand.

"Let's go—you can tell me what's been going on, and then we need to decide exactly how we're going to do this." The ship was already heading to Trakis Seven. He'd sensed the change in direction as soon as Venna's shuttle had docked.

He waited for Tannis to lead the way, but she stood there, hand resting on her laser pistol, that icy-cold look in her reptilian eyes. A shiver ran through him.

"Well?" he asked.

"Well, what?"

"Are we moving? Or are we going to stand here all day?" What the hell was wrong with her?

She shrugged but then headed up the ramp out of the docking bay. Venna raised her eyebrows at him, but he ignored the implied question and followed Tannis. Venna fell in beside him.

Tannis led them to the large conference room in the center of the ship decorated in the usual black and silver with small tables and chairs scattered around the large area. They took seats around one of the tables.

"Okay," he said to Venna. "So what's been going on?"

She gave Tannis a quick glance and then started to give him a rundown on the past few days. But he found it hard to concentrate. There was definitely something wrong with Tannis.

She didn't appear to be paying attention to the conversation. Instead, she gazed at the ceiling, one booted foot swinging, her fingers drumming on the arms of her chair.

"Are we boring you?" he asked.

She turned her head to look at him, her eyes cold and yellow, the pupils narrowed to mere slits. "Yes."

Then she got to her feet and stalked from the room without looking back.

Tannis kept her pace slow until she heard the *whoosh* of the door closing behind her, and then she headed toward her cabin at a run. Her mind whirled, a whole load of disjointed thoughts and memories swirling around her head.

Venna looked like an angel. A fucking goddamn angel and something had clicked in Tannis's head when she'd seen the other woman.

She recognized her immediately as the Collective woman who had visited the research center all those years ago.

Her angel.

The woman who had given her chocolate and awoken a dream.

Rico had asked her the other day what the woman had been doing there, and she'd replied she didn't know. But since he'd asked the question, it had festered in her mind. Demanded that she come up with an answer.

So what would Callum Meridian's head of research have been doing at a privately owned research station?

She slammed her palm into the panel, and the door slid open. Stopping just inside her room, she thought for a minute, finally hurrying over to a closet behind the bed. In the bottom, she found a box with a small scrap of material inside. It was stained brown with old, dried blood and a shiver ran through her at the memory of that day.

She smoothed the cloth out, every cell hoping she was wrong. Her fingers ran over the writing—the insignia of the research company. And everything went cold inside her. CM Research.

She crumpled it in her hand and then sank down onto the bed.

Just about all her life she had yearned to become one of the exalted Collective. She'd imagined she would be like that beautiful angel of mercy who had given the children chocolate and patted their heads. While all the time, she had been responsible for the torment they endured every day. Why hadn't she made the connection before now?

Because she'd been only six years old and such things had been beyond her understanding. She'd grown up isolated from the world, only knowing what they told her, which had been very little. She'd needed something to cling to, some hope of a better future, and she'd picked on the Collective, idolized them in her mind. When she'd left that place with Rico she'd needed a goal, so she had clung tenaciously to that dream.

But maybe all along, deep in her subconscious, she had known the dream was flawed. That's why she had put away thoughts of revenge, because if she'd gone after those behind the research center her dream would have shattered into a thousand pieces, leaving her with nothing.

She'd told herself she would get her revenge, but later. After she'd gotten the Meridian treatment and become one of them, one of the angels.

Shit. She was pathetic. And blind. And stupid.

And there was a good chance that Callum fucking Meridian was responsible for everything.

She flung the scrap of material across the room. Then she hurled anything she could reach until there was nothing left, and she threw back her head and screamed. Black fury filled her. She recognized it, her old friend from the research center. The emotion that had kept her going as, one by one, her friends disappeared. Her sister.

She wanted to go out and kill Callum and Venna, blast them until they were no more than smoking ashes. She leaped to her feet and paced the room, slammed her fist into the wall and cursed at the pain. But it cleared her mind and an icy rage settled over her.

What should she do? First, she had to check out her facts.

Maybe the dream was within her grasp. Just a bit altered from the original version. She could still get the Meridian treatment and her immortality, then say good-bye to them. Permanently.

The buzzer sounded, and she crossed the room and peered into the monitor, relaxing when she saw Rico standing outside.

"What do you want?"

"To come in perhaps?"

She pressed the panel. "Actually, I was just leaving. Why are you here?"

"Callum said there was something wrong. He asked me to come and check on you."

"Did he? How sweet." She forced a smile. "Well as you can see—I'm fine."

Head cocked on one side, he studied her. "No, you're not." He peered around her into the room, his eyes widening, and she followed his gaze. The room was a tip; she'd thrown just about everything that was moveable.

"I was just doing some clearing up."

"Really? What's the matter?"

She thought about telling him. Rico had suffered in that place as well, and he had a right to know. But she wanted some proof first. "Just a moment."

She crossed the room and searched among the debris for the scrap of material. She found it and stuffed it in her pocket, then returned to Rico.

"Where are they?"

"Who? Callum and his blonde girlfriend?" His eyes narrowed. "That's not what this is about, is it? You're jealous?"

"Hah. Did Callum suggest that?"

"No, I thought of it all on my own. There's no need. I was just winding you up. They don't have the look of a couple—my guess is the relationship is strictly business."

"And you're mistaking me for someone who gives a shit."

His frown deepened. "Yes, I was. What's going on?"

She sighed and ran a hand through her hair. "I'll tell you once I've checked something. Are they still in the conference room?"

"Yes."

"And Janey?"

"In her cabin, I think."

"Good."

She stalked off down the corridor, Rico following. At Janey's door, she pressed her palm to the panel and heard the buzzer. Janey appeared a moment later.

"Can I come in?" Tannis asked.

Janey yawned. "Of course. What do you need?"

"Some information. I want you to try and get me some background stuff on a company."

"Sure, should be no problem. Come in."

They both entered. Rico leaned against the wall just inside the door, his arms folded across his chest. Tannis sat down in the chair by the bed, pulled the material from her pocket, and handed it to Janey.

"Ugh. What is this?"

"The company insignia. Will it be enough?"

"Might be." Janey sat down and flipped on the console. She placed the material on the desk beside her and smoothed it out. "CM Research."

"What is that?" Rico asked.

"The badge I took off the guard I killed in the research center."

"Really? And I'm guessing that CM stands for Callum Meridian."

"You don't sound surprised."

"I did wonder when you told me there had been visits from the Collective. But that's hardly conclusive evidence."

"That's what I'm hoping Janey can come up with."

Gripping her hands together, she watched as Janey's fingers flew over the board. "What do you want to know?" Janey asked.

"Could it stand for anything else? Can you find any proof that Callum Meridian is behind the company?"

"Well there's only one company coming up. Closed now by the looks of it—in fact it closed fifteen years ago."

"Really?"

"Let's see if we can't find out who's behind it."

She worked in silence for the next five minutes. Tannis sat and tapped her foot on the floor and tried to curb her impatience.

"What is this company?" Janey asked, her fingers not slowing.

Tannis considered ignoring the question, then she shrugged. "I was brought up in a research center."

"You were born there?"

"No—I think I was sold to them when I was four or so. Most of my family was killed, I presume by the Church, though I don't remember the attack."

"Most?"

"My sister and I survived."

Janey glanced over her shoulder, a small frown on her face. "I didn't know you had a sister."

"I don't. Not anymore." A wave of sadness washed over her as she remembered Thea, her baby sister. "She died. They did some sort of experiment on her and she . . ." She broke off.

"I'm sorry."

"Nothing to be sorry about. It was a long time ago. I thought the center was run by the Church or at least funded by the Church—looking for new and better ways to kill us off."

"No, there's no Church connection. At least not in the ownership. There are large payments going out to the Church though. Could be buying children like yourself." She sat back in the chair and gestured at the screen. "Come and look."

Tannis pushed herself up and stepped closer, her legs strangely heavy, and she realized she didn't want to see this. Didn't want confirmation that Callum was behind the horror of her childhood, the death of her baby sister. Rico came up behind her, put a hand on her shoulder, and squeezed. He so rarely touched her, as though he was aware she found it hard. She took a deep breath and allowed a mask to fall over her features. The same mask she had worn every day in the center.

The screen blurred for a moment, and she made herself concentrate and read the words. She was expecting it, but all the same, a jolt of shock ran through her at the sight of Callum's name clear on the screen. She read the information slowly, making sure she understood.

"So it was privately owned, not by the Collective."

Janey nodded. "Yup, owned by our good friend Callum Meridian. There's no connection at all to the Collective, except—there." She pointed at a line on the screen. "Venna

Harkness, chief research officer. She's Collective. There's a flag by her name."

"I take it that's Callum's friend, currently sitting in the conference room," Rico said.

"Yeah, and my fucking angel."

"What?"

He sounded shocked, and she turned to glare at him. "How did you think I knew to look? Venna fucking Harkness is the fucking bitch who visited the center when I was a kid." The rage rose up inside her again. "She gave me fucking chocolate."

She slammed her fist into the metal wall and then winced at the pain to her already abused knuckles.

"What are you going to do?" Rico asked. "You want me to deal with it?"

"How?" She sounded suspicious.

"I'll toss them out of the airlock."

"They're immortal. It won't kill them."

"No, but they might spend most of eternity floating in space."

"Nah—they're telepathic—they'll just call up for help." She shoved her hands into her pocket.

"Well, we do know how to finish them off for good. Jon's done it before, I'm sure he'd do it again if you asked him nicely."

Jon was the only person to ever permanently kill one of the "indestructible" Collective. He'd ended up in the high-security prison on Trakis One as a result, waiting for transport to the Meridian mines, until the crew of *El Cazador* had broken him out. He didn't like the Collective. Hell, he didn't like many people, though he'd mellowed a lot since he'd come on board. Falling in love would do that to you.

Tannis had no doubt that he would kill Callum if she asked. But she wasn't sure yet what her plan was.

"Well?" Rico asked.

Rico sounded impatient and she frowned. "You're awfully keen to finish him off. Why?"

"You forget I spent three months in that place as well. I would have died there if you hadn't gotten me out."

That was true. Tannis paced the room as she tried to think through the rage that clouded her mind. She realized she still wanted the Meridian treatment, though it was becoming increasingly clear to her that she wanted nothing to do with the Collective afterward. And to get the treatment she needed to go to Trakis Seven, and she needed Callum alive. She would worry about the rest later.

So for now, she had to curb her impatience and not set her resident assassin on him and his blond friend. There would be plenty of time for that, and she'd enjoy it all the more for the wait.

What to do?

While she might be willing to put off her revenge, she needed some sort of immediate retribution or she might explode. She ran her tongue over the sharp points of her incisors.

"Don't do anything," she said.

"What are you planning?"

"Nothing permanent. I want my Meridian treatment, so they live—for now."

When she entered the conference room, the two were sitting close together, reading something from a palm screen Venna had opened. They were so engrossed, they didn't notice her, and she stood just inside the doorway and watched them for a minute. They made a beautiful couple, Venna's blond beauty the perfect foil for Callum's dark good looks. Hatred coiled inside her, but Tannis kept her face expressionless as she coughed to make her presence known.

They both jumped and glanced up guiltily. A flash of annoyance crossed the blonde's pretty features, and she snapped the screen closed as though to hide it.

Callum looked pleased and then a puzzled frown settled on his face. "Are you okay?"

She pushed herself away from the wall and sauntered over. "Sorry, I had to run out there," she said, pasting a sugary smile on her face.

"Is everything all right?"

"Everything is fine."

She'd never done this before, but there was a first time for everything. She lowered her lashes and peeped at him through half-closed eyes. Her tongue flicked out, and she moistened her lower lip. His gaze followed the movement, and his eyes darkened.

Good.

She moved a little closer and put her hands in the pockets of her pants pushing her small breasts forward. His gaze dropped.

Even better.

"Callum!" Venna's tone was impatient, but he waved her away with a careless gesture of his hand, his gaze never leaving Tannis.

"Could I talk to you a minute?" Tannis murmured.

"Of course."

Her gaze flicked to Venna. "Alone."

He almost jumped to his feet. "Definitely."

She pivoted and walked from the room, trying to make her hips sway the way Janey's always seemed to do. She sensed Callum coming up behind her. Casting a quick glance over her shoulder, she saw Venna still seated, her mouth open. Then she dismissed the woman from her mind. Her time would come. Once out of the room, she turned to Callum and placed a hand on his chest. His heart rate was fast beneath her palm.

She leaned in close. "Let's go to your room," she whispered the words against his throat, then stepped back and looked up into his face.

"Why not yours?" he asked.

"Because yours is nearer." She stroked her fingertips down his chest and over his belly, to hook in the waistband of his pants. "And I really don't want to wait."

His breath caught in his throat with an audible groan. He grabbed hold of her hand and almost dragged her along the corridor. They were at his door in seconds, and he slammed his palm to the panel and hustled her in as the door slid open.

Once inside, he crowded her against the wall so she could feel the cool metal through her shirt at the back, and his hot body pressed the length of her front. She gasped as she felt the hard length of his erection prodding her belly.

"Were you jealous?" he asked, his tone smug.

She had to bite back a bitter laugh at the question. Of course, that's what the egotistical bastard would think.

"I didn't like seeing you with her." Well, that was the goddamn truth.

"She's an employee, that's all. No need for you to be jealous. It's you I want."

"And I want you." Yeah, she wanted him all right. Wanted him rolling about on the floor in agony.

She reached up and stroked her fingers over the rough skin of his cheek, then curled her hand around his neck and pulled him toward her. Her mouth opened for his kiss, and his tongue thrust inside. His lips hardened on hers, deepening the kiss. For a few seconds, she allowed herself to relax against him. Then she took his lower lip between her teeth and bit down hard. The warm, metallic taste of blood flooded her mouth. Callum made to pull away, but she held him tight with the hand at the back of his neck, while she pumped him full of the venom from the glands at the base of her incisors.

He went still, and then the first spasm racked his body. Tannis released her hold and shoved him away. He stumbled as she leaned against the wall to observe. She'd never seen the full effects of her venom before, and she watched with interest.

"What have you—" He broke off as another spasm ran through his body. Swaying, he put out a hand, then stumbled again and gripped onto the back of a nearby chair. His face leached of color, his legs buckled, and he crashed to the floor, dragging the chair with him. He landed on his wings and rolled so he came up on all fours.

His head hung down and he retched, vomiting up a mixture of blood and his stomach contents, and she grimaced.

"Nasty," she said. "You see, *that's* why I didn't want to go to my room."

He continued to vomit until nothing further came out, then he collapsed to the floor on his belly and lay still.

Tannis waited a couple of minutes, but when he didn't move, she stepped closer and nudged him in the ribs with the tip of her boot.

His head rolled to the side, and he peered up at her out of half-closed eyes. "Why?"

"Maybe I was *very* jealous. Don't worry—I'll send your friend in—she can mop your fevered brow."

A faint sheen of sweat glossed his skin. Shivers ran through his body and his huge wings fluttered feebly. Finally, he closed his eyes, and the tension went out of him. Presumably, he'd lost consciousness. Pity—she would have preferred the pain to go on a little longer.

For long moments, she stood looking down at him, and then she drew the scrap of material from her pocket and tossed it to the floor by his nose. She whirled around and stalked from the room. Rico was waiting outside; he peered in through the door as she exited.

"What did you do to him?"

"I bit him."

"Really? He doesn't look too good."

"He'll live. More's the pity." One more thing she wanted to do. She pressed the comm unit on her wrist. "Daisy, there's a woman in the central conference room. Can you pick her up and show her to Callum's cabin?"

She leaned against the wall, her hands clenched at her side, and tried to ignore Rico while she waited.

Daisy appeared with Venna in tow a couple of minutes later. The blonde had a pleasant—if entirely insincere— smile plastered on her angel face. That would soon go.

Tannis waited until Venna was level with her, then she straightened, drew back her fist and punched her right in that smile.

"That's for the fucking chocolate," she snarled and stalked away.

# CHAPTER 9

For the first time in his life, Callum wished he wasn't immortal, and he could just die quietly and the pain would stop. He lay very still, because if he moved, he hurt. His wings hurt, his arms and legs ached, his stomach felt like he'd been disemboweled and the hollow filled with molten metal. His head thumped, his mouth tasted disgusting, and a thick, sour stench filled his nostrils.

He would have liked to whimper but that would involve moving, and he really didn't want to do that yet. Maybe not ever.

"Callum?"

He opened one eye at the urgently spoken word. Then closed it again.

"Callum?" The tone was sharper this time.

"What?" He pushed the word out through his torn lips. He must have bitten through them, because they hurt as well.

"Are you all right?"

*Stupid fucking woman.*

The words sounded loud in his head, but he decided to

keep them to himself. He suspected he was going to need her help any minute now, when he finally got the nerve to try and get up. No point in alienating her completely. He settled for a "No."

"Oh. Because we have to get out of here. That woman is crazy."

What woman? And what was Venna doing here anyway? In fact, where was here? And what the hell had happened? He opened his eye again—the one that wasn't glued to the floor—and peered around the room. His room.

It came back to him slowly. He'd come here with Tannis. She'd kissed him, then she'd . . .

Bloody hell—she'd bitten him. On the mouth. That's what was wrong with his lip; the sadistic bitch had bitten him, then injected him with some sort of poison.

But why?

A pair of legs came into his vision, high heels, and slender ankles. Then Venna crouched so her face appeared in his line of vision. Her nose wrinkled in an expression of disgust. "Ugh."

Very useful.

There was something wrong with Venna's lip as well. It looked like somebody had punched her.

Obviously, she must have realized she was being less than sympathetic, and she reached out a hand and gingerly stroked his forehead. "Oh, you poor thing. What happened to you?"

He preferred the earlier approach—at least it had been sincere. When he failed to answer, she continued.

"They told me you had some sort of fit. They said I needed to look after you. And then I got here and that woman hit me. And nobody did anything to stop her. And really, Callum, you'd be better off with someone else looking after you. I'm not good at this touchy-feely stuff." She gestured to him and to the room in general. "And I think I'd better go to my shuttle." She gave the door a nervous glance. "*She* might come back."

He presumed "*she*" was Tannis. But why had she hit Venna? And why had she bitten him?

Time to get out of this pool of vomit and find out. Taking a deep breath, he placed his palms flat on the floor and pushed. Nothing happened. He closed his eyes, counted to ten, and tried again. This time he managed to lever himself onto all fours. He rested for a minute, his breathing ragged. Heat flushed his skin one moment. Shivers raced through his body the next. He wanted to throw up again, but knew there was nothing left in his stomach.

"You don't look well."

"Really? What a surprise," he said. "Look, why don't you do something useful and get me a glass of water."

He waited until she'd disappeared before pushing himself up onto his knees. Something lay on the floor in front of him. He picked it up, studied it, a frown forming on his face. It was a scrap of material and looked like it had been torn from a shirt.

He didn't recognize the insignia, but it said CM Research, so he presumed it must have something to do with Venna and the work she'd been doing for him. He'd pretty much given her a free hand and a lot of money. And gotten not much for it. She reported regularly but had yet to tell him anything of interest or use.

He needed a shower, but the thought of actually standing up didn't seem much of a possibility right now. Instead, he dragged himself onto the bed and collapsed facedown, his head buried in the soft pillow.

Someone prodded him between the shoulder blades, and he groaned.

"Callum. Your water."

He wanted to tell her to go away, but he also wanted to

ask her about this company. Was it somehow connected to Tannis and *El Cazador*? But how? Could they have done work for Venna? A job that had gone wrong? Something had seriously pissed Tannis off.

If he hadn't been immortal, he would be dead.

He rolled over and pulled himself up so he was half sitting. Venna handed him a glass, and he sipped the water, wincing when it hit his stomach.

"So this fit you had," Venna said. "You think it's another change? Something to do with Meridian?"

"No." He touched a fingertip to his lip, felt the jagged puncture marks.

"So . . . ?" She sounded impatient, and he shrugged.

"Tannis bit me."

"What?"

"She must produce some sort of venom. She kissed me—"

"What?"

Christ, she was getting repetitive. "She kissed me, then she bit me, and then she injected me with some sort of poison."

Her brows drew together. "Why? I mean she didn't seem very friendly, but I just thought she was unstable and jealous." Her finger touched her swollen lip. "But that seems a little excessive. Is it some sort of assassination plot?" She glanced at the open door. "We need to get off this ship."

"Not an assassination attempt—she knew it wouldn't kill me."

"So, why?"

"I think she's unhappy about something." That was the understatement of the century. "I just don't know what." He held out the piece of material. "What do you know about this?"

Venna took it from him, but then dropped it on the bed with a grimace of disgust. For a minute, she stared at it, her lips pursed. "It's the badge from the uniform of one of your companies."

"One of *my* companies?"

"CM Research. I set it up about thirty years ago, to do some experimentation into Meridian. The research came to nothing, and I closed the company down about fifteen years ago."

Callum ran a trembling hand through his hair, but he could feel his body fighting the poison and slowly throwing off the effects. He took a sip of the water and considered what she had told him, trying to work out how it could fit in with Tannis.

"What sort of experiments?"

"Genetic mostly, mixing some of our altered DNA with human and other . . . things, seeing if we could get it to take. But as I said—it came to nothing. Most of the subjects died, a few lived, but they never assimilated the altered DNA."

"Subjects?"

"The subjects of the experiments."

"People?"

"I suppose." She frowned. "What are you getting at? You've never questioned the way I do my research before."

No, he hadn't, had he? Hadn't been interested enough—all he'd wanted was results. Now, he had an uncomfortable feeling that he was about to come face-to-face with some unpleasant truths. He wasn't sure he wanted to continue with this, but he forced himself to go on with the questions.

"Who were these people? Where did they come from?"

"How do I know?"

"Then find out. And now. You must have access to the records."

Her face took on a mutinous expression, and for a moment, it looked like she might refuse. But obeying him was too inbred, and she opened the palm screen on her left hand and started flicking through the files. "What is it you want to know?"

"The subjects, where did they come from and what happened to them?" The ones who survived at least. He waited, impatient for her to give him the answers he knew he wasn't going to want to hear.

"Well?" he prompted.

She shrugged. "They came from different places. Some were prisoners heading for the Meridian mines—we just borrowed them for a while."

"Some? What about the others?"

"We bought some from the Church."

He shook his head, then wished he hadn't as pain shot through him, piercing his skull. "How can you buy people from the Church?"

"They weren't people. They were GMs." She sounded defensive now.

"Since when have GMs not been people?"

"Since we condoned the Church's purge for political reasons," she retorted.

They hadn't condoned it, just done nothing about it. They'd needed the Church's support. He'd not been involved in the negotiations, and he presumed his Council hadn't been aware of the consequences when they'd agreed to downgrade GMs to nonhuman status. The purge that had followed had torn the universe apart. He'd eventually managed to put a stop to the overt slaughter of GMs, though the nonhuman status had never been reversed. But that was politics.

He swallowed and drove himself to go on. "Where did they come from—these GMs?"

"The Church still kills them if they believe they can get away with it. It goes on all the time on the outer planets. When they knew we'd pay, they would often keep the children alive and sell them to the research center." She must have seen something in his expression. Her lips thinned. "They would have died anyway."

"Yeah, no doubt you were doing them a favor."

"Don't you mean *we*? You paid for this, so don't go all sanctimonious on me now, Callum. You never asked for the details. You never wanted to know how I got results."

Christ, children. He felt sick again, and this time it was nothing to do with the poison. "What happened to them?"

"Some died during the experiments."

"And the rest?"

"Any survivors were sent to the mines. It was part of the agreement with the Church."

So Tannis couldn't have been there. "Everyone? There were no survivors?"

"What are you trying to get at?"

"You asked why Tannis poisoned me." He gestured at the piece of material, with its incriminating mark lying on the bed between them. "This was on the floor when I woke up. She left it there for me to find."

Enlightenment washed across her face. "She's a GM." Sinking onto the mattress beside him, she closed her eyes for a minute. "Jesus, we're fucked."

"What is it? What have you remembered?"

She examined the palm screen for a few moments, nibbling on her lower lip, her eyes narrowing as she read the information. Callum bit back his impatience as he waited for her to continue.

"Just before we closed down the facility, there was an escape. One of the subjects killed a guard and managed to escape. They freed another prisoner."

"Another GM?"

"No—this was someone our forces had captured and delivered—they thought he might be an interesting study. Would you believe a suspected vampire?"

"Yeah, I'd believe it."

"Anyway they both escaped on this guy's ship. They were never recaptured, but then we didn't try very hard. They had no real value. The GM was scheduled to be shipped to the mines the next day.

"Who was the subject?"

"Wait a second. A GM—shit—designated reptile/human DNA. Double shit. You think Captain Tannis is . . ."

He nodded. "Tell me about her."

"She was bought from the Church—estimated age four. Two siblings, she was the older."

"What happened to the sibling?"

She tapped into the pad. "Terminated after an adverse reaction to one of the experiments."

Callum rested his head against the wall behind him and closed his eyes. She must hate his guts. Along with the rest of him. "How long was she in that place?"

"Fourteen years."

"Jesus."

Venna was right. It was his fault as much as hers. More his, really. But all the same, he couldn't bear to look at her right now.

"Go to your shuttle. I suggest you lock the door and don't come out again. I doubt you're any more popular than I am around here right now."

"Shouldn't I stay and look after you?"

"Thanks for the offer—but no."

She looked at him. "They weren't badly treated. They had food and shelter."

"And they died from the experiments."

"This is science. We need to make sacrifices."

"Just go, Venna."

He watched until the door shut behind her. He wanted to weep, but that wouldn't change things.

Venna had said they weren't badly treated, but they must

have known what was in store for them. To live with the threat of death hanging over you constantly. No wonder Tannis was obsessed with getting the Meridian treatment. Well, at least he could give her that.

He remembered Rico's comment that she was scared of sex. Was that a hang-up from her time at the center? What had happened to her there? He could guess and nausea rose up sharp and bitter in his throat.

*Callum?*

He felt the word like a tap on the door to his mind. The colonel. About time.

*You okay? You feel off.*

*I'll live.*

*You want me to send a ship to pick you up?*

*No. Everything is fine. I saw Rosalie.*

The colonel was silent for a moment. *How was she?*

*Good. Old . . . but happy.*

*Thank you.*

*And I've got Venna—*

*I know. She contacted the Council about five minutes ago. She seems to think you're in danger.*

*I'm fine. If they were going to kill me, I'd be dead by now. The captain will keep me alive—she wants something from me.*

*And that would be . . . ?*

*I've promised her the Meridian treatment if she takes me to Trakis Seven.*

*Ah.*

*What does "ah" mean?*

*There might be a problem with that.*

Callum's head ached viciously. His body was still racked with tremors and his mind weighted down by something he could only guess was guilt. He hardly recognized the emotion, but what else could it be? He had so much to feel guilty for.

All the same, couldn't one thing just go right for him today?

*Are you going to tell me what the problem is? I heard the Church is heading there to destroy the Meridian stocks, but I'm hoping we'll beat them to it.*

*It's more than the stocks they plan to destroy. I just got new intel in from my people inside the Church. They've sent a ship to blow up the whole planet.*

Shock hit him in the gut.

*Why the hell would they want to do that?*

*To destroy the evil once and for all, I guess. Temperance Hatcher is hardly known for his rational behavior. And they're getting a big following. There's a lot of anti-Collective feeling right now. People believe we're holding onto the Meridian in order to push prices up.*

*What are the Council doing about this?*

*Absolutely nothing. I don't understand it. They could at least try and stop it from happening, but they refused to even consider my plan. It makes no sense.*

Actually, it made perfect sense to Callum. Only the Council knew that Meridian was all but finished. Maybe a few others like Venna, who were involved in the running of the planet, might suspect, but they didn't know for sure.

The Council's reasoning would be that if they allowed the Church to go ahead and destroy the planet, they could blame the Church for the loss of Meridian. It would give them valuable propaganda to use against the Church.

But Callum knew the Council would love to see the planet destroyed. They were terrified of what Callum might find there, terrified of the truth.

*It makes sense to me,* he told the colonel.

*And are you going to share? I need to understand what's going on, Callum. I can't help you if I don't know what I'm up against.*

*The Meridian is finished.*

*What?*

Callum could feel the shock reverberating through the colonel's mind. *We've found no new Meridian for over ten years. It's finished. There is no more.*

*Jesus.* He was silent for a moment. *So they really don't care.*

*Oh, they care. They'd like to see the planet destroyed and any secrets it holds with it—the Church is doing them a favor. Is there any way you can stop this from your end?*

*None that I can see right now. We're still under siege here, and the Council has called in just about every ship in range to try and break the Church's hold around the planet. I'm free but only nominally in charge. They've given me the title of strategic advisor, which doesn't necessarily mean they're doing anything I advise.*

Callum rubbed the point between his eyes, trying to relieve some of the tension.

*Okay, I'll see what we can do from here. Can you do something for me though?*

*Of course.*

*Send the intel you have on the Church through to this ship so they can see what we're up against.*

*Sure, Callum.*

*Right, I'll be in touch.*

Once the colonel was gone, Callum lay on the bed and tried to work out what this meant. It was impossible to think of a plan of action until the intel came through and they knew what they were up against, but he supposed he'd better give them a heads-up on the situation.

If Tannis would see him. She might even decide to finish the job, though he didn't think so. She wanted the Meridian treatment too much, and he was the only one who could give it to her. Though even that was looking doubtful, right now.

He put his feet to the floor and found, with a little effort, they would support him. He staggered into the shower and washed the sweat and grime from his body. His stomach still felt hollow, but that was no doubt because it was empty. He needed food.

But first, he was going to have to apologize.

Again.

It was becoming a habit.

# CHAPTER 10

"I'm sorry."

Tannis glanced around at the softly spoken words. Callum stood in the doorway to the bridge. And he looked sorry.

Well, in a sorry state anyway.

Beneath the gold, his skin had a sickly green tinge, and dark circles shadowed his eyes. He leaned one shoulder against the doorway for support.

Good.

But he was upright, which was impressive considering the state he'd been in when she'd left him. And he'd obviously showered, his short hair was still damp and he wore clean clothes, black pants and a black sleeveless T-shirt. He was beautiful, and she hated him.

"You want me to get rid of him?" Rico asked from beside her. "He can be out of the airlock before you can say, 'piece of shit Collective bastard.'"

Tannis considered the question. Would it help if he died? Would she feel better?

"Or I can do it for you," Jon said. "It's easy if you know how."

Yes, if anyone could do it, Jon could.

"And I wouldn't mind having a go." Janey glanced up from her console where she compared data on Trakis Seven, looking for the best way to get safely onto the planet and away again. *El Cazador* couldn't go in—Tannis couldn't expose the rest of the crew to the poisons of the planet—so they would have to take one of the shuttles.

"And me," Alex said. "I'll do it. I wonder what would happen if a Collective member got eaten by a wild animal."

"You mean like a wolf?" Jon asked with a grin.

Tannis held up her hands. "Nobody do anything. If anyone's going to kill him, it's me." But she was warmed by their support. They would do it for her. Even if they risked the enmity of the powerful Collective.

They'd all been very careful around her, trying to act normal, but she could see the pity in their eyes. Or maybe not pity. Maybe compassion, which was a whole different thing, but still she wished they would hide it a little better. She didn't do emotional. Not in public anyway.

She wondered who had told them. Maybe Rico, but she doubted it. More likely, Janey had pieced something together from the information. She was about the brightest person Tannis had ever met, and she'd probably have had no trouble putting together the clues.

The truth was she'd had a crap childhood. But so had a lot of people. Alex for instance, had been a priestess, and grown up in an abbey having to pray every day—that must have been far worse.

And just because she'd had a bad start, did that mean she should go through her whole life hating everything and everyone? She could do that, or she could put it behind her.

She couldn't forgive him, this went too deep, but she also couldn't put revenge before getting what she really wanted. So they would go to Trakis Seven, and she would get the Meridian treatment.

And then maybe she would kill him.

"So, are you going to kill me?" he asked quietly, breaking into her thoughts.

"I haven't decided."

"I think you have. If you wanted me dead—I'd be dead already. Now, if you're not going to kill me, I have some information you need to hear." He gave a brief flicker of a smile. "Afterward, you may want to change your mind."

That didn't sound good. She wondered whom the information had come from. Venna? Or had he been in contact with someone else?

"No, I'm not going to kill you. Yet. But I need a drink. Rico, go get some of your whiskey and let's meet in the conference room in five. Janey, are you finished?"

"Yes, I've got a couple of options for the best approach."

"Okay, bring the data. And somebody tell the Trog to get up there, I want everyone in on this."

Callum stepped aside to let the others walk past him. He seemed oblivious to the dark looks and muttered comments he received, though he winced at something Janey said as she exited the room.

Tannis should leave, but she hesitated. Callum leaned against the wall, hands shoved in his pockets as he regarded her.

"I know it's not an excuse, but I didn't know."

"Well, maybe you should have known." She hadn't meant to talk about it, but the words were out before she could stop them.

"Maybe you're right. But do you know how many things I have to deal with every day?"

"No."

"A lot. I don't have time to do everything. So I delegate."

"Big deal. But I really don't care."

"Yes, you do."

"No, I freaking don't."

"I'm not making excuses. The truth is I should have known. But I didn't."

Tannis sighed. Suddenly, she felt weary. She waved a hand in his general direction. "Forget it. And you can tell your girlfriend it's safe to come out. No one will harm her while she's on *El Cazador*. Or you either."

"She's not my girlfriend. And later?"

"Who knows? Let's go find out what other good news you have for me." Without waiting for him to say anything further, she walked away.

Rico was already in the conference room when Tannis arrived, sitting at one of the small tables, a bottle and a bunch of glasses in front of him. She took the seat next to him.

Callum came in behind her and collapsed into a chair opposite, leaning back his head, and closing his eyes.

Rico grinned. "You look like shit."

He peered through one half-open eye. "I feel like shit."

"Good."

Rico sounded amazingly cheerful, considering he'd suffered in that place as well. He'd once told her it was the closest he'd ever come to dying. But then one of the first lessons he'd tried to teach her was not to bear a grudge. He poured the golden liquid into the glasses and pushed a couple toward her. "Here, and maybe you'd better give your boyfriend one of these?"

"He's not my boyfriend."

"Really? Looks like someone gave him a love bite."

Callum's lower lip was swollen where she'd bitten him. It looked nasty. She told herself she hoped it hurt, but couldn't get up any conviction. Instead, she picked up one of the glasses and held it out to him.

His brows drew together as though surprised, but he took the glass and swallowed the whiskey in one gulp, wincing as it stung his cut lip. He held out the glass, and Rico reached across and refilled it.

The others entered the room, grabbed a glass, and took up seats around them. The Trog came in last. He didn't bother with a drink. While he was happy to make the stuff down in his engine rooms, Tannis had never seen him actually consume it.

She presumed he didn't want the loss of control. The Trog was hiding something, she'd known that when they took him on, but he was also the best engineer she'd ever come across, and if he wanted to keep his secrets, that was fine by her.

"Okay," she said when everyone was seated. "How are we going to do this? Janey?"

"Actually, maybe I'd better go first," Callum said. "As what I have to say affects what we do next. If we do anything."

Tannis didn't like the sound of that. As far as she was concerned there was only one course of action right now. They go to Trakis Seven, she took the treatment, they get the hell out of there, and she would live forever. She really didn't want to hear about anything that would interfere with that plan.

"What do you mean, if anything? You'd better not try and weasel out of our deal, or I might kill you after all."

"I just heard that the Church don't plan on just destroying the Meridian stocks. They're sending a force to destroy Trakis Seven."

Stunned, Tannis sat back in her chair. "Is that even possible? To destroy a whole planet?"

"With enough firepower, you can blow up anything."

"Why?"

"Presumably, to cut off our power base. People support us in the hope of one day getting the Meridian treatment. If the source was destroyed, why follow us?"

"Why exactly?" Tannis muttered. "Great . . . just great." She swallowed her drink and slammed the glass onto the table, jumped to her feet, and paced the room, unable to sit still any longer. "So do you actually know anything useful?"

"The colonel promised to forward the intel here. It should be in your systems by now."

"I'll check," Janey said. She opened a palm screen and her fingers fluttered over the keys. "It's here," she murmured, "and it doesn't look good. Wait, I'll put it up on the main screen."

She rose to her feet and crossed the room to the console, pressed a few keys, and a screen emerged on the far wall.

Tannis stopped her pacing, stood in front of the screen, and read the information with increasing dismay. It was a frigging army. "Where the hell has the Church gotten an army from?"

"Does it matter?"

She turned to Rico. "Can we stop them?"

"Not a chance in hell. There's too many of them."

"What are your lot doing?" she asked Callum.

"Nothing."

"What? They're just going to sit back and let them do this?"

"Yes. I'd say they're more than happy about this move. I told you—the Meridian is finished. There's nothing else on Trakis Seven worth saving. Except maybe answers. And the Council don't want answers." He sipped his drink. This time he didn't wince. He must be healing fast. "No, they're probably rubbing their cowardly little hands in glee at this turn of events."

"Damn. Damn. Damn." Tannis kicked the table. She was so close. Trust the Church to try and blow her dream out of the sky. "There must be something we can do."

"I can help."

At first, she didn't realize who had spoken. Then the Trog raised his shaggy head.

"You can?" She didn't mean to sound skeptical, but it came out that way. For a second, she thought she saw a glimmer of humor in his blue eyes, but it was gone before she could be sure.

"So, how can you help?"

"I think I can get someone to take the ship for you."

"The Church's ship. The really big Church's ship that's going to Trakis Seven?"

He nodded.

"The one guarded by a whole load of other ships?"

"Yes."

Tannis glanced around the room, curious to see what the others would make of this.

"You mean the Rebels?" Rico asked the question, and the Trog nodded again.

Tannis flung herself into the nearest seat, while she tried to make sense of what was going on. She turned to Rico. "What do you know about the Rebels? And what have they got to do with the Trog?"

"That's up to the Trog to tell you."

"But you know something, and you didn't tell me?" She'd thought Rico told her everything. Obviously not.

"Not my place," he replied.

She sighed; he was right. It had always been her policy that peoples' secrets were their own. As long as they didn't endanger the rest of the crew. She presumed Rico must have suspected that the Trog's secret might do just that and so questioned him.

"Tell me," she said.

Rico nodded to the Trog, and the engineer stood. He usually slumped and now, standing up straight, Tannis realized how tall he was, appearing even taller with his lanky build. He had dark blond hair, which looked as if it hadn't been cut in a long time, and which usually fell over his features, hiding his expression. Now, he pushed it back, revealing high cheekbones and blue-green eyes slanted like a cat.

"So," Tannis said, "why would the Rebels come and help us?"

"Because I'll ask them to."

"And why would they do what you ask?"

"Because the leader of the Rebel Coalition is my brother."

Alex leaped to her feet. "Holy Meridian. I know who you are."

The Trog turned his wary eyes on her. "Tell them then. They might as well know the worst."

Alex stared at him with something close to horror stamped on her expressive features. "Ten years ago, there was an attack on the Cathedral on Trakis Four. Some sort of explosive device went off. It was Christmas Eve and the place was packed. Over two hundred people died, mostly children. For once, the Rebels didn't try and crow about it—instead they claimed it was a mistake—that the explosives had gone off early."

Tannis turned to the Trog and frowned. "You did that?"

"I built the device. Someone tampered with the timing mechanism. It was supposed to explode later that night, when the priests were taking Holy Communion." The Trog's tone was flat, expressionless. He put his hands in his pockets, hunched his shoulders, and paced the room. "I found out later that there had been a dispute among the leaders—some wanted to cause maximum casualties and didn't really care who they were as long as they were Church followers."

"What happened?" Tannis asked.

"I killed the man who'd done it. Then I left. I'd lost my taste for rebelling. But the Church was after me—I was pretty well known, and the explosive device was my specialty. So I changed my identity."

Tannis turned to Rico. "You knew all this?"

He nodded. "Pretty much."

"Anyone else?"

"Me," Janey said.

"Rico suggested I tell Janey. She helped me with my new identity, and she's been keeping track of anyone who might be coming after me."

Tannis rubbed a hand over her face, then pressed her eyes.

"We would have told you, if you needed to know," Rico said. "But you didn't."

It came back to her now—the news of the explosion had been splashed all over the comms at the time, but she hadn't taken too much notice. She shook her head; she needed to forget that half her crew had kept a whopping secret from her and get on with the matter at hand. That's what was important right now.

"So I take it your brother is still with the Coalition?"

The Trog nodded.

She had a thought. "Hey, what is your name?" She couldn't remember from the news reports.

"Starke, but the Trog is fine."

Skylar had been leaning on the back of Rico's chair. Now she straightened. "So that would make your brother, Devlin Starke?"

He nodded, looking wary.

"Wow." Skylar sounded impressed, and Tannis dug in her mind for anything she could remember about the name but came up blank.

"Wow?" she asked.

"Devlin Starke is about the most wanted man on the

Corps's most-wanted-men list. He's a legend. Supposed to be a real hard bastard."

"He's had to be hard." The Trog sounded defensive. "Our parents were killed by the Church—"

"They were GMs?" Tannis asked. She couldn't see any sign of obvious genetic engineering in the Trog, but some just didn't show and were able to hide what they were.

"Our mother was—that was enough for the bastards. Dev was only fourteen. I was six. He looked after me."

"He also apparently went after the Church's extermination squad and killed every last one of them," Skylar added. "My God—he was only fourteen—that wasn't in the files."

"They deserved to die," the Trog said, his tone harsh.

"Hey, I doubt you'll get anyone arguing with that here. What was your mother's GM mix?"

"She was part jaguar. It was obvious in her, and in Dev. Not so much in me though, which made it easier to hide. I don't remember her that well, so I was never as bitter as Dev. Anyway, after he'd killed the Church's people, he went in search of the Coalition and told them he wanted to join. He made it his whole life, dedicated himself to destroying the Church, and he rose quickly through the ranks."

"And where did he stand on killing little children?" Alex asked.

"He was against it. He's a good man."

"Hmm." Tannis knew you had to be ruthless to get to the top of an organization like the Coalition. Ruthless and dedicated. "Have you been in touch with your brother?"

"Not for ten years. But that won't matter. He told me to come back when I was ready."

"And are you ready?" Tannis asked.

"I was never very interested in the fighting. It was always

engines that interested me." A smile flickered across his face. "You know, Dev's a brilliant engineer as well, but he got a little sidetracked—he taught me everything. Then I made the explosive device that blew up those children, and that act made us as bad as them. I couldn't stay. But I do believe the Church has to be stopped." The Trog glanced at Janey and shrugged. "Am I ready to go back? The truth is—I don't know."

Janey crossed to him and laid a scarlet nailed hand on his arm. "It wasn't your fault."

"It was as much mine as anyone's."

The look that passed between the two of them was interesting, but Tannis decided she would think about it later. Right now she needed to work out if this was a legitimate plan, or whether it was likely to get them all killed.

"But your brother is still dedicated to the cause?"

"As far as I know. I doubt he'll ever give it up—he hates the Church." He cast a glance toward Callum. Tannis followed his gaze. Callum still appeared a little green, but he looked a lot better than when he'd first arrived. "Dev hates the Collective as well. He says they're as responsible as the Church for the purge."

"How does he figure that?" Tannis asked.

"The Collective allowed the GMs to be downgraded to nonhuman status, which allowed the Church to kill us without legal repercussions, and they did nothing to stop the purge."

Callum sat absolutely still in his seat, his expression blank, but he didn't defend himself or the Collective.

"Yeah, well, perhaps their leader was too busy to know what was going on," Tannis suggested. "No doubt, you weren't important enough for his illustrious attentions, and he delegated. I've heard he does that a lot."

"Dev said one thing at a time, first the Church and then the Collective."

"Hmm, so do you think he will help us? Maybe he'd like to see Trakis Seven destroyed."

"Maybe. But he'd rather blow a few of the Church's ships into space dust. Plus, if what he"—he waved a hand at Callum—"says is right and Meridian is finished, then it doesn't matter, does it?"

That was true. "Okay, so how do we do this?"

"I have a code we set up when I left. I need to send it out and hopefully he should answer me straightaway." He sat at one of the consoles and Janey stood at his side, one hand resting on his shoulder.

Tannis forced herself to relax. She sat down but couldn't prevent her foot from tapping on the floor, her fingers drumming on the arm of the chair, while she waited. She cast a sidelong glance at Callum, just as he leaned forward and picked up Rico's bottle, topping off his glass. He caught her gaze and held out the bottle.

"Why not?"

He filled her glass and pushed it toward her.

"Anything yet?" she asked the Trog.

"It's been less than a minute. I don't even know where he is, whether they've been active."

Tannis turned to Skylar. "What about you? You said this guy was on your most-wanted lists—you must at least try and keep track of what the Rebels are up to."

"Small stuff, as far as I know," Skylar said. "They've been quiet for a while. The consensus within the intelligence section of the Corps was that they were building up to something big. But we had no clue what. That was before I left, but I haven't heard anything on the comms about them since then."

Tannis took a sip of her drink. "And how well do you know this Devlin guy?"

"Well, I've read the files. You know we nearly caught him once?"

The Trog turned from where he stared at the screen as though willing it to give him something. "No, I hadn't heard."

"About five years ago. We nearly killed him, but he somehow gave us the slip. We're pretty sure he was injured though."

"Maybe he's dead," Tannis said, peering around the Trog at the blank screen.

"No. I'd know if he were dead."

"Hey, something is happening."

The screen was blinking. Tannis jumped to her feet so she could see the words flashing up.

*Welcome back. Where and when?*

The Trog turned around so he could see her. "Well?"

"It needs to be soon, and we don't know where your brother is. Can you ask him?"

"I'd rather not. They tend to be a little touchy about giving away their location. Give me a time and a place and we'll see if he can make it."

"Janey, can you bring up that intel on the Church's ship—we don't have much time and we need to work out where to intercept it."

Janey flicked a few keys and a 3-D screen came up in front of them. The planets of the Trakis system popped up one by one, the *El Cazador* appearing somewhere between Trakis Two and Seven. A second group of ships showed up close to Trakis Four. Tannis studied the configuration and tried to work out where would be the best place to intercept. She didn't want to leave it too late, but on the other hand, they needed time to plan.

They also had no clue where the Rebels were based, so they might have to give a few locations before they hit one that worked. "Janey, can you put in the variables and give us a few suggestions to start with. Begin with the closest, and we'll work our way out."

\* \* \*

Okay, so he was feeling like shit. Physically, the symptoms were fading, and he'd been starting to feel better when they hit him with the guilt thing again. He hadn't thought he could experience guilt anymore. He'd actually believed it was part of the whole Meridian thing, a bit like the lack of sexual urges. But just like lust, the guilt had been in hiding, waiting for someone to wake it up with a few well-pointed comments.

Like he was responsible for the near genocide of a whole species.

Though the GMs weren't really a separate species. They were as much human as . . . well, as he was. Maybe more so, because he was still changing. Who knew what he would end up in another five hundred years? The idea excited him more than it scared him. Though it scared him, like the fear he'd felt going into combat when he was a pilot on Earth. Fear of the unknown.

But back to the guilt. It was beginning to dawn on him just how much he had to be guilty about. The GM purge had been wrong, but the Council had referred to them as collateral damage, acceptable to maintain their precarious hold on power. The world thought they were all powerful, but it didn't take much to sway the balance, and the Church had the masses behind them. All those people who knew they would never have the means to obtain immortality through Meridian. And it wasn't only money that was required—the selection process had become strict when it was obvious that even at the exorbitant prices, there were still many more people applying than there were Meridian available.

But the need to maintain power didn't justify anything. Why should they be in charge anyway? What made them believe they should rule the world just because they were immortal? All that meant was they could make the same mistakes over and over again.

They had forgotten that people mattered. Half the time, he hadn't thought of them as people at all, just pieces in this game he was playing—the let's-rule-the-universe game. He'd become distanced from everyone. Even his own people.

Christ, he was a self-pitying bastard right now.

Or maybe he was just drunk. On Earth, he'd been able to drink everyone under the table. But it had been a long time, and he could feel the alcohol like a buzz in his brain. He liked the feeling. Relaxing back in his chair, he sipped his drink and watched them all through half-closed lashes.

Tannis fizzed with energy; she was one of the most alive people he had ever encountered. At least she hadn't tried to kill him again, though the poison thing hadn't been a serious effort—she'd just let him know very effectively that she wasn't happy.

He wasn't sure about this whole Rebel thing. He'd always considered them an unorganized rabble and not capable of being a serious threat. Look at the Trog and the balls-up that had ended with him hiding on *El Cazador*. They couldn't even agree *who* to blow up.

But they didn't have a lot of choices here.

"So," Tannis broke into his thoughts, "while we're waiting, what does everyone think about this? Anyone have any comments or concerns—vent them now."

She stood in front of them, hands in her pockets, legs braced while she waited for answers. She was a good leader. She asked for advice and her crew would probably follow her anywhere, trusting her to do what was best for all of them. Unlike his Council, who hadn't trusted him one little bit. And with good cause. For the first time, he realized he hadn't actually given his Council's wishes any thought. He'd merely disregarded them because their ideas weren't in line with his own. Yes, they were scared and that had irritated him. But only because they disagreed with him, and he'd gotten used to doing exactly what he wanted.

"I've always thought the Rebels were a load of undisciplined amateurs," Jon said. "But if the Trog vouches for this guy, then I'll trust him."

"Janey?" Tannis asked. "What about you?"

She glanced up from the console. "I'm with Jon—if the Trog thinks they're okay, that's good enough for me."

Callum was getting the distinct impression that there was something between Janey and the reclusive engineer. Maybe not consummated yet but simmering just under the surface.

"Alex?"

Callum waited to hear what the little priestess had to say—she'd been part of the Church all her life, they were her people, presumably people she had known well, she must have strong feelings about this.

"I think they need to be stopped. Temperance Hatcher is a fanatic. The current guy in charge might be an asshole—" She waved a hand at Callum, and he winced. "But if he makes mistakes, it's through laziness and stupidity not through evil, which is what Temperance is."

He winced again at the stupidity comment, but he reckoned he deserved it.

"Fair enough," Tannis said. "Rico?"

"Let's go for it. Any chance of blowing a few religious types into dust is my idea of fun, and we can't do this alone."

"Well, looks about unanimous. What about you?" She was staring straight at him, and he realized with surprise that she was actually asking his opinion.

He sat up straight and placed his glass on the table in front of him. "You mean I have a say in this? I'm just a lazy, stupid asshole."

Tannis smiled sweetly, with her mouth at least, her

yellow eyes remained cold. "Yes, but you're our lazy, stupid asshole employer, after all."

He'd asked for that. "I say we go for it. Unless you want to say good-bye to that Meridian treatment—it's our only hope."

"Yeah, but don't try and convince me you're doing this for me, because I won't buy it. I think you've blown your chance at the Mr. Caring award. You want to go to Trakis Seven as much as I do."

For a minute, they stared at each other. Callum had an almost overwhelming urge to defend himself, to say it wasn't his fault. But that would be a lie. Or maybe that he would try and do better in the future. But perhaps that was a lie as well. The truth was he'd always been a selfish bastard and done exactly what he wanted. Back on Earth, they'd called him a hero, but really, he'd only been doing something he loved. But he *wanted* to do better, and the thought surprised him. He just wasn't sure he was capable of it, so he kept his mouth shut. Anyway, he reckoned words would be meaningless. He'd have to show her somehow.

"Okay, Captain," Janey said. "I've got five coordinates where we could meet and still have time to intercept the ship before it reaches Trakis Seven. You want me to send them."

"Go ahead."

Tannis sat down opposite him, while they waited.

Five minutes later, Janey glanced up and grinned. "Okay, looks like we're on. Second option. Hmm, they must be quite close."

"Where and when is option two?"

"Twenty-four hours from now, on our most direct course to Trakis Seven."

"So we meet in space."

"Yes. Is that okay?"

"It's fine. Better really, we can see what we're up against—less chance for them to take us by surprise."

"Dev won't do anything underhanded," the Trog said.

"Maybe, but you haven't seen him in ten years, and I'm not taking any chances." She rubbed her hands together. "Looks like we're back in business."

Callum tried to feel enthusiastic, but all he really wanted to do was lie down.

# CHAPTER 11

Tannis paced the floor of the large meeting room while they waited for Devlin Starke to appear. He'd been dealing with something when they'd boarded and would be with them as soon as he could. Tannis tried to curb her impatience, but she'd never been any good at that.

So far, she was impressed with what she had seen. The ship was immaculate and appeared to be well run. She was a Mark Three cruiser like *El Cazador*, though her design and decor were more functional, less luxurious, but that was Rico's influence.

They'd decided to keep the boarding group small, plenty of time for the Rebels to meet the rest of the crew if they agreed to help. And she was by no means convinced they would. She could only hope that they would see enough benefit in destroying the ship and hindering the Church's plans for ultimate power.

So it was just her, Rico, and the Trog. Callum had wanted to come, but she had pointed out, quite reasonably—well reasonably for her anyway—that he might not be one of Devlin Starke's favorite people, and their chances were better if he stayed in the background. He'd agreed—albeit reluctantly. She didn't think Callum was a background sort of person.

Callum had been acting a little weird. If she hadn't known him better, she would have presumed he was feeling guilty. He mostly remained in his cabin, but did join them for meals, where he stayed quiet and just watched them, usually with a slight frown on his face as though he didn't know what to make of them. His girlfriend hadn't shown herself, whether through choice or because Callum had ordered her to stay out of the way, Tannis didn't know. But she was glad. Venna and her "angel" face might have been a little too much to stomach.

The door slid open, and she turned to look at the man who stood in the entrance. He hesitated a moment, spoke a brief aside to somebody behind him, then entered the room alone. He bore very little resemblance to the Trog. His hair, mainly black with streaks of blond, was pulled into a ponytail showing off his sharp cheekbones and slanted blue-green eyes. Cat's eyes—they were the only thing he shared with his brother. He was a handsome man, but with a hard, ruthless stamp to his features, further enhanced by the scar that ran from his right eyebrow, down his cheek to the corner of his mouth, giving him a perpetual sneer. She wondered why he had never had it corrected; maybe he knew it gave him an amazingly sexy and dangerous look. The thought surprised her. Since when had she noticed that men were sexy?

He strolled toward them. Where the Trog was lanky, he appeared perfectly proportioned, with long legs and broad shoulders. He moved like a cat, on the balls of his feet, graceful for such a big man. The Rebels didn't wear a uniform, but he was dressed in khaki pants tucked into combat boots, and a short-sleeved T-shirt. A weapons belt was strapped to his waist, and his hand rested lightly on the grip of his laser pistol.

"You're staring," Rico murmured from beside her.

Luckily, it didn't matter. Devlin Starke's attention was all on the Trog. He came to a halt in front of his brother, and suddenly his deadpan expression melted and he grinned. "Welcome home, Tris."

Tannis turned to Rico. "Tris?" she mouthed the question.

"Tristan Starke," he murmured. "You didn't think his name was really the Trog, did you?"

She hadn't actually thought about it at all, but now that she did, it did seem unlikely.

"I'm not actually home as such . . ." the Trog replied.

"It's good enough for me. I missed you, bro." He wrapped his arms around his brother, hugging him tight. After a moment, the Trog's arms came out and he hugged him back.

"I missed you, too. I just thought it was easier this way. If you knew where I was, you might have come after me."

"I always knew where you were."

"You did?"

Devlin nodded and stepped away, turning his gaze to her and Rico. Tannis did her best to keep her features expressionless.

"So, Tris, are you going to introduce me?"

"Sure, this is Tannis, captain of *El Cazador.*"

Devlin held her gaze. His green-blue eyes had little flecks of gold in them and a dark green circle around the iris. His lips curled into a slow smile, banishing the sneer.

"Snake-lady . . . nice." His voice was a rough purr, and a shiver ran through her. When he held out his hand, Tannis slid her palm into his warm hard one. He clasped it for longer than necessary, and Tannis didn't pull away.

Rico coughed loudly. Devlin released her hand, but slowly, his fingers sliding against hers, before focusing on the vampire. His eyes narrowed as though he couldn't quite place who or what he was. Which was unsurprising. Not many people had come across a vampire before, and even less knew what they were facing. A few sensed the difference, that there was something not quite right, but most assumed he must be some form of GM.

"This is Ricardo Sanchez," the Trog said. "Owner and pilot of *El Cazador*."

"Rico is fine," Rico said and thrust out his hand. Devlin took it but the contact was brief, and Rico raised an eyebrow. "Aren't you going to tell me *I'm* nice?" he asked.

Shit, Rico was going to be an asshole. Tannis sighed and waited, not even considering trying to deter him. When Rico wanted to be a dick, nothing was going to stop him.

But Devlin just smiled. "I suspect 'nice' isn't a word used to describe you often." He studied Rico, his head tilted to one side. "What are you?"

Rico grinned, flashing the tips of his sharp white fangs. "Guess?"

"Jesus," Devlin muttered. "Nice friends you've got, Tris."

"They've been good to me," the Trog said.

Devlin pursed his lips but then nodded abruptly. "Why don't we sit down and you can tell me just what you think we can do for you, and why the hell we should do it."

He sank into a chair and rested one booted foot across his thigh, leaned back, and gestured to the empty seats around him.

Tannis took the seat opposite, Rico sat beside her, and the Trog took the chair next to his brother. Tannis tried to get her ideas together. Having met the man, she had to decide what was the best approach.

Direct, she decided as his fingers started tapping on the arm of his chair.

"We want you to help us intercept a ship."

"And why should I do that?"

"Because it belongs to the Church, and you hate the Church."

"Indeed I do. Tell me the rest."

"There's actually more than one ship. There's the one we want destroyed and then five more guarding the main target. They're all Mark One cruisers and heavily armed."

"Where are they heading?"

"To Trakis Seven. Their aim is to destroy the planet, and the Collective's source of Meridian."

"And so destroy their power base and no doubt wrest control from the Collective. I heard they're in chaos. Callum Meridian is missing and . . ." He broke off and frowned, then pressed the switch on his wrist and a small screen appeared. He read for a minute and then turned back to them. "I thought I recognized the name, *El Cazador*. It's the ship that supposedly kidnapped Callum Meridian from Trakis Four."

"We did not kidnap Callum Meridian."

"Pity. I would have liked a chance to get at the bastard."

*Great, just great.*

She decided to move past the subject of Callum for now. Time enough for that later. "So will you help us?"

"I might." He got up and paced the room, moving with a feline grace that Tannis found very easy to watch. "I'll need to get my inner circle to sign off on this, but I think they'll go for it." He glanced at his brother. "But I'm getting the distinct feeling that you haven't told me everything yet. Tris? Anything else you want to add?"

The Trog glanced toward her, a question in his eyes, and she nodded. There was no point in trying to keep secrets if they wanted this man's cooperation.

"There are two members of the Collective on board *El Cazador*," Tris said.

Actually, there were technically three, if you included

Venna, though if she stayed on her own shuttle . . . she supposed two was accurate enough.

"One is an ex-intelligence officer with the Corps—"

"Ex?" Devlin interrupted. "I thought once in, they never left."

"Skylar's different. But I trust her, she's good people."

Devlin ran a finger down the scar on his cheek. "You do know how I got this, don't you?"

Tris shook his head. But Tannis had a good idea.

"The fucking Corps. Set an ambush and nearly finished me off. They're not my favorite people." He shoved his hands in his pockets and scowled down at them. "And the other?"

The Trog grinned. "The other is Callum Meridian."

"What? I thought you said you didn't kidnap him."

"We didn't kidnap him. We're working for him."

His eyes narrowed, the greeny-gold icing over, and for the first time she saw the man who was the Collective's "most wanted dead" terrorist. A little shiver ran through her.

"Let me get this straight," he said, his tone equally icy. "You want me to help you do some sort of job for Callum Meridian?"

"Not exactly."

"So explain."

Tannis shrugged one shoulder. "Callum Meridian has employed us to take him to Trakis Seven. We're not going to be able to do that if the Church blow the planet up before we get there. So we're not asking you to help us take him there. We're asking you to stop the Church from blowing up Trakis Seven. And you get to kill a few Church people in the meantime. What's the big deal? Who do you hate the most, the Church, or Callum Meridian?

"It's a toss-up."

"No it's not," the Trog said. "And you know it. The Church came after you because of what you are. The Collective are after you because of what you've done. I always remember you telling me you have to be willing to take the consequences for your actions. You broke their laws."

"The same stinking laws that said we were animals and the Church could do what they liked to us."

"Maybe. That doesn't change things."

Devlin stared beyond them for long moments, and then he nodded abruptly. "I'll take it to my people."

"We're on a timetable here."

He gave her a long, measured look. "I'll take it to my people . . . quickly."

Tannis realized the meeting was over. Beside her, Rico pushed himself to his feet. As she got up to follow, Rico touched her lightly on the arm.

She glanced up into his face. "What?"

"You might want to hold off on the hand-holding if there's a next meeting with this guy."

"Why?" she snapped. "It was a perfectly normal greeting."

"He was practically drooling over you, and you did nothing to discourage him."

"Your point is?"

"Well, I'm guessing neither our new friend over there, or Callum for that matter, are the types to cope with jealousy very well. So don't stir up trouble. You're pissed off at Callum right now, but this is a complication we do not need."

"I can't believe you're saying this to me."

He grinned. "I can't believe it myself. But seems I'm turning into something of a relationship counselor these days."

"I do not have a relationship, and I do not need counseling."

"Just giving you the benefit of my experience."

"Thanks," she said sourly.

"I thought you were on a timetable?" Devlin stood in the doorway, clearly waiting for them.

Tannis shrugged off Rico's hand and headed toward him, pushing past and out of the door. Then she came to a halt.

A woman stood on either side of the entrance. As Devlin emerged, they moved to stand on either side of him. Dressed similar to Devlin, in khaki pants and tight T-shirts, weapons at their waists, they looked like Amazons, beautiful but fierce.

"Aren't you going to introduce us?" Tannis asked.

Devlin grinned. "My bodyguards. Shawna and Mara. They go everywhere with me."

"Everywhere?" She fell into step beside him as they headed down the corridor toward the docking bay.

"Yup. They sleep at the bottom of my bed. And they think you might be a threat to my person."

"Well, I'm not."

"No?" He cast her an amused glance. "Pity."

They arrived back at the shuttle, and he held out his hand again. She took it and allowed him to hold it longer than necessary just to rile Rico. Who the hell was he to give relationship advice? Before he'd met Skylar, Tannis had never known him to have a relationship that lasted more than a couple of hours. And most of those "relationships" had been paid for. He'd always said he preferred whores; he knew what he was getting and so did they. Well, maybe they hadn't known exactly what they were getting.

"I'll contact you as soon as I have an answer." Devlin dropped her hand and turned to the Trog. "Will you stay and talk a while, Tris? I'll see you get back to your ship whatever our decision."

The Trog nodded. "That okay, Captain?"

She nodded. "Of course. We'll see you later."

Rico was already on the shuttle readying for takeoff and she hurried after him.

Devlin contacted them less than an hour after they got back to *El Cazador*. Tannis had been pacing the floor of the bridge. She knew she was driving everybody crazy with her nerves, but she couldn't help it.

"So what's this guy, Devlin, like?" Skylar asked Rico. "Is he as bad as his reputation?"

"Ask Tannis," Rico said. "She was holding hands with him."

Skylar's glance shot to her, and she raised her brows. Tannis ignored the look, and Rico's comment, and the stare she received from Callum, who was slumped in a chair watching her pace. She could feel his eyes on her, hot, intense.

She hadn't forgiven him. She doubted she ever would, but her rage had drained away. He hadn't made any more attempts to justify himself, and she liked that, mainly because there was no justification.

"It's the Rebels calling," Janey said. "You want to talk to them? Or you want to pace a bit more?"

"I want to pace a bit more," she snapped.

"Okay, I'll ignore them."

Tannis stopped her pacing and growled.

Janey grinned. "I'm putting them on speaker."

"We're on," Devlin said. "I'm bringing Tris back and a few of my people for a meeting. We'll be there in thirty."

And he was gone.

"Sounds like an asshole," Callum said.

"He sounds hot," Janey countered. "Is he anything like the Trog?"

"Nothing," Tannis said. The tension seeped from her. They were back in with a chance. She looked up to find

Callum still watching her, his eyes narrowed. "He's definitely hot," she added, though she wasn't sure who she was trying to piss off with that comment. Rico or Callum. "I'm going for a shower. We'll all meet in the central conference room as soon as they arrive."

Her step felt light as she hurried from the room, despite the weight of the stares that followed her.

Callum studied the other man as he entered the conference room at the head of his people. He reckoned he was predisposed to hating Devlin Starke, nothing was going to change that, however fucking "hot" he was.

Tall and lean, the man moved with the controlled grace of a highly trained fighter. In his time as leader, Callum had learned to sum up people quickly, and he was rarely wrong. Dangerous, was the first word that sprang to mind. Starke gave the impression of leashed-in power that could explode at any moment.

He stared around the room, his gaze settling for a second on Callum. His eyes widened a little, no doubt taking in the wings. Callum held his stare and the expression didn't change, the cold sneer remaining firmly in place. He moved on and his expression warmed. Callum followed his gaze. Tannis.

She'd showered and changed into tight black pants tucked into knee-high boots that made her legs look impossibly long and a bright red shirt that hugged her small breasts. There was something different about her. He frowned and realized she was wearing makeup—subtle but there—black smudged around her eyes so the yellow stood out stark, and her lips were red to match her shirt. And earrings, long glittering drops that swung against her slender white neck.

Something ugly stirred to life inside him. If she'd done this for Devlin Starke, there was going to be trouble. He looked away, straight into the vampire's dark eyes. Rico raised one eyebrow. Callum ignored him and slunk lower in his seat, folding his arms across his chest. Amusement flashed across Rico's face, and Callum scowled. He got the impression the vampire knew exactly what was going through his mind. Well, at least he was providing amusement.

But in truth, he couldn't ever remember being jealous. How was he supposed to know how to behave?

Tannis was obviously still upset with him. She couldn't really see anything in that guy, just because he had a cool scar and no wings, and hadn't actually been responsible for torturing her during her childhood and indirectly murdering her sister.

Rico pulled a silver flask from his pocket and tossed it over. Callum caught it and nodded his thanks. After unscrewing the top, he lifted it to his mouth and took a deep pull. At least he was just about recovered from the poison.

He lowered the flask as Venna appeared in the open doorway. She didn't look happy to be there, but then who could blame her? She must have realized she was far from popular on this ship, and she wasn't used to that—she liked to be liked. She'd been skulking in her shuttle, but he'd ordered her to be present at this meeting. He still wanted her with them on Trakis Seven; she had done more research on the planet than anyone. If he was going to find some answers in the limited time they had before the planet's bloody nature drove them away, then he needed her expertise. She scuttled around the edge of the room, took a chair at the rear, and tried to make herself small.

Tannis was whispering to Starke. Finally, she nodded, headed over, and took the seat next to him, which surprised him. He held out Rico's flask, and she frowned but took it and sipped delicately. Who was she trying to impress? He'd seen her drinking, and she could drink even Rico under the table. Probably didn't want to smudge her lipstick.

Starke turned to face them.

"My brother reckons we can trust you. The rest of my people aren't so sure. But fuck with us, and you'll regret it."

"Oooh, I'm sooo scared," Jon said from the seat behind him.

Callum grinned. It appeared there was someone else the werewolf didn't like, besides him.

"Shut up, Jon," Tannis snapped.

"Right." Starke ignored both comments. "So we have that out of the way. We need a plan."

"What we need is some serious firepower," Rico said. "Can you provide that?"

"We have enough to take on those Church ships."

"And win? You know the Rebels don't have that good a reputation when it comes to seeing things through."

Tannis glared at him.

Rico shrugged. "I'm just pointing out a few truths."

"Like we've got so many other options," Tannis said. "Do you mind not screwing this up."

Starke leaned against the wall and watched them. "Finished? Yes, we can win."

"Good, that's all I needed to know."

It took an hour to hammer out the plan.

"Right, we'll aim to intercept them here." Rico pointed at a spot on the monitor. "Devlin's guys will take out the guard ships, while *El Cazador* concentrates on the main target. Afterward, Devlin and his pals can go off and do whatever he does, and we'll continue on to Trakis Seven. We'll get as close as we can, then whoever is going will have to complete the journey in the shuttle. I've heard Trakis Seven isn't a pleasant place to visit."

"No, it's not pleasant," Callum said. "Though *you* might survive. I don't think a vampire has ever landed there."

"I'd prefer not to test it." He shuddered. "I've heard it's not a good death."

No. Callum had seen most of his crew die from exposure to Trakis Seven, and it had not been pretty. He tried not to think of all the people who had been sent there since they'd discovered Meridian. Sent by the Collective to work the mines and die on that hideous lump of poisoned rock.

He'd justified it by telling himself that they were criminals, but now he'd learned that innocent people had also died in the mines, their only crime being they were not entirely human.

With a start of shock, he realized that Tannis would have been one of those people if she hadn't escaped from the research center. They would have taken her to Trakis Seven, and she would have died, in a week, maybe not for a year. He had heard of people who lasted two years, but he was sure at the end of that time they'd been desperate for death. An image of her body ravaged by poison flashed through his mind.

"What's the matter?" she asked

He glanced up to find her watching him, her brows drawn together.

"Nothing." What could he say? He was running the complete gamut of emotions these days. Guilt, jealousy . . .

Maybe it would be best if the planet was destroyed. He hadn't allowed himself to consider that option. But what if they were to just allow this to take its course and let the Church destroy Trakis Seven once and for all. Except he had promised Tannis the Meridian treatment, and he wanted to give that to her. Maybe it would make up in some small way for the past.

But there was more; he needed to find out the truth about

what he was, what he was becoming, and every instinct told him the answers were to be found on Trakis Seven. Somehow, he had to find a way to get the planet to give up its secrets.

"Okay, so we have four days until we intercept the ships," Tannis said. "That long enough for your guys to get there?"

Starke nodded. "I'm still getting the numbers in, but I should know later tonight."

"Then I think we're finished for now, not much else we can do until we know what firepower we have on our side. We'll meet again tomorrow and go over the details."

The meeting was obviously over. Callum got to his feet, meaning to get close to Tannis and stick close while that slimy bastard was on board. Hopefully, that wouldn't be for long. No doubt, he'd be heading back to his own ship now that they were done. And good riddance.

Starke approached her, and Callum's eyes narrowed on the other man. "Captain, can I speak with you for a moment?"

Callum shifted closer so he could hear the conversation.

"Callum?" Venna spoke softly from beside him, and he turned away impatiently.

She shifted from foot to foot, casting furtive glances around the room. "Will you walk me to my shuttle?"

"Why?"

"I don't think they like me." She nodded toward the small knot of people by the door. The crew didn't look too friendly.

He glanced at Tannis, who stood way too close to Starke, but Rico was still seated, so he reckoned it was safe to leave them for a minute. And it was his fault Venna was here. He supposed he couldn't just abandon her, much as he would have liked to—it wasn't part of his new caring image. All the same, he hustled her out of the room as fast as he could.

* * *

Tannis was conscious of Callum leaving with Venna and had to keep her feet firmly placed to stop from following. She sighed and looked back at Devlin.

"Is it okay if I stay on board?" Devlin asked. "I want to spend some time with Tris."

"No problem. Though we're pretty pushed for space right now."

"That's okay, I'll bunk in with Tris." He gave her a slow smile. "Unless I get a better offer."

He was flirting with her, and she wasn't sure how she felt about that. He was such a contradiction. The deadly terrorist who'd killed hundreds, and this man who wanted to spend time with his brother. She had a thought. "Your bodyguards aren't staying, are they?" There certainly wasn't enough room for them.

"No, I've sent them back. They weren't happy—they don't think I'm safe with you. They think you'll take advantage of me." He gave her a slow smile that banished the sneer from his face. "Will you take advantage of me, snake-lady? If I ask nicely?"

She was aware the rest of the crew had left, even Rico who had loitered as though he didn't want to leave her alone.

She studied him for a moment, a small frown pulling her lips. "The Trog said you were obviously GM, but I can't see it."

He raised his brows, then turned his back on her. She frowned, wondering what he was doing. Then he gripped the hem of his T-shirt, pulled it over his head, and tossed it onto the chair.

"Wow." The word slipped out. She glanced at the open doorway where everyone had disappeared, not knowing whether she wished somebody would come back, or she was glad they were alone. She returned her attention to Devlin. He was very easy to look at.

He was broad at the shoulders, tapering to a narrow waist. His skin had the sheen of good health, though that wasn't what held her attention. Faint rosettes of color, black on gold, marked his back. Jaguar rings.

He turned, and she found herself very close to the smooth swell of his chest. The jaguar markings tinged his skin around the sides, fading to leave his chest a creamy gold. A line of hair dissected his ridged belly, the same gold, disappearing into the waistband of his pants.

"There are also these." He took her hand in his and moved her fingers so they pressed against the pad of his. A sharp claw emerged.

"Retractable claws—cool."

He stroked the sharp claw lightly across her palm, and a shiver ran through her. But when he reached up to grasp her shoulder, she backed away.

"I have things to do," she said.

And ran.

# CHAPTER 12

Callum was racing back to the conference room when he
bumped into Rico. Literally. He hadn't been looking where
he was going, and it was like running into a blaster shield.

"Shit."

Rico grinned. "In a hurry?"

For a moment, Callum peered down the corridor. "No."

"Then come with me," Rico said. "I have something
for you."

"Really? A present? How nice but—"

"She's only pissing you off. Don't rise to it."

For a second he hesitated, then said, "Lead the way."

He followed Rico the way he had come, down into the
docking bay, intrigued despite himself. The area was large
and empty except for the two shuttles parked at the far side.
Rico ignored them and crossed the room in the opposite
direction, coming to a halt beside a large cabinet with
double doors. He pressed his palm to the panel and the
doors slid apart revealing an extensive stash of weapons.

Callum watched in silence as Rico studied the contents.
He didn't think the vampire meant to shoot him, but all
the same, his gut tightened. Rico selected a weapons belt

and handed it over. Callum didn't ask, just fastened it around his waist. Next, Rico picked up a laser pistol and weighed it in his hand, then put it down and tried another. He glanced at Callum.

"I take it you do know how to use one of these things?"

"It's been a while."

"I'll bet it has. How long a while?"

Callum couldn't remember when he had last worn a weapon. There was no need when you spent your whole life in meetings, had an army at your disposal, and a set of personal guards at your back.

"Three hundred years, give or take."

*"Christos."* Rico studied him as though he were something curious. "Oh, well, just make sure you learn how to use it. I don't want you shooting anyone by accident."

He tossed the pistol to Callum, who caught it easily and slid it into the weapons belt. The grip felt good in his hand, and he flexed his fingers. But he needed to understand one thing. "Why?"

"Starke is staying on board, and this is my ship. If anyone gets to kill you, it's going to be me. Or the captain. I might let her if she still wants to and she asks me nicely."

"Why's Starke staying on the ship?" He had a few ideas, but he really hoped he was wrong.

"He says he wants to spend time with his brother, and he's probably telling the truth."

"So why give me the gun?"

"His brother isn't the only one he wants to spend time with. He's got his eyes on the captain, and she's still pissed enough with you that she might just think it's worth leading him on. In which case, seems he's got a gun, it's only fair you have one as well."

"Good. I think."

"Besides, I don't know him, and I don't trust him."

That was good news. "Why?"

"Because he's an idealist. He sees things as black and white, and I'm guessing, to his eyes, you're as black as they come."

"But not in yours?"

"I'm no idealist. Besides . . ."

"Besides?"

"I lived on Earth. The place was a mess, much worse than here. You lot might not be perfect, but you're doing an okay job. Except for the GM thing, but you're going to put that right. Right?"

"It's at the top of my list."

"Good. And while I might not think much of the Collective as a whole, you're a damn sight better than the alternative."

"Thanks. I think. By 'alternative' I presume you mean the Church. Why do you hate them so much? Is it the whole vampire thing?"

"No. I hated them before I became a vampire. You could say I became a vampire because I hated them." He sighed. "I grew up in a time when the Church was powerful, even more powerful than today."

"I take it you were never a believer."

Rico cast him an incredulous look. "Do I look like an idiot? Though strangely I've come to believe there's something out there, just not the crap the priests spout." He shrugged. "They killed my wife. Claimed she was a witch and burned her at the stake."

"And was she? A witch, I mean?"

Rico glanced at him sharply. "You know, you're the first person to ask me that. Most people assume not, but in fact, by the rules of the day she was. Enough—it was a long time ago and in a faraway place." He nodded at the laser pistol at Callum's waist. "Let's give you a go with that thing— see just how bad things are." He flicked a switch and a target appeared on the far wall.

Callum drew the weapon, flipped the power on, and shot a blast. Once he'd been good at this—the best—and he swore softly when he only clipped the edge of the target.

"I guess you're more used to the old-fashioned type with bullets."

"Ha-ha."

"But you're not completely without hope, you just need some practice. With these things, it's not enough to be able to shoot and hit a target. If you're good you can deflect the incoming blasts, even direct them back at the shooter. Janey has some training programs on file somewhere. Ask her nicely, and she'll dig them out for you."

Callum sent him a look of complete disbelief. "Is this the Janey that offered to murder me presuming Tannis didn't want to do it herself?"

"If Tannis wanted to kill you, you'd be dead. If she didn't when she first found out, then chances are she's not going to now."

Callum had an idea the vampire wasn't always so talkative and he had a thousand things he wanted to know. "What was she like when you met?"

"What do you think she was like? Fucked-up." He considered Callum for a moment. "Let me give you a word of advice: get the crew on your side."

Callum snorted. "Is that even possible?"

"Maybe not, but you can try. For a start, you might tone down that massive superiority complex you've got going."

Callum grinned. "That'll be hard."

"I'll bet—but try." He leaned against the wall as Callum tried a few more shots at the target, hitting it this time. He holstered the pistol.

"So, the crew?" Callum asked.

"Most of Jon is just talk. He's been acting mean for so long, it's become a habit."

"Yeah, I can see that underneath, he's just a big fluffy dog. What about the little priestess?"

"Alex knows what it's like to be in a position of power and not be able to totally control things. Play it right, and she'll sympathize. Plus, she has this whole 'to forgive is divine' thing going on. She wants to forgive—all you have to do is ask nicely."

"Janey?"

"Janey likes to flirt, but she doesn't really like men."

"Why?"

"Her business, but you'll get points if you don't flirt back. And don't try to manipulate her—she's got the best brain I've ever come across, and she'll see right through you."

"The green girl?"

"Daisy? She's already half-infatuated with you. You can fly, and to Daisy, that puts you on a whole different level from the rest of mankind. Be her friend and she'll love you forever." He gave Callum a sharp look. "Just don't take advantage of that."

Callum was actually shocked at the thought. "It never even crossed my mind."

"No, your mind—not to mention the rest of you—is somewhere else." He grinned. "Good luck with that."

"What about Skylar? How do I get her on my side?"

"You don't." Rico drew his laser pistol and placed three blasts in the center of the target. "You stay away from Skylar."

Callum decided that however hard it was going to be, he was going to have to give Tannis some space. He was sure if she spent time with Starke, she would soon realize what a tosser he was.

Meanwhile, he was going to attempt to follow Rico's advice and get the rest of the crew on his side. He wasn't expecting it to be easy. He decided to start with Janey and found her at her console on the bridge. She glanced up, her expression vaguely hostile as she caught him watching her. He tried a smile. She didn't seem impressed.

*Humble. Think humble.*

"Rico gave me a gun," he said.

"So?"

He frowned. Wasn't she supposed to be flirting with him? "I haven't shot anyone in a long time."

She raised one arched elegant eyebrow.

"Rico said you might have some training programs you could set up for me."

"He did?" She frowned. "Why do you want to learn? Aren't you a politician? Who do you want to shoot?"

Janey sounded suspicious, and he tried to think what would be a good answer. He reckoned one of the reasons the crew was so against him was because they were protective of Tannis. He could work with that. "I'll be going down to Trakis Seven with Tannis. I might need to protect her."

"From what? There's nothing alive on Trakis Seven."

"Maybe someone will follow us down there."

"This is Trakis Seven we're talking about. Somehow, I doubt you'll be inundated with company. Besides, the captain is quite capable of looking after herself."

He resisted the urge to follow his natural inclinations and order her to give him the stuff. Instead, he took a deep breath. There were some occasions when only the truth would do. "Okay, the truth?"

"A novel idea, but why not?"

"I suspect, at some point in the near future, I'm going to want to shoot Devlin Starke. Unfortunately, he's essential to our plans, so I want to make sure that I don't kill him by accident."

Janey grinned. "Great reason. You'll find a headset

underneath the console in your cabin. I'll send the files through there."

"You know, you should think about joining us," Devlin said.

Tannis hadn't been paying attention. Instead, she'd been playing with her food and watching the doorway. Now she turned to the man at her side. "Sorry?"

"I said, I think you should consider joining the Rebels. We need good captains."

The comment took her by surprise. She wondered why. On the outside, she supposed she was ideal rebel material. She was a GM and an experienced captain. Still, anyone who knew her well could have told him she wasn't one for causes, and she certainly wasn't a joiner. Rico's influence.

"I don't think so."

"Why?" He reached across and stroked a finger down the back of her hand, and she twitched with the need to pull away. She didn't like unsolicited personal contact. But maybe Devlin didn't realize that. After all, she'd hardly been standoffish with him. She was just unused to this sort of situation, so she left her hand where it was and tried to control her twitching. He obviously took that as positive and stroked her again. She analyzed the resulting feeling: not unpleasant, but not wildly exciting either. Her gaze strayed to the door.

"We'd be good together," Devlin murmured.

She realized he was still on about her joining the Rebels. At least she hoped that's what he was talking about. She turned to face him. Close up, he really was very good-looking.

"No, we wouldn't," she said. "You like to be in charge and so do I. Besides, you're an idealist and I'm not. You want to save the world, and I just want to earn lots and lots of money."

"You don't come across as the mercenary type."

Tannis grinned. "Believe me, I love money."

"Is that why you're working for that bastard? For money."

She presumed he meant Callum. "Yeah, for money. Mainly."

He frowned. "Maybe you need to open your eyes and see what's going on in the world. GMs are suffering. It's our duty to stop this, to bring down the government—"

"Yeah, yeah, and make the world a better place," she interrupted his sermon as irritation nipped at her nerves. "My eyes are open, thank you, and I think I know what's going on, probably better than you. I just don't want to make that my life." She pulled her hand free and picked up her spoon, starting to eat and hoping he would get the message.

Callum was late for supper. Where was he?

He'd left her alone for the last couple of days, and she didn't blame him. After all, she had poisoned him. At first, she'd tried to tell herself that she liked it this way, but her deep-rooted self-honesty wouldn't allow her to accept that. She missed him.

But the one time he turned up unfailingly was mealtimes. The first couple of times, he'd sat in silence, obviously listening. He hadn't attempted to sit next to her, usually taking a seat opposite. She occasionally found his gaze on her, but he would just smile politely and go on with his food.

Then, after the first couple of meals, he'd started joining in with the conversation. Making the odd comment. Asking questions. Last night, he and Rico had gotten into an argument about an old program they had both watched back on Earth—*Star Trek*—and which season was the best. But the argument had been friendly—it looked like Rico had forgiven him for his time in the research center.

Afterward, she'd asked him, and he'd shrugged. "We've

all done things we should probably be ashamed of. Hell, I changed Bastian, and look how that turned out."

Now, she played with her food and waited for Callum to appear.

"So once you get rid of your client," Devlin said from beside her, "why don't you give it a try and join us?"

Jesus, he was still on about that. "I'm not getting rid of Callum."

"You're not?"

"No, I'm going to Trakis Seven."

Devlin sat back in his seat, a frown on his handsome face. "No one survives Trakis Seven except the Collective."

"He's paying me with the Meridian treatment." Devlin would know she was going to Trakis Seven soon enough. They had a strategy meeting scheduled for after supper. It would be obvious then.

At that moment, Callum appeared in the doorway. Alex was at his side like some exotic flower in her burnt-orange jumpsuit with scarlet piping. Alex had spent most of her life in the black robes of a priestess, and now she loved color, the brighter the better. Callum's head was bent toward her as he listened to something she was saying, and Tannis strained to hear.

"Thanks for hearing me out," he murmured. "I needed to get that off my conscience. You're a good listener."

Alex patted his arm. "I'm glad it helped." She gave him a sweet smile and went and sat beside Jon. Tannis frowned.

Callum nodded at the room in general and glanced around. There was a free seat on the other side of Tannis, but he ignored that and sat down next to Daisy. Tannis pretended to eat as she eavesdropped.

"I wanted to ask you a favor," he said.

Daisy looked at him, her emerald eyes wary. At least she hadn't been won over—yet. "What sort of favor?" she asked, her tone suspicious.

"Janey has sorted out some training programs for me. I need to brush up on a few skills. I'm way behind most of you, and if we get into a fight, I don't want to let you all down."

Tannis gave up the pretense of eating, put down her spoon, and listened openly. What was he doing? She glanced around the table and caught Rico's gaze. He grinned at her, and she turned her attention back to Callum and Daisy. Daisy was twirling a strand of long green hair around her finger as she listened.

"So how can I help?" she asked.

"One of the programs works better with two. I wondered whether you could spare a little time to work with me."

Daisy's eyes brightened until they sparkled with green fire. "Of course. I'd love to."

Tannis rose slowly to her feet. "I'll see everyone later," she said to the room in general. "We have a meeting in thirty minutes."

She didn't wait for anyone to answer, just pushed her chair away from the table, and strode from the room.

She paused outside the door.

"What's it like to fly?" Daisy asked and now her voice was tinged with hero worship.

"You want me to show you?" Callum replied. "There's probably enough room in the docking bay."

At that point, Tannis decided she'd heard enough. The thing was, Callum wasn't flirting. He was just being . . . nice. Why did that make her feel as though there was something not quite right with the world?

# CHAPTER 13

Tannis was sitting alone in the meeting room, brooding, when Rico turned up. He kicked out the chair opposite and sat.

"What's going on with Callum?" she asked.

"You think something's going on?"

"Hell, yeah. And who gave him the gun?"

"I did. I didn't like the idea of him being unarmed with Starke on board. He's promised not to kill anyone." He grinned. "At least not on purpose."

"Well, that's a relief. So why's he being so nice?"

"That's down to me as well. I suggested that if he wants a chance of getting into your pants, it might be a good idea to get the crew on his side."

Tannis glared. "He's never going to get into my pants. And I don't want him to try. I hate him." But she could hear the lack of conviction in her voice. "So it's all an act? The nice-guy, humble thing?"

"Who knows? I doubt even he does anymore. But does it matter? He's doing a good job. And it's not so much that he's humble—no one actually believes that—but they appreciate he's trying. It's obviously not easy for him."

"No, I'll bet it's not."

The others started coming in then and she put the thoughts aside—she needed to concentrate. Well, except for the thought about Callum getting into her pants; that one kept creeping back into her mind.

He wandered in and sat down at the edge of the room, where she could see him if she turned her head a fraction. Which she did. Her gaze drifted down to his hands with their long, elegant fingers. She had a flashback to the feel of those fingers, and a wave of heat washed over her. Glancing up, she caught him watching her, his eyes sleepy, heavy-lidded, and she had the distinct notion that he was thinking about the exact same thing. She squirmed in her seat, and his lips curved up in a slow smile.

"Tannis!" Rico spoke sharply from beside her.

"Yeah?"

"Meeting."

"Oh, right." She looked at him, and he shook his head, then leaned in close.

"You need to get laid. And soon. It's messing with your mind."

"My mind's fine." Maybe he was right. If living with Rico had taught her one thing, it was that sex was no big deal. Or it didn't have to be. Then again, it was obviously a big deal for Rico with Skylar. And Jon and Alex. This whole sex thing was doing her head in.

She took a deep breath and stood up. "Okay, so let's work out how we're going to do this. Janey, can you give us the intel?"

"They have the main target, which as far as we're aware is unarmed except for the weapon intended to destroy Trakis Seven. It's a Mark Two cruiser, but heavily modified."

"Crew?"

"Four, we think."

Tannis frowned. "How reliable is this intel? Where are we getting it from?"

"Mostly from Callum's friend, the colonel. He'd been feeding us information as he receives it."

"And he's getting it from?" She looked at Callum.

"The colonel is head of intelligence. He has people everywhere. I presume he has someone on the inside."

"Okay. Go on, Janey."

"There are five vessels guarding the ship. All Mark One cruisers, but the new design, top of the line."

That didn't sound good. But expected. "So when are we due to intercept them?"

"We could reach them in two days."

"Okay. Devlin—what do we have from your people?"

"Six ships that can reach us here in time. But none with the firepower of the new Mark One cruisers."

Six sounded good, even if they were smaller. They could work with six. She'd been worried that the Rebels were going to turn out to be all mouth and no ships; she was glad that wasn't the case. She had a good feeling about this and only just resisted rubbing her hands together—it didn't do to appear too confident.

"That's seven with *El Cazador*. Should be plenty," she said. "So how do we do it?"

"Well, the easiest thing would be to blow them out of the sky, including the weapon," Rico said. "That would get rid of the threat."

Sounded good to her. They'd get rid of the weapon, then *El Cazador* would take them as near to Trakis Seven as was safe—no doubt that bitch Venna could tell them where, and then she, Callum, and Venna would continue on to the planet in the shuttle and arrange to rendezvous with *El Cazador* when their business was done.

Their business—getting her the Meridian treatment.

She was finding it hard to believe that it was going to

happen at last. It had been her dream for so long. She glanced across at Callum, who watched her out of his inhuman violet eyes. How long would it take her eyes to change color?

The thought made a little shiver run through her. She looked from Callum to Skylar with her identical eyes. Skylar had told her the Collective were a sort of gestalt, all part of a larger being. Tannis didn't know whether she liked the sound of that. When she had just been dealing with Skylar alone, it had been easy to ignore the fact that she was part of something, but seeing them together sent a prickle of unease down her spine. She pushed the thought away. She would worry about that later.

"So that's the plan. Sounds simple enough. I like straightforward—less to go wrong." She looked at Devlin where he sat on the opposite side of the room from Callum. "You happy with that?"

"Straightforward sounds good to me."

"Well, I think we're done here then. What's our estimated time until interception, Janey?"

"Forty-six hours, give or take."

"That enough time for your people to join us?" she asked Devlin.

"They'll be with us within the day."

"Good. We'll have a meeting with the captains tomorrow."

"Just one thing," Devlin said.

"What's that?"

"I'm in charge."

Tannis pursed her lips as she considered that. Did she trust him? Did it matter? He'd be on board his own ship by then and she'd be here on *El Cazador*. She'd follow his lead as long as he didn't tell her to do something she didn't want to do. But she would worry about that if it happened.

It occurred to her that there was a lot of worrying she

was putting off. She just hoped it wouldn't all catch up at once and bite her on the butt.

She nodded. "You're in charge."

People began to drift away. Callum left with Daisy after sending her a long look that made her toes curl. She tried to remember the research center, and all he had been responsible for, but she couldn't bring it to mind.

Rico left with Skylar, his arm draped across her shoulder. Jon and Alex left together. She felt edgy and restless.

Janey was chatting with the Trog and Devlin, and she watched him covertly. Then turned away to pace the floor.

Maybe it wasn't Callum. Maybe it was just a natural progression. Yeah, she'd been put off sex, but that was understandable. She'd come away from the research center with a total aversion to being touched and to being held. But a lot of time had passed since then, and she was a healthy adult woman. On top of that, and the whole ship had turned into some sort of knocking shop since Skylar, and then Jon, had come aboard. There were probably a whole load of pheromones or whatever just floating around on the air waiting to zap her. So it was hardly unexpected that her own libido had decided to wake up at long last.

And perhaps it was pure coincidence that Callum had arrived at the exact same time her sex drive had decided to return from the dead. That combined with the fact that Callum was Collective, and she'd always had a fascination for anything Collective, she was predisposed to fall for him—it wasn't only not unexpected, it was probably inevitable.

She just needed to prove that.

Prove that Callum wasn't the only man who could make her heart beat faster and her insides melt. Somehow, she just needed to trigger her brain. She peered across at Devlin. In his own way, he was as gorgeous as Callum.

As if sensing her stare, he glanced over and held her

gaze for long moments. Then he broke the contact and spoke to the Trog, who nodded and left with Janey. The door slid shut behind them, leaving her alone with Devlin.

He strolled over to stand in front of her, a small smile on his face. One hand reached out and he cupped her jaw. "I go back to my ship tomorrow."

"I know." She stepped in closer and looked up at him from under her lashes. Tried a little flutter and felt like a complete asshole. Shit, she didn't know how to do this. How did you get a man to kiss you?

She licked her lips, and at last, he seemed to get the message. His big hand slid from her jaw to the back of her neck, and he pulled her closer.

At the touch of his mouth, she swayed toward him, her breasts brushing against his chest. His lips were warm and hard, and he pushed hers open and thrust his tongue inside. Tannis waited for the rush of heat to overwhelm her.

It never came.

There was no revulsion. It appeared that particular reaction had been banished, and she was glad. But there was also no burning need. No urge to meld her body with his, to push herself close until they were one.

After a minute, he raised his head, a rueful expression in his eyes. Dropping his arms from around her, he stepped away. Head cocked on one side, he studied her, and she had to prevent herself from squirming under the intense scrutiny. "Callum Meridian?"

She started at the name. "Callum Meridian what?"

"You tell me."

For a few seconds, her lips tightened and she considered the idea of telling him to mind his own goddamn business. But she supposed it was his business in a way. She had just come on to him. "Sorry, I didn't mean to . . ." She broke off not really knowing what to say, because she had meant to get him to kiss her. And she'd always been crap at apologizing especially when she was in the wrong.

Devlin shook his head, disgust clear in his expression. "Jesus. Callum Meridian. Well, I wish you luck with that—you'll need it." He gave her a long look. "So what was this—trying to make him jealous?"

"No!" She bit her lip, and then her innate honesty made her go on. "Well, maybe a little, but not really. I just wanted to see whether . . ." She really wished she had never gotten herself into this.

He chuckled at her discomfort. "Don't worry. I don't think I'm up to warding off your protectors anyway."

"Protectors?"

"So far, I've had Rico, Janey, and Jon come and tell me that if I harm you in any way, they'll—"

She gritted her teeth. "They'll what?"

"Actually, it varies from drain me dry, to rip my throat out, to slicing off my dick with a blunt knife and tossing it out the airlock." He shuddered at the last one. "So maybe it's for the best. You know, you have a good crew—you obviously inspire loyalty. The Coalition could use you."

"Thanks, but no thanks."

He shrugged. "Well, the offer is open. At least until you become one of those bastard Collective monsters. Though come to think about it, it might be useful having a member of the Collective as part of the Coalition."

"No."

He laughed, easing the harsh lines of his face. "Okay, I guess it's time for bed. You do know the Trog snores, don't you?"

"So you were only coming on to me for the chance of a quiet night?"

"Yeah."

Tannis paused just outside the room, wanting to thank him for not making a big deal out of her kissing him. She reached up to touch his face. "Thank—" Her words were cut off as a fist came out of nowhere and slammed into Devlin's mouth, hurling him to the floor.

"Keep your hands off her, you bastard."

Tannis spun around in time to see Callum leap at the other man. He landed on top of him in a flurry of wings, and for a moment, she couldn't make out what was going on.

They rolled. Devlin came out on top, and he smashed his fist into Callum's face. Callum heaved him off and pounced on top of him, pummeling his chest.

Tannis stood watching, hands on her hips. She considered walking away, going to bed, and forgetting the pair of them. Let them beat the shit out of each other. But there was work to do tomorrow, and she could do without either of them being incapacitated. So she drew her laser pistol, flipped it to stun, and thought about what or who to shoot.

A noise down the corridor made her glance away—it looked like the rest of the crew had come to watch the fun—just as Callum and Devlin rolled again and nearly slammed into her legs. She swore loudly and took aim. She wasn't planning on shooting either of them, but she wasn't perfect—she might make a mistake and actually hit someone. It was tempting. Callum was immortal. He would heal quickly. Devlin wasn't. She waited until Devlin had the upper position and aimed the laser at the floor by Callum's head.

Sparks shot out as the blast hit the metal floor, and the two men sprang apart. She put a booted foot on Callum's chest and aimed the pistol at his head.

"You making trouble on my ship?"

Amusement flashed in his eyes. "No, Captain."

"Good."

She swung the laser around to point directly at Devlin. "How about you?"

He actually grinned. So she was funny now, was she? Her finger tightened on the trigger, and the grin was replaced by a look of alarm. Much better.

"No, Captain."

Someone sniggered, and Tannis backed off a step and turned to face the crew. She studied them with narrowed eyes. "And you lot," she said, waving her weapon in their general direction. "I do not need protecting." She pointed the pistol at Jon. "Right?"

"Of course you don't, Captain."

"I can protect myself." She took a pace toward them, jabbed the pistol into Rico's stomach, and met a solid wall of muscle. "Right?"

He grinned. "Yes, Captain."

Vaguely mollified, she turned away. "I'm going to bed." And with that, she stalked down the corridor, pistol still in her hand.

She was back at her cabin when she realized Callum had followed her. Whirling around, she raised the gun and shoved it into his chest hard.

"Back off, Callum."

"I want to talk to you."

She sighed and holstered her weapon. "What?"

He considered her a moment. A bead of blood welled on his lip where Devlin had got in a punch. He licked it away, and her gaze followed the movement. Then back to his eyes.

"You might not be willing to accept me in your bed, just yet," he said. "But while you're working for me, you don't sleep with anyone else either."

"Really?"

"Yeah, really. You're captain, and in everything else, I'm willing to take your orders. But in this, you'll take mine." He pushed up close to her.

"And how are you going to make me?" she asked, genuinely curious.

"I'm going to ask nicely."

She was backed up against the wall now with nowhere left to go. The heat of his body pressed against hers, his hips thrusting into her, so she could feel the rigid line of his erection against her belly, and flames burst into life inside her.

"How nicely?" she asked, and her voice sounded weak and thready.

"Very."

His lips lowered to hers, and her breath caught in her throat. She stared into his eyes. "Aren't you scared I'll bite you again?"

"Yes."

Her hand came up to press flat against his chest and beneath her palm the thud of his heart beat a rapid tattoo.

He leaned in closer. "But I'm willing to risk it."

*Just one kiss*, she told herself. No doubt she'd feel absolutely nothing, just like with Devlin. But she was already way beyond feeling nothing. Need coiled up tight inside her, and she knew it would snap with the first touch of his lips.

She tried to remember the research center but couldn't bring it to mind, then Venna, her "angel," but again the image refused to materialize. All she could see was Callum's violet eyes drawing her in. His lips slightly parted.

"You're sure?" he said at the last moment.

"Jesus!" Her fingers hooked in his shirtfront, and she dragged him the last few inches. The first touch of his mouth was almost tentative, gentle, and she didn't want that.

Her lips parted beneath his, and she thrust her tongue into his mouth, tasting the smoky sweetness of whiskey. She was drowning in the taste of him, intoxicated. Her breasts ached, and her insides were melting. Her hand slid up over his chest to curl around his neck and hold him close while she rubbed her body against his, trying to get some relief for the strange sensations building within her.

"Slowly," he murmured against her mouth. But she didn't want it slow. She didn't know how she wanted it. How could she?

At last, he deepened the kiss, his lips hard, his tongue urgent. At the same time, he slipped a thigh between hers, raising it so it pressed against her sensitive core, and sensations flooded her body. She whimpered deep in her throat as every cell yearned toward him. He must have sensed her need, and he pushed his hand between them, cupping her sex. She went instantly still and didn't move as his fingers shifted against her. Even through her clothes, the feeling was exquisite, and her thighs parted as one long finger rubbed against her.

Her breathing turned hard. She'd pulled back from the kiss unable to focus on anything but the hand between her legs. Her eyes clamped shut as the pleasure built inside her. She felt out of control, and she hated that but there was no way she could stop this now. Then he found the exact spot and rotated his finger, and at last she exploded, pleasure radiating out from that point between her thighs. For an age, her body spiraled out of control, and she realized he was holding her upright with one arm around her shoulder. The other hand was still between her thighs and as the shivers subsided, he pressed upward, and she came again.

Pulling her against him, he stroked her back, the touch strangely soothing, and after a few minutes, the shudders that racked her body died away.

He released his hold on her and stepped back. Tannis pushed her heavy lids open to find Callum watching her, head tilted to one side. His expression was blank, and she had no clue what he was thinking. Then he gave a slow smile, and her heart rate picked up. Her legs were shaking, and she locked them. She'd never known her body could feel like that, could react like that.

He remained silent, and she bit her lip. Then coughed, opened her mouth, and closed it again. She had no clue what to say. Tearing her gaze from his, she peered around and realized they were still in the corridor outside her cabin. She'd lost all track of where they were.

If anyone caught her canoodling with their client, she would never live it down. Luckily, the corridor was deserted.

She licked her lips and took a deep breath. "Would you like to come in?" She nodded at her door.

He shook his head. For a moment, she didn't understand, and then he took another step back as though distancing himself.

"I honestly never meant for anything to happen tonight," he said.

"You didn't?"

"I just meant to make sure nothing happened with anyone else."

Her eyes narrowed, and his lips twitched.

"I was trying to give you some space." His hand came up to touch his lip and he winced as though at a memory. "I decided you needed time to forgive me, before I tried again."

"I'll never forgive you." That was the goddamned truth, but she wasn't sure forgiveness was what mattered anymore.

"Well, maybe not forgive but at least see past what happened. Then I thought a kiss wouldn't hurt, and we both got carried away. But I'm guessing this whole sex thing is new to you, and I don't want you coming back later and claiming I took advantage of your innocence."

"I am *not* innocent."

"No? Maybe not innocent in some things, but I'm guessing that's the first orgasm you've ever had."

She so didn't want to be here right now. Her hands fisted at her side as she fought the urge to punch him in the nose.

Been there. Done that.

She was supposed to have moved on. But he was infuriating, and she wasn't used to holding back. "Look, if you're not coming in, maybe you'd better piss off. Go practice your Mr. Nice Guy disguise on someone else."

"I will. If I practice enough maybe it will sink in. Anyway . . ." He nodded at her door. "When this is over, ask me again."

He was a total fucking idiot.

What had possessed him to walk away?

She'd come so sweetly for him. He could have been in there with her now, buried deep between her thighs. At the thought, his cock jerked in his pants and his balls ached.

He was taking this nice-guy thing way too far.

He got to his own door and hesitated. Should he go back?

In the end, he slammed his palm to the panel before he could change his mind. Once in his room, he leaned against the wall and closed his eyes.

His cock was still hard, and he shoved his hand down his pants and gripped it in his fist, tried not to think it could be Tannis's hand around him. Or her mouth.

He groaned at the thought and a minute later, he came.

# CHAPTER 14

On the monitor, Tannis could see Devlin's ship, *The Black Cat,* with an array of smaller ships fanned out behind him. His job was to coordinate his people, annihilate the Mark One cruisers guarding the weapons ship, and to protect *El Cazador.*

*El Cazador* was positioned slightly to the rear and side where Tannis had a good view of what was going on. Their job was to destroy the weapons ship.

They'd had a meeting of the captains earlier that day on board *El Cazador.* It hadn't taken her long to figure out that Devlin had been right: the Rebels were definitely in need of some "good" people. She guessed it wasn't Devlin's fault. You could only do so much with training if the raw material was crap. And the ships were a mixture of old and ancient, no match for the sleek, new Mark One cruisers of the Church.

Still, this was hardly a plan that required brains to see it through. They were going for a straight-up attack. Just blast them all out of space. How difficult could it be?

Obviously, too difficult.

"They're good," Rico murmured, and she knew he wasn't

referring to the Rebels. The Church was managing to fend off the attack. Not only that, but they had arrayed themselves in front of the weapons ship and were effectively deflecting any shot *El Cazador* sent toward her.

And now, as if things couldn't get worse, it looked like they were using the shield of the other ships to just continue on their way.

"Shit, Rico, they're getting away."

"Do I look like I'm blind?"

"Well, do something."

He turned and snarled at her with a flash of fangs. "Shut up, sit down, and strap yourself in. That goes for everyone else as well."

Tannis opened her mouth. Rico snarled again, and she clamped her lips together and did as she was told. There were some occasions when it just didn't do to cross the vampire.

Callum took the seat next to her, and she watched him struggle to fasten the harness—those wings made things awkward. He glanced up, caught her gaze, and grinned.

He looked far more relaxed than he had when he'd first come on board over a week ago. Which was odd as right now things were going to shit. She could see the weapons ship getting smaller on the monitor as they stood around doing nothing.

"Janey," Rico said. "Get Devlin on the comm."

"Okay."

"This isn't working," Rico said.

"No shit," Devlin replied.

"I want to change tactics."

"What do you need?"

"We need to turn this around literally. I want your lot to concentrate everything on the central ship. Bring her down, ignore the others for now."

"And what then?"

"I want you to create an opening we can get through. We're going after the weapon. Once we're through, you follow us, turn around, and make sure they don't come after us."

There was a minute's silence. No doubt while Devlin considered the plan. But the plan was a good one. Well, actually the only one.

Callum leaned across while they waited. "Did you sleep well?"

She had actually, like a baby. "Okay."

"I didn't. I tossed and turned and told myself I was all kinds of stupid that I hadn't taken you up on your offer. I had a hard-on all night. Couldn't shift it."

Her gaze shot to his groin, and he chuckled. "Don't worry, I got myself under control eventually. At least I did until I saw you all strapped up in that harness. When this is over, you, me, and that harness are going to get together."

She shifted in the seat and warmth stole through her body. He must have caught the movement, and he grinned. "You like that idea? Get you all naked first, then strap you down . . ."

Holy moly, she was melting, and he wasn't even touching her.

"Tannis!"

She jumped as Rico snapped out her name, and she turned guiltily to face him.

His eyes narrowed. "If you could put off the foreplay until later—we're going in five."

Jesus, she hadn't even heard Devlin reply to them. "I'm ready."

"Yeah, I bet you are, but ready for what?" He turned back to the controls. "Okay, we're off."

Rico had switched on the main screen, showing Devlin's forces. They were grouping together, tightening up, turning so they all focused the central ship. Then as one, their blasters flared. Skylar punched *El Cazador's* guns at the same time and the ship exploded with flashes of light. But the Church's ship maintained position, and Rico swore.

"And again," he said.

This time when the shots hit the ship, she rolled. The blasts kept coming now, hitting her vulnerable underside, and she lost control and spun. She hit the ship next to her, and together they tumbled through space.

"We're off," Rico said. "Hold on."

He punched the main thrusters, and *El Cazador* shot forward, heading for the gap between the ships. Skylar kept hitting the guns so a steady stream of blasts shot out. Tannis closed her eyes as the speed built up until she was pressed into her seat by the force.

A blaster from one of the ships caught them in the side and they rolled. For a minute, the lights went out, and Tannis hung upside down from the harness. Then they flickered back, and the ship righted herself. She blinked and then stared at the monitors. There was nothing to be seen but space. They were through.

"What's happening behind?" she asked.

Rico flipped the monitor and the screen filled with flashing lights. She stared at it, trying to make sense of the chaos of ships.

"Looks like they pulled it off," Rico said. "They're between us."

It did, and Tannis grinned. "Janey, can you get Devlin?"

"No problem." She flipped the comm unit to speaker. "He's on speaker."

"Thanks, Devlin."

"My pleasure. You take care of my little brother."

"Will do. See you around."

"Remember that offer is always open."

"I'll remember. Okay, shut it down, Janey. Let's get after that ship."

It took them an hour going at full speed before they picked up the weapons ship on their scanners. Callum stayed in his seat and watched the crew. They worked well together. There had been no sense of panic, well except for maybe Tannis. But she had more at stake here than any of them.

She was up on her feet now, stalking the bridge, fizzing with energy. "Any sign yet?" she asked for the fifteenth time—he'd counted.

"Captain, sit down," Janey said. "I promise I'll tell you when they show."

She ignored the request and continued pacing, hands shoved in her pockets, and Callum sat back and admired her sleek, sinuous figure. If all went well, they would be there and back within twenty-four hours.

"There she is," Janey said.

"How long until she's in range?"

"Ten minutes."

Tannis flung herself into her chair, fingers drumming in the armrests. "Well?"

Janey sighed. "Nine minutes and thirty seconds."

"Okay," Rico murmured. "Let's get ready to blast the bitch out of the sky."

"Just hold on a second," Callum said. He'd been considering an idea while they caught up. Now, he was interested to know what the others thought. "Janey, are you getting anything from them?"

Janey glanced at Tannis, and she nodded her permission.

"I'm picking up a lot of chatter," Janey said.

"What sort of chatter?"

"I think it's the Church, but I don't think they're communicating. It's more like the steady pulse from some sort of tracking device—a beacon perhaps."

Tannis swiveled in her seat to face him. "What is it?"

"I have an idea."

"A good one?" Tannis sounded as though the notion of a good idea coming from him was unlikely.

"Well, obviously I think so."

"Spit it out then."

"Why don't we not blow her up?"

"That's an idea? It sucks."

"Why don't we take her instead?"

"Board her?" Rico said.

"Why would we want to do that?" Tannis asked.

She was being slow. He presumed Tannis wasn't thinking straight. He hoped it was because of his proximity, but suspected it was more that she was close to getting the Meridian treatment she had dreamed about for so long.

"At the moment," he said, "we're planning on taking the shuttle down to Trakis Seven. But the shuttle is small for the three of us, and I'm not sure I trust Tannis and Venna in a small, enclosed space together."

"Good point," Tannis muttered.

"Plus her range is short. *El Cazador* is going to have to stay relatively close in order to pick us up after we've been on planet."

"And," Rico said, "we have to presume that if we blow up that ship, then they'll come after us. Either the ones who survive the Rebels—and having seen their performance I'm presuming some will—or they'll send someone else to intercept us."

It looked like he had Rico on his side. "But if we take the ship," Callum continued, "and use her to get to Trakis Seven, the beacon will show her going exactly where she's supposed to go."

"And *El Cazador* can get out of the way until we need to rendezvous."

Tannis sat for a minute, chewing on her lower lip. "Hmm, won't they just comm the Church when we try and board?"

"Not necessarily." He turned to Janey. "Can you set up a jamming frequency? Stop any comms getting through, but keep the beacon functioning?"

"Of course."

He turned back to Tannis. "So, what do you think, Captain?"

"Rico?"

"I'm for it. Can't believe I didn't think of it myself."

"Skylar?"

"I'm with Rico. It's obvious, really."

"Okay, Janey—jam them."

"I'm on it."

"So how do we do this?"

"Daisy can take the controls on *El Cazador*," Rico said. "She can send them a few blasts from the front to keep them busy while we sneak around the rear in the shuttle."

"Who's going?" Skylar asked.

"I reckon you and me, Jon and Tannis. That's four against four—it's probably overkill, but no point in taking chances."

Callum was starting to feel as though he didn't exist. Whose idea had it been anyway? "Five against four," he said.

Tannis swung around to face him. "*You* won't be fighting. You'll be staying in the shuttle with that woman until it's all clear." He opened his mouth to argue, but she continued without giving him a chance to speak. "You're the only one who knows how to find that Meridian—you're too valuable to risk."

"I don't think so."

Tannis smiled sweetly. "Who's captain?"

Shit. Had he really said he'd take her orders? He hadn't

meant it literally. She stood staring at him, hands on her hips.

"You're the captain."

"Thank you."

The shuttle was a squash with six people. Rico got the seat as he was flying. Skylar stood behind him, her hand resting on his shoulder. Jon stood off by himself, arms folded across his enormous chest, a scowl on his face. Alex had put up a fuss when she'd realized they were not taking her, and for someone so small, she knew how to make her feelings clear. Callum knew exactly how she felt.

Venna stood on the far side as though trying to keep as much distance as possible between them.

Tannis lounged against the curved wall just inside the door, and Callum inched around toward her, his wings making it difficult in such a confined space. Everyone else faced the monitor at the front, and he pulled her toward him, wrapped his arms around her, and reclined against the wall. For a moment, she stiffened, then relaxed into him.

He leaned close and whispered in her ear, "Be careful in there."

"I'm always careful."

He let out a small bark of laughter, and all heads turned in their direction. He waited until they'd turned back. "Darling, I bet you've never been careful in your entire existence. For someone who wants to live forever, you picked a dangerous way of life."

Callum's words made her stop and think. For once, his touch wasn't sexual, it was comforting, and she turned his words over in her mind.

The truth was she'd spent her time in the research center terrified of death, every day an ordeal to be gotten through.

But however terrible it had been, she hadn't wanted to die—had clung to her dream of living forever.

But since then, though she hadn't courted death, she hadn't been afraid to put her life on the line while doing a job. In fact, she'd enjoyed pitting herself against almost impossible odds. It made her feel alive.

She decided he didn't need an answer. Resting back against him, she closed her eyes and relaxed.

# CHAPTER 15

Callum paced the shuttle and tried to ignore Venna.

He couldn't hear anything and the wait was driving him insane. He wanted to comm Tannis, but if they were in a fight, he might distract her.

"For God's sake, relax," Venna grumbled.

She'd sat down in the pilot's seat and was studying him as though he was one of her specimens. "What's with you and the captain?" she asked.

"What?"

"All that lovey stuff?" Her tone held intense distaste.

"Mind your own business."

"Actually, it is my business. You told me you'd lost your libido years ago. You said you thought it was another side effect of the Meridian. It's in my files. So I'd really like to know if it's not the case."

That sounded like Venna—her mind focused solely on the science. He thought back to the extremely uncomfortable night he had spent, with a raging hard-on that had refused to subside. Nothing wrong with his libido.

"Yuk," Venna said. "Get that sick smile off your face. I'll delete the entry from my records."

"Good idea." He peered into the monitor, but could see nothing in the docking bay. "Where the hell are they?"

"Don't worry. She's obviously impossible to kill. Meridian is wasted on her." She got up and paced for a minute, then sat down again, and started gnawing on her fingernails. She was driving him nuts, but she was obviously stressed out, and he decided to take her mind off the whole thing.

The thought brought him up short. Maybe he was turning into a nice guy after all. He was actually feeling pretty good; things were on track, and while he was sure Tannis would never forgive him, she was starting to see beyond the past. He felt a grin tug at his lips.

"Let me repeat it," Venna said. "Yuk."

Back to Venna. The one thing that could be guaranteed to focus her mind was talk of her research. "Tell me about the planet," he said. "What's my best chance of finding anything?"

"We've been over and over this."

"Tell me again."

She took a deep breath, and he saw her brain click into action. "I reckon you'll have about six hours before the sickness makes it impossible to function."

It didn't seem very long to discover "the truth." Why was he so sure that he would find his answers when Venna had spent years hunting and come up with nothing? Maybe it was just a gut feeling, but he'd learned to follow those. Then he realized that wasn't the case. The feeling wasn't in his gut, but in his mind—in that part of his mind changed by Meridian, where he could communicate with the other members of the Collective. Could it be some sort of ancestral memory? Or was there something on the planet calling to him, drawing him there. But they had never found any living organisms on Trakis Seven or any sign that there had ever been an indigenous life-form. One of their theories had been that an alien spaceship could have crash-landed like they had, although they'd found no evidence.

"We'll land close to the Meridian site," Venna said, breaking into his thoughts. "But it's still half an hour beneath the planet's surface, that's an hour there and back plus at least an hour for the treatment to take. That leaves you less than four hours."

"Doesn't seem long."

"It will when you're down there, believe me."

He did. He could still remember the time he had spent on the planet—it had not been a pleasant occurrence.

"So we go for the Meridian first?"

"No. I suggest you leave that until last—the place messes with your brain but you don't need much mental capacity to get to the cache."

"So where do we start?"

"There's a chamber close to the place where the Trakis Seven crash-landed and luckily quite close to the final cache of Meridian. It's the center of the radiation—though it's not really radiation—more like some sort of poison. I reckon that's your best bet. I've been there a couple of times. It's a weird place, but there's something . . . I don't know."

"You still think it's some sort of alien?"

It was something they had discussed many times, but Venna refused to commit to a conclusion that wasn't firmly based in scientific fact.

"Yes."

He'd been gazing at the monitor, but at her answer, he whirled around to face her. "Well, that's a change."

"I can't see what else it could be. I'm hoping you'll find some proof where I've failed. Go to the chamber, open your mind, and see what happens."

He nodded. His comm unit flashed, and he reached across and flipped the switch.

"We're done," Tannis said. "Just clearing up, so you can come out now if you want to. We're on the bridge."

"Come on," he said to Venna. "The place is ours. Let's get on with this." A sense of deep excitement rose inside him. What would he find? The truth?

The ship was built like *El Cazador* but on a smaller scale, and once out of the shuttle they headed up the ramp to the upper level. She was obviously new, still gleaming, with the smell of fresh clean air. They found the bridge, and he paused in the doorway. His gaze went straight to Tannis. She stood to one side, talking to Skylar. She appeared unharmed and some of the tension inside him eased.

It was obvious a fight had gone on in here. Scorch marks from laser blasts scarred the walls, and a couple of bodies lay on the floor.

Jon pushed past him from behind, entered the bridge, and picked up the nearest body, tossing it over his shoulder with ease. He grinned at Callum as he passed, carrying the dead crew member—presumably they were just dumping the bodies out of the airlock.

The last body lay on the floor, eyes staring. There was no obvious cause of death, but when Callum looked closer, he could see the puncture wounds in the throat. He glanced up to where Rico paced the deck at the far side of the bridge. As though sensing his gaze, he turned Callum's way. He appeared totally wired—his eyes glowing crimson, blood staining his lips, and a shiver of primordial fear skittered down Callum's spine.

"I'd stay away from him for a while if I were you." Tannis came up beside him.

"That was my plan. Are the crew all dead?"

"Yeah. We did give them the chance to surrender."

"How much of a chance?"

"Not much. It may have escaped your notice, but Rico isn't too fond of the Church."

"It hadn't escaped me."

"He was sort of blinded by the light flashing off the crosses around their necks." She shrugged. "They chose to do this, so they must be willing to take the consequences."

"If you live by the sword, you should expect to die by it."

"Something like that. And look on the bright side—at least they died believing they were going to heaven. But the good news is none of the systems have been damaged—she's fully functional and ready to go as soon as we've cleaned up."

Jon came in and picked up the last body, carted it out like so much rubbish.

Tannis glanced at him. "This is really bothering you, isn't it?"

"Maybe."

"You sent God knows how many men and women to their deaths in the mines, you've probably given orders that have killed thousands without blinking an eye. But faced with a few bodies and you go all squeamish."

She was right, in a way. He'd always killed from a distance. Even when he'd been a fighter pilot on Earth. But dead was dead, whether it was under your nose or a million miles away.

"Take responsibility, Callum."

His anger flared. "You have no idea of the responsibility I take every day. You don't think I know that my decisions can lead to deaths? But they also sometimes lead to life. Not every order I make gets people killed." He'd actually done some good in his time as leader, but he was past defending himself, because the truth was he had done things that were indefensible. He hoped the good outweighed the bad, but he was in no way sure.

"Okay," Jon said, returning to the bridge. "We're done, and we're out of here."

Callum glanced away from Tannis and saw that the others were standing by the door. Rico came forward, and he'd come down from the high a little, though he still looked twitchy.

He stalked over, wrapped his arms around Tannis, and hugged her. She stiffened in his arms—Callum reckoned she wasn't really one for hugs—then she relaxed and returned the gesture. When she stepped back, she looked vaguely embarrassed.

"Come home," Rico said. He turned to Callum. "You keep her safe, or we'll be looking for you."

He nodded. "I will."

Skylar smiled. "Hey, when we see you again, I'll be able to get inside your head," she said to Tannis.

"You'll keep out of my freaking head," she replied.

"Good luck," Jon said. "Call if you need us."

Tannis nodded. "We'll see you at the rendezvous. It should be no more than three days."

"We'll be there. Don't be late!" Rico swung around and headed out the door. At the last minute, he paused, dug his silver flask out of his pocket, and tossed it to her. "To keep you company."

Then they were gone. Leaving her alone with Callum and Venna.

# CHAPTER 16

Tannis watched them go with a vague feeling of unease. It was that old, everything-is-changing feeling that had plagued her for the last few weeks, maybe longer. Probably since Skylar had come aboard with her offer of work.

She felt the change in vibration under her feet as the shuttle fired up. There was no turning back now.

Venna stood just inside the doorway. Tannis still couldn't look at the other woman without a feeling of betrayal, which was crazy. While she hadn't forgiven Callum, she could see past it. At least Callum was honest. He wouldn't go around offering little children chocolate if he meant to do horrible things to them.

Tannis stalked toward her and stood staring down at the woman. She did bear a strong resemblance to an angel— all blond curls and big violet eyes.

"Why the fuck did you give me chocolate?"

Those enormous eyes stretched even wider. Venna tried to edge away, but came up against the curved wall of the bridge and visibly jumped. Her gaze darted to Callum, who had followed Tannis over. "Callum, get her away from me."

"I just want to know why," Tannis ground out.

"She gave you chocolate? When?"

"Nearly thirty years ago. She came to the research center, and she handed out chocolate to the children, and I want to know why the fuck she did that when she was responsible for us being there." She looked from one to the other of them. "I thought she was a goddamn angel. She was the first person in that place to show any kindness, and I want to know the fuck why."

Venna opened her mouth. "I . . ." She trailed off, licked her lips.

"Venna likes to be liked," Callum said. "It's a weakness."

"Jesus," Tannis snarled.

"She could come there and see you, but only if you didn't hate her to her face. She can't take it. She likes to think she's a nice person, and the only way she can make believe that is if other people think she's nice."

"I am nice." Venna finally found her voice.

"No, you're not, but you're good at your job."

Tannis was overcome by weariness as the adrenaline from the fight drained from her system. She turned away. There was no such thing as angels anyway; she'd always known that.

Glancing over her shoulder, she spoke to Callum. "You want to fly this thing?"

"Hell, yeah."

Callum took the pilot's seat and rubbed his hands together. Tannis took the seat behind him and fastened the safety harness—she had no clue what Callum was like as a flier. But it was a pretty safe bet that he hadn't done it for a while, and she didn't want to die just now.

Venna had very wisely disappeared. She'd obviously realized her chances of being "liked" were about zero in the present company. Tannis rested her head against the back of the seat and watched Callum as he familiarized himself with the controls. After a few minutes, when she'd assured herself he was competent enough to head in the right direction, she closed her eyes and let herself drift off into sleep.

When she opened her eyes, he was sitting in the seat next to her, watching her.

"We're on automatic," he said.

He stretched his long legs out in front of him, folded his wings close against his shoulders, and sat back as best he could.

"You know," he murmured, "I'm tired. I can't remember feeling tired in a long while. Fed up, bored, but not actually tired."

"Sleep then. Find a cabin and sleep."

"Can't. I'm too wound up. I've been waiting for you to wake up so you can talk to me."

"About what?"

He shrugged. "Anything."

She thought for a minute. There was something she would like to know. "How about you talk instead?"

"What about?"

"Tell me about Meridian. About how you found it, what happened when you landed on Trakis Seven."

"We didn't actually land as such—we crashed. Machines don't work well on Trakis Seven."

"So how will we get down?"

"You have to shut down the engines and let the planet pull you in, then switch them back just before landing. I've not done it—but I had a crash course before I left."

"What about getting off again?"

"As long as you're quick, there's time to make safe distance before the engines cut out. Just no dawdling on take-off."

"Great," she muttered.

"It will be fine." He settled in his chair. "Okay—so the story of my life. Are you sitting comfortably?"

She nodded.

"When we reached the Trakis system, each ship was allocated a planet to check out for viability. We'd already lost contact with Trakis One—we know now that she disappeared into a black hole, but back then she just went dead."

Tannis shuddered. "Holy moly. What a way to go."

"I'd forgotten. You've been to Trakis One, haven't you?"

"When we broke Jon out of the prison."

"You were lucky to survive."

"No, not lucky—Rico's a brilliant pilot. Even so, it was a little hairy."

"Anyway, the crew was already on edge. And the planet was far from inviting—as you'll soon see."

"How many of you were there on board?"

"Awake? Twenty, plus ten thousand or so in cryo. We orbited the planet for a while, then, when I couldn't put it off any longer, we went in. I lost control almost immediately. I remember thinking *this is it*. And what a way to end after five hundred years in space."

"What happened? Obviously you all survived the crash."

"Something slowed us down, some force field before we hit the ground. We still sustained a lot of damage, but the main systems were repairable. So we set about doing the repairs and exploring the planet."

He stared into space for a few minutes obviously remembering the past, and if his expression was anything to go by, the memories were not happy.

"We'd heard from the other ships by then. Trakis Four and Five had found habitable planets. We knew we had a safe place to go if we could get the ship fixed. So I made the decision to wake some of the Chosen Ones. There were scientists, including an environmentalist. While I was sure Trakis Seven wasn't suitable for colonization, I wanted to find out if there was anything we could use in the future. It was a mistake."

"You couldn't have known."

"Maybe not. It seemed fine at first, the planet actually has a breathable atmosphere though it's a little thin, tiring for doing anything physical. But it was good to be off ship even on that hellhole."

"How long had you been captain?"

"Ten years. It wasn't too bad. There was space on the ship. Books to read, plenty of entertainment, which was just as well as the ship ran itself. I was redundant except for in an emergency. And when we did have one, I very nearly failed."

"But you didn't." Why the hell was she trying to comfort him? What was it about Callum Meridian that touched her as no man had before?

"Well there are relative stages of failure. People died because of decisions I made, and back then I wasn't nearly so comfortable with that idea as you believe me to be now."

"So what happened? How did you find Meridian?"

"It was more like it found us. The planet's a strange place, as you'll see when we land. I never returned after that first time, but even after five hundred years, I can remember it clearly. I took a team out to explore." He closed his eyes as if he was remembering. "It was as though something was calling to us. I found myself in a sort of cave. No light but the place glowed violet. Eerie." He opened his eyes and stared at her. Violet. Inhuman.

"There were these growths, like tentacles, hundreds of them, emerging from out of the walls. I touched one, and it reacted almost as if it was alive, wrapped itself around my arm and needles cut into my skin. I've never felt such pain, like fire through my blood. I blacked out. When I came to, the rest of my team was unconscious on the ground around the chamber. The thing that had attacked me had shriveled to nothing. And there were others the same next to each of the crew members." Callum jumped to his feet and started pacing the confines of the bridge. "They awoke shortly after me, and it was immediately obvious that we were changed. We could read each other's thoughts."

"And the rest," Tannis said.

"Well, we didn't know about the immortality then or the fact that we could repair just about any damage to our bodies. Though the damage thing we found out early. One of the six, Tyler, was injured in a fall. We thought he was dead, it should have killed him but it didn't, and he recovered quickly—far too quickly to be normal—but we'd already left the planet by then."

"Why did you leave? Didn't you want to stay and explore?"

"No. You'll understand when we reach Trakis Seven. The place has an unfriendly feel. But it was more than that. The rest of the crew, and the Chosen Ones we'd woken from cryo, began to get sick. Then the first one died, and we knew we had to leave."

"I thought it took two years to die from the radiation poisoning."

"The planet can kill you quick, or it can kill you slow but it always kills you unless you undergo the treatment. But we didn't realize we were immune at first. Not until we got clear of the planet, and then it took a long time for us to understand. While the six of us felt immediately better as soon as we were away, the others only got worse. We took the ship to Trakis Five and settled there. Within two years, all those who'd been on the planet's surface were dead. Worse than that, even the ones who had been in cryo became sick and eventually died."

"And you were all fine?"

"We never got sick. As the years passed, we didn't age." He shrugged. "The rest is history. That's enough storytelling. Why don't you go get some rest? It's a big day tomorrow."

"What about you?"

"I'm fine. Another side effect—we don't need much sleep."

"Okay. I'll go find somewhere to lie down—enjoy sleeping while I still can."

He grabbed her hand as she went past and tugged her toward him. She didn't try to pull away, just looked down into his eyes.

"Are you absolutely sure this is what you want?" he asked.

Tannis frowned at the question, unsure why he was asking her at this point.

"Once we're on the planet," he continued, "there is no more choice. You take the Meridian, or you die."

"I know. And I want it. I've always wanted it. Why ask now?"

He shook his head. "Telling how it happened has brought it all back. And I suppose Aiden's suicide affected me more than I thought. Then the way the Council members are behaving . . . I just want you to be sure."

"I'm sure."

"Good. Go sleep." He raised her hand to his lips, kissed her palm, and then released her. Tannis closed her fist around the kiss and stepped back. For a minute, she hovered, not sure whether she wanted to go or stay. In the end, she whirled around and left the bridge.

Tannis stumbled as she stepped off the ramp and onto the planet's surface. Callum reached for her, but she shook her head.

"I'm fine." Breathing in deeply, she blinked a couple of times. "I think." She swayed and then righted herself.

"You can stay in the ship," Callum said. "I'll come back for you after we've been to the chamber."

"No, I want to come."

He studied her for a moment, then nodded. The planet affected people differently. Some were almost incapable of functioning without antinausea drugs. Strangely, and unhappily for them if they had been brought here to work the "mines," they were the ones who lasted the longest. The people who reacted the least to the planet, tended to die the quickest. Venna had done a detailed study of the subject. He remembered reading her report, but it had meant nothing to him—merely numbers. Now, he couldn't help but think of the vast amounts of suffering reflected in those statistics. When had he become this person who didn't care? He shook his head. Now was not the time to contemplate his past inadequacies as a human being.

Tannis had gone pale and a fine sheen of sweat coated her face, but she appeared perfectly capable of functioning. It was just as well she was getting the treatment, because she wouldn't last long.

"Let's get going, then. You'll only get worse.

Callum felt the old, familiar fog in his brain, the nausea in his stomach, but this time, he didn't fight it. He allowed it to wash through him, and a sense of peace stole over him. Something whispered through his mind, not a voice—there were no words—but the need to move filled him, and a deep sense of excitement stirred in his gut.

He didn't know why he was sure he would find his answers here when Venna had searched for years and come up with nothing. But he had always been the strongest of their kind, even among the inner Council who had all been changed with him on that day. He was the first to get the wings. And his telepathic powers were the strongest, though he still got nothing from Tannis.

She appeared strangely subdued. He'd expected her to be fizzing with excitement, even taking into account the sickness. Maybe he shouldn't have told her about the pain, but it was better to be prepared. Besides, he didn't think the thought of pain would dampen her spirits.

He'd asked her yesterday if she wanted to back out. He hadn't wanted to ask, and he'd silently prayed she wouldn't say yes. Whatever journey lay ahead, he wanted Tannis to share with him.

Maybe he was a little scared of what he might find after all. Maybe he wanted someone to hold his hand through whatever eternity would bring. He'd never believed in love, wasn't sure he did now, but something drew him to her. And he knew she felt the same, otherwise he had a notion he would have been dead days ago.

Behind her, Venna appeared composed, if a little green. She was coming with them to the chamber, in case she could cast any insights into what he found there, but then she would return to the ship—no need for her to accompany them to where Tannis would get the treatment.

"Can we get on with this?" she snapped. "I hate this place."

Callum realized that he didn't. This time felt different. His head was clearing and his stomach settling. It was around midday and the light was bright, showing the harsh, hostile landscape. No vegetation grew on the planet, or at least nothing they recognized as vegetation. The rock that formed most of the landscape was a dull, gray green.

But despite the obvious lack of any familiar forms of life, the planet had always seemed curiously alive to him. He turned to Venna.

"Lead the way . . ."

As she set off, he allowed Tannis to go in front of him so he could monitor how she was doing, and he followed slowly. But with every step he took, a voice in his head screamed at him to stop. He tried to ignore it, but then wondered why. Should he trust Venna, who had so far found nothing? Or should he trust his instincts? Even as the thought entered his mind, he realized instinct wasn't the right word. This was more than instinct. Something real and tangible was trying to communicate with him. At the thought, a sense of wonder filled him, and he came to an abrupt halt.

Some sentient being was trying to talk to him. They didn't share the same language, and he could sense its frustration. He opened that part of his mind where his innermost thoughts were hidden, the place where his telepathy arose, and knew immediately what was wrong.

Venna must have realized he was no longer following. She glanced over her shoulder. "What?"

"We're going the wrong way," he said.

Irritation flickered across her face. "No, this is the way to the chamber I told you about."

"That's not where I need to be." He turned around, closed his eyes, and allowed the inner voice to guide him. "This way." He cast Tannis a brief glance. "You okay?"

She nodded but didn't speak, and he set off, quicker this time. His steps sped up without conscious thought, and he knew he was leaving the women behind. That didn't matter; they would catch up. In this wide-open landscape he was impossible to lose and need drove him on.

Finally, he came to a tall cliff face of gray-green rock and paused while he waited for the knowledge to come to him. Placing his hand flat against the rock, a sense of rightness filled him, almost like coming home, as though he somehow belonged here. He followed the line of the wall and came to a crack only an inch across, but as his hands learned the shape of it, the fissure expanded until it was just wide enough for him to slip through. He didn't hesitate, but stepped into the opening and found himself in a narrow passageway. After a few feet, the light vanished, and he walked through darkness until, up ahead, an eerie violet glow lit the way and the tunnel widened into a large cavern.

In the center was a huge glowing mound. Violet, like his eyes.

He stepped forward and for the first time a flicker of fear ran through him.

What would he find?

What was he?

What would he become?"

The questions ran through his mind as he inched closer. This was the center of power. This was where the voice in his head came from. He could feel it now like a buzzing in his brain.

As he placed both hands flat against the mound, a tingle ran up his arms and through his body. Then the buzzing vanished and his mind was clear. He banished all thoughts and opened himself.

Blackness closed around him, but he wasn't afraid; he welcomed it, and then he was flying through the darkness toward the truth.

# CHAPTER 17

One minute, Callum stood outlined against the gray-green rock, and then he vanished.

Tannis felt like crap, but she pushed herself to stumble after him and came to a halt in front of the narrow fissure. It was dark inside, and the place pulsated with energy that seemed to simultaneously draw and repel her. She edged forward, her stomach churning as she got closer.

A last step took her inside, and she stopped abruptly, backing away as nausea rose in her throat. She whirled around, dropped to her knees, and vomited. For long minutes, she remained, head hanging down, while she gathered her strength.

When she finally looked up, it was to the realization that she was alone. Had Venna returned to the ship? Tannis had been too focused on just keeping up to notice the other woman. Every step a challenge. What must it have been like to be brought here and made to work? She'd come so close to that very fate, and a shiver ran through her.

How did they get the slaves to keep going? What possible motivation could they give to make someone go on, when this would be all they would ever know? Surely, death would be far easier.

Then she realized that wasn't true. The will to live was amazingly strong, and the human mind resilient.

Still, she wanted to be away from here and back on *El Cazador* so badly it was like a pain in her chest. Or maybe that was just another shitty reaction to this shitty planet.

She dragged herself along the edge of the cliff a good distance from the gap and leaned against the smooth rock. Alcohol probably wasn't a good idea right now, but she needed to wash the sour taste from her mouth, so she pulled Rico's flask from her pocket. Taking slow sips, she relaxed as the warmth spread through her, her stomach settling a little.

Had Callum found anything? Did she want to know? She tried to think of anything that would stop her from going ahead with the Meridian treatment, but came up blank. So what if she would be part alien? She was hardly pure human anyway, and she had always liked the idea of being part snake—something different, unique.

Her dream was so close. Soon she would be truly immortal. One of the exalted Collective.

Where was Callum?

A roar sounded from within the gap, and she startled. She pushed herself to her feet, feeling stronger now after the rest, with the whiskey warming her insides.

Still, she hesitated at the gap. When the sound came again, she swallowed her fear and stepped between the rocks. The darkness closed around her. Each step was as if she pushed through glue, but the noise was continuous now. She knew it was Callum, and she forced herself on.

Finally, a faint, throbbing light flickered up ahead. She followed the glow until she found herself in a wide cavern. As she stumbled into the open, her gaze locked on Callum. He was on his knees, his hands flat on the mound in the center of the cave, a mound that pulsated with violet light.

"Holy freaking moly," she whispered.

At the words, Callum's lids shot open. Eyes the same violet as the light that pulsated through the cavern stared at her, blazing with triumph. He appeared revitalized, buzzing with energy, the same energy she could feel wrapping itself around her. She had to get out of there before it sucked her under.

Callum was alive; he could take care of himself. And from the look of him right now, probably a damn sight better than she could. She whirled around and headed down the tunnel, not stopping until she burst out into the open and the bright sunlight.

Leaning against the wall, she breathed deeply, and a moment later Callum emerged. He looked totally wired, a huge grin on his face.

"What is it? What did you find?"

He stopped and she glanced at him. His brows drew together in concentration.

"What is it?" she asked.

"Come on, I'll tell you on the way." He looked around. "Where's Venna?"

"I have no clue. I lost her somewhere along the way. I'm guessing she's gone back to the ship. But to be honest, I don't really care if one of your aliens came down and ate her."

He grinned again. "I get the impression you don't like her."

"Really? Actually, I think she's a fucking bitch. But is it a problem she's not here?"

"No. I have the coordinates of the last cache. We don't need her to find it." He seemed to pull himself together. "Let's go get that Meridian treatment for you."

Taking her arm, he hurried her away. Tannis did her best to keep up, but there was no way. "Slow down, Callum."

He glanced at her. "Sorry, I feel . . ."

"Good," she finished for him. "I can tell. That's just great, and I'm glad for you. But I don't."

He slowed his pace. She waited for him to speak but he appeared deep in thought, gazing around him, eyes filled with wonder.

"Tell me," she said.

He waved his hands around the landscape. "The planet's not just a planet."

"I don't understand."

"We thought some alien species might have landed here at one point. Left something behind when they went. But that's not what happened."

Impatience gnawed at her. "So are you going to tell me what did happen?"

"The alien came but never left. As far as I can tell, they're immortal. The physical body couldn't sustain itself—it faded, but the consciousness remained behind, absorbed into the very structure of the planet. It's sentient. Maybe not how we define sentient. But it communicated with me. It showed me."

"Showed you what?" Though from his reaction, it wasn't anything too bad, and she tried to force down her unease.

"It's reproducing."

Shock brought her to a standstill and she turned to face him. "What?"

"We always thought what happened to us was a mere coincidence. That we'd stumbled across Meridian, and it was just chance that it reacted that way with us. But this is how it reproduces, or at least, one of the ways. It was no accident. This life-form has the ability to combine its DNA or the equivalent of DNA, with other species. We didn't stumble upon it—I think it drew us in, probably from a long way off. It was lonely and it was no chance that brought us to the Trakis system, after all."

Her unease returned with a vengeance. She'd liked the stumbling and the chance theory much better. She hated the thought of being controlled, manipulated.

"So are there more of these things?"

"Not here. At least I don't think so. It came here a long time ago, thousands of years. I got the impression it was lost and couldn't find its way home."

"But you don't know where it came from?"

He stared into space for a moment. "It came through the black hole at Trakis One."

"I can't believe there's life on the other side of that thing."

"I saw it in my head. It came through by accident and couldn't get back, probably injured on the way through."

"Well, I can believe that. I've been there. I've stared into that black hole." She walked in silence for a moment as she thought of what this meant. Glancing down at her feet, she studied the ground. Was it thinking?

"They can fly through space," Callum said. "I was with them—in its memories—flying above their home planet. It was beautiful." He flexed his wings as though imagining what that would be like. "It's lonely. Where it comes from, there are others and they can communicate across space. Here it's so alone. For so long."

"Aw, and now it's got you."

"And you soon. Come on."

She drove herself onward. Each step was painful now. Each breath an effort that was almost too much. And all the time this new knowledge tumbled through her mind. But the effort of thinking and moving was too much, and she pushed the thoughts aside and concentrated on putting one foot in front of the other.

Finally, Callum came to a halt in front of a tunnel that led underground.

"Not much farther now."

"How long?"

"Half an hour, that's all. Are you going to be all right?"

"I'll make it."

The tunnel led down steeply. She stumbled, and Callum picked her up in his arms and carried her. She wanted to protest, but she was beyond that. Instead, she relaxed against him. His strong arms felt good around her, and she rested her cheek against his chest. She had a flashback to the last time she had been held like this, when Rico had carried her on to *El Cazador* and the start of a new life. Well, this was the start of a new life as well. Would Callum be part of that life? Or would he go back to ruling the universe and forget all about her? But something told her he wouldn't. Whatever his failings, she believed he was coming to care for her, and strangely, to care for the rest of the crew as well. He wouldn't abandon them lightly.

Maybe he wouldn't return to his old life at all. Maybe he would stay with them on *El Cazador*. Though it was getting pretty crowded on board—perhaps they should consider upgrading to a bigger ship. She had money now that she no longer had to save for the treatment, and Rico was loaded. So was Jon for that matter—he'd been very successful in his time as an assassin. They could all chip in. Get a new, improved *El Cazador 2*. She smiled at the thought, then a spasm of nausea racked her, and she clutched at Callum's shoulders.

With his free hand, he stroked her hair. "You'll be fine as soon as you get the treatment."

She had an unpleasant thought. "Hey, so you're saying this whole treatment thing is actually reproduction? Please tell me I'm not about to have sex with an alien."

He laughed so she could feel the rumbling in his chest against her cheek. "No. Any sex you have will be with me."

"Oh."

"And soon."

She closed her eyes and just concentrated on getting through the next minutes. Callum came to a halt, and her lids flickered open.

"Are we there?" She didn't think they could be. Her mind might be a blur, but no way had they been going for half an hour.

"No." His brows drew together in a frown.

"What is it?"

"Skylar. She's trying to get through to me. The comm units don't work down here—it must be the only way they can get in touch."

"Well, answer her."

"Maybe we should wait. After the treatment."

Unease shivered through her. Why would *El Cazador* try to contact them now? What had gone wrong? Tannis struggled in his arms. "Put me down."

His grip tightened for a moment, and then he gently lowered her to her feet. She leaned against the wall and stared at him. "See what she wants. Now. It must be important."

For a second, she thought he would refuse. Then he closed his lids, though she could see the rapid movement of his eyes. His mouth tightened, and his fists clenched at his side.

"What is it?" she asked.

"They have *El Cazador*."

Shock hit her in the gut. "Who has *El Cazador*?"

"The Church. They were waiting in ambush at the rendezvous point."

"What's happening? What do they want?" Frustration welled up inside her. She needed to know what was going on.

He closed his eyes again. "They want you to destroy Trakis Seven."

"What?"

"They want you to use the weapon on the ship we took and destroy the planet. If you do that, then they will release *El Cazador* and her crew.

"And if we don't?"

"Then they'll execute them one at a time."

Her mind whirled. She needed to think this through, but her brain refused to function properly.

"We can finish this, Tannis. Half an hour, that's all we need. The Church isn't going to do anything in that time. Your crew will be safe for that long. And they'd want you to do this. They know how much it means to you."

She licked her lips. Was he right? She had to decide, and now.

Callum looked at her face, must have seen her inner turmoil. "Let me decide. You're not up to this." He picked her up and hurried in the direction they had been going. Tannis tried to relax, but fear was a tight knot inside her.

He was right. Another half an hour and this would be done. Her dream realized, they could leave Trakis Seven forever, destroy it from Orbit. The Church would never know of the delay.

Callum stumbled. "Shit."

She looked up and saw the blood drain from his face.

Dread filled her mind, coating her nerve endings. "What is it?"

"Janey."

For a moment, her mind refused to process the words. Then her mind filled with a scream of denial. "Tell me."

Callum's face leached of color. "She's dead. They're monitoring the beacon on the weapon ship. When the ship didn't take off, they executed her. Jon will be next. We have half an hour."

"Oh, God, Janey." Tannis bit her lip, tasted blood as she almost suffocated under the wave of guilt that washed over her. "We have to go back."

"We don't. You're what matters. We can still do this. I'll tell Skylar we're on our way. That will buy us some time." His eyes were wild, mesmerizing as he stared into hers as though he could somehow convince her. His arms tightened around her, and she knew he meant to continue on. That he would ignore her wishes if she didn't convince him.

"Not enough. Not if they're monitoring the ship. If you do this and Jon dies, I will never forgive you."

"Why? Why do they mean so much? More than the chance of living forever. Living with me, forever?"

His words tore into her, but she didn't have to think about the answer. "Yes—they're my family. We have to go back."

"Do we?" He sounded bitter but resigned.

"How could I exist if I bought my life at the price of my friends? You must understand that, because whatever else you are, you're still at least part human." She reached up and cupped his cheek. "Take me back, please. Help me save my friends."

"You'll die. You've been exposed. Without the treatment, you'll die."

"I know." She forced her lips into a smile. "But we all have to have something that's worth dying for. Even you."

He nodded once, and then he whirled around in the opposite direction. He ran up the tunnel, and she held on, her fingers digging into the flesh of his shoulders, her face buried against his chest as she tried to fight down the waves of panic that clawed at her guts.

"It's too far. It will take too long. We can't let him die."

"We won't. Hold on."

Tannis only had a second to tighten her grip, and then Callum spread his wings. A waft of cool air shivered across her face as he launched into the sky, and then they were flying. The ground sped by beneath them. All she was conscious of was the flap of those huge wings as Callum powered them back. Soon she spotted the ship beneath them. "Please, please," she found herself muttering under her breath. They couldn't be too late. They couldn't lose Jon. She was trying her hardest not to think about Janey right now, as she would disintegrate from the pain. She was cracking up, and she needed to stay strong. She had failed Janey. She had to save the rest of them. Otherwise, what was the point? What was the point in anything? She might as well have died all those years ago.

Callum lowered them to the ground in front of the ship. The double doors slid open, and Venna stood framed in the doorway. She looked from one of them to the other, a frown forming on her pretty, vapid features.

"Is it all done? What did you find?"

"Shut up, Venna. We're leaving now."

"What's the hurry?"

"The Church has captured *El Cazador*."

Venna's eyes narrowed. "So?"

"So we're leaving now."

Venna's right hand had been behind her. Now she raised it, revealing the pistol she held pointed straight at Tannis. "No, we're not."

# CHAPTER 18

"What are you doing?" Callum's tone was icy, but the laser pistol didn't waver in Venna's hand.

As she stared at the pretty blond woman blocking her way, something occurred to Tannis. She turned to Callum. "You said the Church was waiting for the ship at the rendezvous point?"

He nodded.

"And only the three of us and the people on board *El Cazador* knew where that rendezvous was going to be."

She saw the moment he understood. His gaze sharpened on Venna. "You gave away the location of the rendezvous site?"

"The Council wanted them dead."

"Since when have you worked for the Council?"

"Since they pointed out that you're unstable. Since they offered me a job in the *new* Council. Since they promised me a chance to go on with my research."

"Idiot," he snarled. "How can you go on with your research if the planet is destroyed?"

For the first time her expression wavered. "What are you talking about?"

"That's the price the Church want for releasing *El Ca-zador*. To use the weapon to destroy the planet once and for all. The Council has played you—they knew all along that's what the Church would demand."

"That won't happen if I keep you here."

Tannis could feel her rage and frustration rising. She took a step forward, and Venna's finger tightened on the trigger.

"We need to hurry," Tannis ground out. She glanced at Callum, and he nodded. The movement was almost imperceptible, but she caught it and readied herself. She didn't know what he planned to do, but she'd be prepared.

Venna gave out a small cry and pain flashed across her features. Tannis lashed out with her right leg. Her foot connected with the pistol and it flew from Venna's hand. She kicked again, and Venna crashed to the ground. But the effort was too much, and Tannis swayed and fell to her knees. She took a deep breath and crawled to where the other woman was coming up on all fours.

Drawing back her fist, she gathered her failing strength and punched Venna in the face. "That's for me," she snarled. She punched her again, heard the *crunch* of bone, and blood spurted from her nose. "And that's for my sister." And for Janey she wanted to add, but thoughts of Janey were too painful. Later, she would have to face them, but first, she needed to save the rest of the crew.

A hand touched her on the shoulder, and she looked up into Callum's face. "We have to go." He gripped her arms and picked her up. "What about her?" he nodded in Venna's direction.

"I want her dead."

He nodded once. "Then leave her."

Venna looked up as Callum strode with her up the ramp. "What are you going to do?"

"We're going to destroy the planet."

"Take me with you." Callum ignored her, and she screamed this time. "You can't leave me here. I was doing my job, my duty. Come back!"

Callum could still hear her shrieking as the doors slid shut behind them. His mind was numb. Everything was in pieces. His euphoria of earlier had vanished completely. He strode quickly to the bridge and lowered Tannis into one of the seats, then fastened her harness. She looked awful, her skin a sickly green, her yellow eyes bloodshot.

"Comm *El Cazador*," he said. "I'll ready us for take-off."

Her hands were trembling, and he reached across and opened the comm link himself. Then he sat down in the pilot's seat and switched on the engines, and felt the vibrations beneath his feet as the main thrusters engaged.

God, he hoped they were in time. He didn't think Tannis could take another death. And it was his fault. If they had turned back as soon as they had heard from Skylar, then Janey would still have been alive. Or maybe not. He didn't know anything anymore.

For a minute, there was no reply. The ship was ready for takeoff now and he turned his attention away. They were lifting into the air, and he had to concentrate on what Venna had told him about leaving the planet. They couldn't do it without the engines, and he had to get out of there fast before they were affected.

He hit the boosters, and they shot skyward. They reached maximum speed within seconds and were beyond the planet's atmosphere. The lights flickered and went out, the thrusters stuttering. Though they lost power, their forward momentum kept them heading in the right direction, then the lights came on and the engines burst into life.

"Come in, *El Cazador*."

Silence. Then the comm unit flashed. "This is Temperance Hatcher, High Priest of the Church of Everlasting Life."

"What do you want?"

"To destroy Trakis Seven."

"And if I do that, you'll let my crew go?"

"I will, but you have five minutes to comply and then the assassin dies."

"How do we know you won't kill them anyway?"

"Destroy Trakis Seven and we will release your ship. I'm a man of God, and the Lord does not allow his priests to lie."

"Sanctimonious bastard," Tannis mumbled under her breath. She was sounding stronger. Already the effects of the planet were wearing off. Callum wondered how long that would last before the sickness started to eat at her.

She was going to die, and nothing he could do would prevent it. Callum Meridian, all-powerful Leader of the fucking Universe couldn't even save the woman he loved.

Because he did love her. If he hadn't, if it had been some lesser emotion, then he would have ignored her demand to abort their plan. He would have carried her there, compelled her to take the Meridian treatment. But he hadn't, because for once in his selfish life, he had followed someone else's wishes instead of his own.

Maybe she would die not hating him. Instead of living forever and hating his guts.

She turned to him. "How long until we're a safe distance?"

He checked the scanners. "We're already there."

"Then do it."

Callum slowed their forward momentum and brought the ship into a smooth turn so she was once again facing the planet. Except it wasn't a planet. It was a huge sentient organism. And he was about to kill it, and with it his chance of discovering more about what he was. What he was becoming. The future stretched out as an endless river of gray.

Tannis would die. And he would live forever.

"I'm sorry." Tannis's voice was soft.

"I know." *So am I,* he added silently—though she didn't need to hear that.

But someone did. Opening his mind, he reached out to the planet. He found Venna's consciousness first. She was still disbelieving, and he decided it was better to leave her that way. He reached out further, found the soul of the plant.

*I'm sorry.*

Then he slammed his palm on the button and released the weapon. The ship shuddered under the force as the blast shot outward. A crimson bolt flared across the sky. It hit Trakis Seven within seconds, and the whole planet exploded in a huge fireball.

A scream erupted in the deep recesses of his mind.

Pain. Fear. Denial.

The organism had lived for maybe a million years, the final years alone and in exile, and it still didn't want to die. The emotions swelled in his head, cramming his brain until he knew his mind would explode. He stared at Tannis, letting her fill his vision, and the last thing he saw before the darkness swallowed him was her face.

Tannis stared in horror as Callum collapsed in his seat. She wanted to get up, and go to him, but she needed to finish this first. The monitor still showed the burning planet, and she pressed the keys needed to send the pictures down the live comm link.

"Are you getting this, you bastard?"

"We are. You have done God's work. The Lord will thank you."

"I don't want the Lord's thanks, just free my fucking ship, you asshole killer."

"They are free to go. God is merciful."

Tannis slammed her hand down, shutting off the comm link. She scrabbled to release herself from the harness and crossed over to where Callum slumped over the console. His pulse was weak, but present, and some of the tension relaxed inside her. She pulled him back, then reached across and adjusted the controls so they once again headed away from the planet.

Then she sat down in her seat and relaxed the hold she had on herself. Now, when there was no one to see her, she allowed the tears to spill over.

She'd failed. Her dream was as dead as the planet behind them. Janey was dead. It seemed unbelievable; she'd been so bright, so beautiful. But the rest were safe—she had to cling to that thought.

Skylar called in, ten minutes later. Tannis wiped her eyes and straightened in her seat. She had to be strong for the rest of them.

"The Trog's dead," Skylar said.

Shock hit her in the solar plexus and the breath left her. "How?"

"He tried to save Janey. He went crazy, and they killed him."

There was more. She could hear it in Skylar's voice. Although she was obviously making an effort to keep her tone blank, the emotions seeped through. Barely suppressed rage but tinged with fear.

Not Rico. Please God, she hadn't brought his death as well.

"Tell me." Tannis forced the words out.

"They wouldn't release Rico. They said he was to be executed for the murder of Hezrai Fischer. He could already be dead. They wouldn't risk keeping him alive. And Alex. They kept Alex as well, said she would have the chance to resume her position as priestess. If not, then she dies as well so a new priestess can be born. I had to knock Jon out in order to get him away; he was going crazy—I was scared he would get himself killed, too."

"Is he okay?"

"He's come around, but he's not good. He's shifted now—it's the best thing. But at least they're unlikely to kill Alex quickly. They'll give her a chance to change her mind, take up her old position."

"We'll get her back. We'll get them both back."

"Maybe."

She'd never heard such defeat in Skylar's voice. She'd always been so strong. Tannis arranged a new rendezvous point and switched off. For a minute, she sat gazing unseeing at the monitor. Then she commed the priest.

"You said you'd release my crew, you lying bastard. Release my pilot or we'll be coming to get him."

"That would be a waste of time. He's already dead, burned in the cleansing fires."

Her mind went blank, refusing to make sense of the words. Rico couldn't be dead. He was the one constant in her life for the past fifteen years. Her friend. Her mentor.

Smashing her fist on the comm link, she squeezed her eyes shut. Beyond tears now, red-hot rage flooded her mind. She wanted revenge.

Tannis set the ship to automatic and put in the coordinates of the new rendezvous point. After that was sorted, she dragged Callum onto the floor, laid him on his side so his wings wouldn't be in the way, and put a cushion under his head. She sat close by, leaned against the wall, and watched him.

On Trakis Seven, he'd told her they could have eternity together. She'd never believed she could hold such a man for eternity, but maybe she could have him for the time she had left.

However short.

# CHAPTER 19

It was hours before Callum regained consciousness. He blinked open his stunning purple eyes but didn't speak.

"How are you feeling?" she asked.

"Empty."

"Me, too."

He dragged himself up, then crossed to where she sat and slumped down beside her. Wrapping his arms around her, he pulled her against him, his big hands rubbing the skin of her back, massaging away the tension.

Tannis realized she didn't want to talk. For a little time, she just wanted to forget. Emptying her mind, she concentrated on the feel of his touch. No one had ever touched her quite this way. Not sexual, just soothing. She closed her eyes and allowed sleep to blank away the memories.

When she awoke, she was still wrapped in his arms. Callum was half sitting, leaning against the wall behind him, and she was in his lap.

He took one look at her eyes. "What happened?"

She took a deep breath. "Rico's dead. And the Trog. And they have Alex—she's alive for now, but I'm scared she'll lose it and shift. Then they'll kill her for sure."

"Bastards." He stroked her hair. "I'm sorry."

"I want him dead. Temperance Hatcher."

"You look so fierce, like a hawk."

"I am fierce." She bit her lip. "Usually. I just can't believe Rico is gone."

"He meant a lot to you, didn't he?"

"He was my friend. Strangely, he taught me how to be human."

"Tell me."

She'd never spoken to anyone about her time in the research station. Even Rico. It had been too painful. Now she knew it was time to let go. Pulling free of Callum's arms, she struggled to her feet. She swayed, weakness washing over her.

Could she be sick already? Then her stomach rumbled and she realized how long it had been since she had eaten. It was strange, but life went on. A few hours ago, she couldn't have imagined ever feeling hungry again.

"I will," she said, "but let's go find some food first."

They checked the autopilot and went to the galley. Callum got them both a bowl of stew and placed one in front of her. She ate in silence for a minute, but after a few mouthfuls, she couldn't face anymore. She put down the spoon and took a deep breath. Where to start?

"I can't remember my life before the research center. Maybe I blanked it out when my parents were killed. Thea, my sister, was younger than I was, and she remembered something, at least at the start. She would ask me when was Mummy coming for us, and I'd look at her blankly."

"What happened to her?"

"She died. I think she was around ten. I was eleven, though that's guessing, as we didn't exactly celebrate birthdays in there. I think because we were siblings they would conduct the same experiments on us, with one of us as the control. It always seemed to be me. She would get sick, and I would be fine. When I realized, I used to beg them to use me, but they never listened, or maybe I was just stronger."

She pushed the bowl of food away from her, as the pain churned in her stomach. "One time she didn't recover. They took her to the medical center and she never came back. The guards told me they had put her down. She was too sick to bother with. No more use for more experiments. I think that was when I decided I wanted to kill them."

Callum reached across the table, took her hand, and squeezed her fingers. "I'm sorry. I never knew, and if it makes it any better, I will know in the future. I'll never use that excuse again. What happened to you after she died?"

"The same, but I went on without her. Actually, it was easier in some ways once Thea was gone. I had no one to worry about but myself. I learned to distance myself from the others, not to care when they died or left. But I knew that it was only a matter of time. There were grown-ups at the center but they were human, not GMs. The GMs were always sent to the mines when they reached adulthood."

"Venna told me it was an agreement they made with the Church when they bought the children. That GMs would be destroyed when they reached maturity."

"I suppose that figures. You know, I've been thinking, and the truth is if the research center hadn't existed then the Church would have killed Thea and me along with our parents. I should probably be thanking you for saving my life."

He shook his head. "How did you get to be so positive?"

"That was Rico." A wave of pain flooded her as she thought of Rico, but she forced herself to go on. "I was pretty messed up, but he straightened me out, told me he might as well drain me dry and put me out of everyone's misery if I didn't cheer up. So I did my best to put it behind me."

"How did you escape?"

She closed her eyes and relived those last hours in the research station. "I'd been planning for a long time. I'd made a knife. But I kept putting it off and putting it off."

"Why?"

"Because however crappy my life was, I wanted to live, and I knew I had zero chance of getting out of there. Even if I took down a guard, got out of my cell, there was no way I could get off the station. I never admitted it to myself outright, but really it was suicide. Still, I figured better than dying a slow death in the mines." She gave a short laugh. "Ironic really."

"But you did get away."

"That was Rico again. He was a prisoner there as well. He called out to me as I ran down the corridor after I killed the guard. He said he could get me away if I released him. So I did, and he bit me. Nearly drained me. Later, he told me he'd been there for three months and hadn't fed in that time. I was lucky to survive. Then he got me away and never bit me again."

"Have you and he ever . . ."

She knew exactly what he was asking. "Never. I think he recognized I was . . . damaged, and he left me alone. He was my friend. The first real friend I'd ever had. When I escaped the research center, I thought I wanted revenge. Rico persuaded me not to focus my life on that. He told me I would regret it, and even if I got my revenge, afterward I would be left with nothing. So I put it behind me, and I built a life, and it was a good one."

"So why did you want the Meridian treatment?"

"Doesn't everyone?"

"Not everyone, no. And some think they do but faced with the reality, they don't really want it."

"You can blame Venna."

"Of course. Venna, the angel."

There was something she'd been meaning to ask. "What did you do to Venna? Back there on the planet."

"Zapped her mind. Sent a wave of energy into her. It hurts."

"I saw—nifty trick. Thank you. She was one of your people. You didn't have to side with me."

"Yes, I did. And she lost the right to my protection when she betrayed us all."

*Us.* She liked that he was identifying with them.

"I'm sorry," he said. "For what happened to you and my part in it. I would take it back if I could, but that's not possible."

"I think I understand that now." Forcing her lips into the semblance of a smile, she pushed herself to her feet. "I'm going to take a walk around the ship, have a shower, get my head straightened."

For a moment, she thought he would argue, and then he nodded. "I'll be on the bridge when you need me."

She found a cabin and showered, then pulled on her clothes. She roamed the ship for what seemed like hours, allowing her mind to wander over her memories of Rico and Janey. The Trog. She didn't cry. The tears had all dried up.

In the end, she was drawn to the bridge where she knew Callum waited, worrying. He was slouched in the pilot's chair, but he straightened as she entered, his gaze searching her face.

"I'm okay," she said to preempt the question.

"No, you're not. But you look a little better." He rose to his feet and held out a hand to her. "Let me try and help you forget some more."

Callum waited to see whether she would take his hand. He wouldn't blame her if she didn't. How could she ever forgive him? How had she turned out so strong after such a beginning? He reckoned he owed the vampire a big thanks for that. Though he'd never be able to deliver that thank you. Rico was dead.

As Tannis soon would be.

He'd shied away from thinking about how long Tannis had left, but he'd been lying when he'd said she looked better. Already, if he looked closely, he could see the faint violet tinge to her skin—the first visible symptom of the poison. He'd never known it to react so quickly. Perhaps she'd been exposed to it at the research center, or one of those experiments had predisposed her to the poison. He didn't know. And did the whys really matter?

He thought she was going to ignore his outstretched hand, but she took the final step, reached out, and slid her palm into his. He pulled her close, lifted her in his arms, and headed out of the bridge and down the central corridor, kicking open the doors as he passed. Finally, he found one with a big bed and took her inside, lowering her gently to the mattress.

He intended to make slow love to her, to make it last, to draw out her pleasure, make her forget the past and the future.

She was exquisite. He couldn't believe he had ever not thought her beautiful. She was the most beautiful thing he had ever seen, her body long, slender, sinuous. Her skin luminous, shot through with iridescent lights.

He stripped off her clothes, kissing each inch of her skin as it was exposed. Then he quickly pulled off his own clothes, dropping them to the floor, before stretching out beside her. He took her mouth in a long, slow kiss, his tongue sliding between her lips to stroke the warm velvet of hers. When he raised his head, her eyes were heavy, languorous. He kissed her throat, nipped the soft spot where her neck met her shoulder. He licked long strokes over her breasts, then concentrated on the dark red nipples until they were tight with need, and she made mewling sounds deep in her throat.

"Please, Callum," she murmured.

"Shh. Trust me."

His tongue dipped into her navel, tasting her, then lower over the flat plain of her belly to the dark curls that protected her sex. He blew a light breath over her, and her hips rose. Parting her legs with one hand, he slid his tongue along the seam of her sex, the taste of her making his cock twitch with need and his balls tighten. He shifted to lie between her thighs, using his hands to part the folds, reveal her secrets. She was glistening wet, and he dipped his tongue inside, holding her still as she wriggled against him. Then he slanted his mouth against her and kissed her, using his lips, his tongue and teeth to give her pleasure, sucking and licking, nipping gently with his teeth. She was pushing against him now, and he finally took her swollen clit in his mouth and suckled. A low, keening cry left her throat as she came. He lapped at her soothingly until the tremors that racked her calmed, then he bit down, and she screamed.

He moved swiftly up her body, to stare down into her pleasure-flushed face.

"You want me?" he asked.

He lowered his hips so the hard length of his erection pressed into her, and her hips rose up to meet him.

"Yes."

Tremors of pleasure rippled through her as his shaft nudged at the entrance to her body. She needed him inside her, and she shifted her hips impatiently against him. One hand came up to cup his jaw, and she stroked the pad of her thumb over his sensual lower lip. His tongue flicked out, licking her fingers, and heat pooled in her belly.

Then his hands slid behind her neck and he pulled her

to him. His lips met hers with a savagery she'd never felt in him before, and she gave herself over to the feeling, allowed her own rage and fury to come through.

For a second, he hesitated, then he deepened the kiss, his tongue thrusting into her mouth with a fierce passion.

He reached between their bodies, opening her with skillful fingers, then stared down into her eyes as he pushed inside her, filling her with one fluid thrust of his hips.

There was no pain, just a feeling of stretching fullness. She needed more, and she pushed her hips in a mute plea.

"I don't want to hurt you," he murmured.

She jerked against him. "You won't. I want this. I need this. Just to forget."

He nodded. Then he pulled out and shoved back inside her. Hard. There was nothing gentle about his lovemaking. It was full of rage and sadness. Fury and passion. She lost herself in the ebb and flow of his huge body moving on her, in her. The glide of his withdrawal, the push of his hips when she whispered to have him back inside her. She wrapped her legs around his waist and pulled her to him but it limited his movement and he growled deep in his throat.

Gripping her knees in his big hands, he bent them against her body, so she was open to him, and then he pounded into her, forcing the memories from her mind. Each stroke drove her closer to release, but she didn't want this to end so she fought the pleasure that built inside her.

His hands shifted to her bottom, pulling her up against him, and he ground into her, rotating his hips, pressing against her swollen clit so however much she fought the pleasure it was too much. She gave herself up to it, her mind blank, her body just a mass of sensations. Then he lowered his head, sucked one nipple into his mouth as he pressed deep inside her, and she exploded in a starburst of pleasure.

He followed her over the edge, his head went back, and his hips pumped against her. She came again, her spine arching from the bed, until finally she collapsed back, sated.

Afterward, she lay with him still lodged deep inside, his arms tight around her. "I'm going to die, aren't I?" she said.

"Yes."

# CHAPTER 20

*El Cazador* was a mess. Tannis had seen the battered hull all scarred by laser blasts as they'd docked the smaller ship. Rico would have hated that.

What was left of the crew were gathered together on the bridge. It looked like there had been a firefight in here as well. But if the ship was a mess then the crew was no better.

On the surface, Skylar looked in the best shape, but her figure was tense, every muscle tight. Jon had shifted back into human form. He paced the bridge as though unable to stay in one place, and his eyes glowed feral. Daisy sat in Janey's old chair, her emerald eyes bloodshot from weeping.

Tannis put her hands on her hips and stared at them all. "I leave my goddamn ship for five minutes and this is what you do to it."

A smile flickered across Skylar's face but didn't reach as far as her eyes. Tannis looked at her closely and realized she must be holding herself together by willpower alone.

"Rico's dead," Tannis said. She was pretty sure Skylar

already knew, but she needed to get the words out in the open.

"I know." Skylar's voice was without expression. "The Church contacted us. They seem to believe that if we know he's dead, then that will be it."

"It won't," Tannis promised. "So, what happened?"

"They were already waiting at the rendezvous point. Almost as if they knew we were coming."

"They did," Tannis said. "Venna told them."

"Fucking bitch. I'll kill her."

"Too late. She's dead. We left her on that planet we blew up."

"Good. Anyway, we nearly managed to fight our way out," Skylar continued, "but there were just too many of them. In the end, they boarded us. They managed to capture Daisy and Janey, and it was all over."

"They made us try and comm you, but there was no answer, so I tried Callum." She looked at Tannis. "We don't blame you."

"Jesus," Tannis muttered. "You should."

"You couldn't know what would happen. Besides, you needed to go on, you had no choice once you were on the planet. You had to get the treatment or . . ." She studied Tannis, stared into her eyes. "Or you're dead. Holy Meridian, you did get the treatment?"

"Do I look like I got the goddamn treatment?" Tannis growled. "We were going to—we were nearly at the site when you contacted Callum. We went on anyway—so don't start thinking I'm some goddamn hero. Then Janey . . . I couldn't risk Jon as well, and there was no time." She ran a hand through her hair. "Tell me what happened."

"They told us they would execute one of us if you didn't comply and then another every thirty minutes after that. When you didn't immediately respond they picked Janey, said she'd be first. I don't think any of us believed they would really do it. I don't know why. It seemed unreal."

"Why Janey?" Janey would have been the last person she would have thought they would pick. Not that anyone else would have been better, but she couldn't understand it. She would have thought Daisy—she was a GM—but maybe the Church didn't think she was worthwhile. Or one of the men. If they'd planned to kill Rico, why not pick him? Janey had been so bright and beautiful.

"I don't know. But they did it so suddenly. They made her go down on her knees in front of us all. She was so brave, but you could see the terror in her eyes."

Tannis almost swayed at the tidal wave of guilt that washed over her. This was her fault. She had let this happen.

"It was quick—a shot to the back of the head. The high priest did it himself. He enjoyed it—you could see it in his eyes."

"And the Trog?"

"He went crazy, absolutely wild. They couldn't hold him. In the end he broke free, leaped for the priest, and the guards shot him as well."

"Where was Rico?"

"He was unconscious. They'd given him something. Maybe they thought he was too dangerous, or maybe he was dead even then."

"No, they'd have to do more than that." Rico had told her once—a stake through the heart, decapitation, or burning and scattering the ashes. But she thought it probably wasn't wise to go into those sorts of details with Skylar right now.

"And Jon was cuffed," Skylar continued. "But they had a gun to Alex's head, he wasn't moving."

"Is Alex okay?"

"She was when we left. At least she was alive. When they picked Jon as the next to die, she lost it. I was sure she would shift and they'd kill her, but she managed to stay human. When we didn't hear from you . . ." Skylar closed her eyes. "Well, Jon was cool, but he was about the only one."

"I'm sorry."

"Stop saying that," Skylar snapped. "They held us until you sent the comm showing the planet on fire, and then they let us go. Except Rico and Alex. I didn't want to leave, but the others were a mess. They'd knocked Jon out as well by then. I had to get them away, and I thought there would be time. I never thought they would kill him straightaway."

"They probably knew we'd come after him."

Skylar blinked and huge tears welled up, intensifying the deep purple of her eyes. "The others, they were falling apart, I had to hold them together. Now you're here, and I need . . ." She shook her head. "I can't believe he's gone."

She whirled around and ran from the room. Tannis made to follow, but Callum stopped her with a hand on her arm. "Let her go," he said. "She's hurting, and there's nothing you can do. Nothing anyone can do. Only time will help her now, and she has plenty of that."

"And getting Alex back."

Jon paused his pacing and came to stand in front of her. He appeared truly scary, his eyes half wolf, and she had to make herself stand her ground. "We'll get her back."

"And kill that priest," Daisy said.

Tannis turned to look at her. She'd never known Daisy to want to hurt anyone, now she looked fierce. Tannis nodded. "And kill the priest."

Exhaustion tugged at her and she swayed. She peered over her shoulder and saw Callum's worried frown quickly wiped clean. She couldn't get ill yet; it was too soon. She'd thought she might have years. That's what they'd told her at the research station. Two years of slow death.

"How long do I have?" she asked Callum.

He shook his head.

"Tell me."

"I don't know—it's different with each person." He held her gaze, and she saw the sadness in his eyes. "But I'm guessing not long."

"What's going on?" Jon asked.

"I didn't get the treatment and I'm poisoned and I'm dying." There was no point in circling around this.

It was ironic. Now when she would have gladly allowed Rico to turn her into a sex-craved monster, he was gone. If only she'd done it earlier. But earlier it hadn't seemed an option, and now it was too late.

Callum studied Jon speculatively. "You saved Alex when she was dying. Could you do the same for Tannis?"

She looked at him sharply. It hadn't even occurred to her, and a little flame of hope burst to light inside her. She thought she'd accepted the fact of her death, but now she realized that was an illusion—she didn't want to die. She glanced at Callum and saw her excitement reflected in his eyes.

But Jon shook his head. "I'm sorry. It doesn't work with GMs. They always go insane, and they always die. At least this way you keep your sanity."

Callum wrapped his arms around her and pulled her against him. Tannis shoved down the despair, she needed to be able to concentrate. They had to make a plan to free Alex. Time to think about dying later. Or not dying. There was one more chance, however remote. If only she could hang on long enough.

"Do we know where they are now?" she asked.

"We're pretty sure they headed back to Trakis Four."

"Shit, that's not good news." Trakis Four was the Church's main headquarters. It would be almost impossible to get in there and out again with Alex.

"It's not that bad," Callum said. "Their forces must be pretty thinly spread right now. I've been in contact with the colonel. They're still under siege on Trakis Five. That must be taking up most of their ships and men."

"Maybe. I still don't see how we can get in and out."

"We need some sort of distraction," Jon said.

"Yes, but what?"

She pulled out of Callum's hold and paced the bridge, trying to get her head around what they could do. On their own, it was a suicide mission, and no way were any more of her crew going down. Could she somehow go in herself—after all, it hardly mattered if she died at this point. Though she didn't want to die now, she wanted to spend what little time she had left with Callum and with her friends.

"Shit. There has to be a way."

"Captain?" She swung around as Daisy spoke. "There's a comm coming through," she continued. "Do you want me to open the link?"

"Who's it from?"

"Devlin."

Crap. She was going to have to tell him his brother was dead. How he would react, she could only imagine. But even as her mind balked at facing him, the thought occurred to her that he could help. He'd want revenge for his brother's death as much as they did, and the Rebels could provide the perfect distraction. She just hoped they weren't too far away.

"Put him on," she told Daisy.

"Devlin," she said.

"I know about Tris."

His words took her by surprise. She hadn't expected them, and for a moment, she was silent.

"I'm sorry, Devlin. He died trying to protect Janey." She frowned. "But how did you know?"

"The Church—the bastards. He's been on their most-wanted list since the bombing. They sent out a comm announcing they had caught and executed him. Showed a fucking goddamn picture of his body."

Tannis glanced up as Skylar entered the bridge. Her face was pale, and she had a pair of Rico's dark glasses perched on her nose, but she appeared composed.

"They must have identified him after we left," Skylar said as she came to stand beside her. "They certainly didn't while we were there, but they wouldn't let us take his body, and besides we had our hands full with Jon."

"What happened?" Devlin asked. "How did they get hold of him?"

"They ambushed *El Cazado*r. Rico and Janey are dead as well, and they have Alex."

"What?" She could hear the shock clear in his voice. "What are you doing about it?"

"We're going to rescue Alex, and then we're going to kill the people responsible."

"Sounds like a good plan. I want in."

# CHAPTER 21

Callum had thought she'd hurt him that day she'd poisoned him. But the pain was nothing to what he felt now.

He'd gotten used to being in control. Now he was faced with something he had absolutely no control over, and he was breaking up inside. She was so brave. Her dream had been to live forever, and now she was dying. How could she go on as though nothing had happened? She was discussing the "plan" with Skylar, tossing ideas back and forth. What did it matter to her whether they rescued Alex or not when she wouldn't be around? And they couldn't save Alex anyway. This was a suicide mission. They would all die.

They might as well have continued on Trakis Seven and gotten Tannis the treatment. At least she would have lived. But she'd chosen these people instead over a chance of forever with him.

And now. Now, there was one last remote possibility. So remote that he didn't even dare talk to her about it. But the longer they put it off the remoter the chance of them succeeding. And they were wasting time.

Anger built up inside him, and he allowed it to rise because it was better than the pain.

"Callum?"

At Tannis's softly spoken question, he looked up. Everyone was watching him with expressions varying from alarm to understanding. "What?" he snarled.

"Chill out, you're scaring people. I know you're hurting—"

"How the hell do you know that?" he growled. "You're not a fucking mind reader, remember? You gave up the chance of that."

She bit her lip. "I'm sorry."

"You seem to be saying that a lot lately."

Anger flashed in her yellow eyes, the irises narrowing to mere slits of black. She stepped up close to him and poked a finger in his chest. "Yeah, and you know what— it's true—I am fucking sorry. I'm sorry that Janey and the Trog are dead. I'm sorry the goddamn Church killed Rico because that would have really pissed him off. I'm sorry that they still have Alex, and I'm really sorry that I'm dying." She poked him again, harder this time, and he winced. "And now, I have to be sorry for you as well, because for once you're not getting what you want. I bet that really hurts."

As her words sank in, he saw himself for the first time as she must see him. They were all hurting, and all he could think of was how this affected him. Why would Tannis want to spend eternity with such a selfish bastard? A wave of pain washed away the anger and left him drained and empty. He looked from Tannis to Jon and Skylar and Daisy. He expected to see anger in their faces at his selfishness, but all he saw was understanding.

Pain squeezed his heart in a vise, and he spun on his heels and stalked from the bridge. Tannis was behind him, but he kept on going, until she came up beside him and slipped her hand in his. They walked in silence, and he didn't notice where they were going until she pulled him to a halt outside her cabin. She released her hold on him and he felt bereft. He'd better get used to it.

Tannis pressed her palm to the panel and ushered him inside where he stood, hands shoved in his pockets. He didn't want to talk. He was scared of what would come out.

A maelstrom of emotions churned inside him. "I don't know what's happening to me. And I'm not sure I can take this. It hurts."

"You're becoming human."

"What?"

"Rico told me that once. He said you might be kidding yourself that you were changing, becoming something else, but it was actually the human part of you that was causing the problems."

"Problems?"

"You've closed yourself off for so long. I bet you've even convinced yourself that you're turning into some sort of alien so the rules of being human don't really apply to you anymore. But they do."

He knew she was speaking the truth. He'd been fooling himself. Whenever he had to make a difficult decision, something his conscience whispered was wrong, he'd tell himself it was the Meridian, not him. He wasn't responsible. He'd been a coward as well as a fool.

The knowledge of her coming death was eating into his soul. If he still had one. If he'd ever had one, for that matter. Maybe this was God making him pay for all his sins. But why should Tannis pay as well?

"Look," she said. "I'm tired. I just want to rest for a while."

She didn't want him here. Why should she? He must be a constant reminder of what she had lost. "I'll go."

"No." The word was torn from her, and she reached out and laid her hand on his arm. "Please stay. I don't want to be alone. Just stay with me. Hold me. Forget for a while that I'm dying and just be with me."

"I don't think I can."

She frowned, irritation flicking across her face. "Well, just freaking pretend!"

He curved his lips into the semblance of a smile. "Let's go to bed."

He undressed her slowly, picked her up, and laid her gently between the sheets, before stripping off his own clothes and sliding in beside her. The lights dimmed and he rolled onto his side and pulled her close to him, wrapped his arms around her.

"We're two great humans, aren't we?" he murmured into her hair.

Tannis raised her head and stared at him so he could see the glow of her eyes in the dark. "Yes, we are," she said fiercely. "Being human is as much about how you behave as what you are. It's looking out for the people you love." She bit her lip. "Actually, there's something I wanted to ask you."

"Anything."

A grin flashed across her face. "Don't be so quick. After I'm gone, will you look after them? Just for a while. *El Cazador* will need a captain. I'm thinking maybe Skylar would like the job in the end, but she's a mess right now. And Jon is no better. If we don't get Alex back, I'm scared he'll revert to the way he was."

"We'll get her back."

"I know you'll return to your old life, but just keep an eye on them until they're over this."

"I promise. Now sleep."

He closed his eyes, sure he wouldn't be able to sleep—he rarely slept these days. But as he lay in the darkness, listening to her slow steady breathing, he drifted into sleep.

He woke in the darkness. For a moment, he thought her gone and panic clutched his heart, threatened to suck him under. Then he felt her soft lips moving over his body, her warm mouth engulfing him. They made love as though it might be the last time ever.

When he woke again, he was alone. This time he didn't panic. He'd gone over what she'd said, and he was determined that if she was going to die, it would be knowing that Alex and what was left of the crew were safe.

He didn't know how, but he could forget the wallowing in self-pity, at least for the present. The future would be soon enough for that.

*Colonel?*

For a moment, he thought he would get no answer.

*Callum? We thought you might be dead.*

He breathed a sigh of relief. He'd kept very quiet since Trakis Seven was destroyed, partly because he was totally pissed off with the Council and their part in the destruction of the planet, but also because if the Council believed there was a possibility he was dead, then they might free the colonel. It was well known where the colonel's loyalties lay. *Well I'm not.*

*I'm glad.*

*So am I. What's happening over there?*

*I'm still being treated as suspect, but they've eased up since Seven was destroyed. I get the distinct impression that this is all part of some plan. They don't appear to have made any effort to break the siege, and there's something else. Your new stealth ship is missing.*

The Endeavor?

*That's the one. I would have expected her to be here trying to break the siege. But she's not around. I think maybe the Council aren't as stupid as they seem.*

Callum thought for a moment. *Hmm—get the Church*

*to destroy Trakis Seven so they get the blame for elimi-*
*nating the only source of Meridian. Then they destroy the*
*Church, and it looks like self-defense.*

How could he use this? *So what's their next move?*
*Where is* The Endeavor?

*I don't know, and I doubt they'll tell me. But if it were*
*me planning this, then I'd be on my way to Trakis Four.*
*Destroy the Church's base. Then return and break the siege*
*when they're leaderless and in chaos.*

It did make sense, but Callum needed confirmation, before he passed the information on to Tannis. He didn't see
yet how they could use this. But if *The Endeavor* planned
on destroying the Church's base on Trakis Four, maybe that
could provide the distraction they needed to allow them
to slip in, get Alex, and kill that bastard Hatcher.

On the other hand, *The Endeavor* could succeed before
they got there and Alex would be blown to bits with the
rest of the Church. He needed some idea of the time frame.

*Thanks, Colonel. Let me know if you find out anything*
*else.*

*Callum?*

*Yes?*

*I know you went to Trakis Seven. Did you find anything?*

*Yeah, I found something. And if I get out of this, I'll*
*tell you.*

He closed off the link.

*Tyler?* He met with some resistance and pushed harder.
*TYLER!*

*Callum.*

*I want to come back in. Can you send a ship to pick*
*me up?*

*You've given up on the crazy hunt?*

*Well, there's not much point in going on now that the*
*Church have destroyed the planet.*

*No, that was a tragedy. Look, Callum, I know you*

*wanted to discover the truth, but maybe some things are best not known.*

Callum gritted his teeth, then forced his face to relax, so his emotions wouldn't come through the link. *You're right. I know that now. Besides, if there had been anything to find on Trakis Seven no doubt we would have found it already.*

*I'm glad you're being sensible.*

Yeah, he was being sensible, and if he ever got out of this, he was going after Tyler and the rest of his weasely Council. *So when and where?*

*Where are you now?*

Callum gave his coordinates and waited while Tyler looked them up.

*You can get a ride on* The Endeavor. *She has a small job to do over in that area, but she can pick you up before heading home.*

*A little job?*

*Just a cleanup. We're going after the Church's Head-quarters on Trakis Four. We have to be seen to retaliate. But I'll inform Captain Harris that he's to rendezvous with you afterward.*

That was no good. Afterward would be too late. He needed to find a way to stop the ship or somehow use the attack to their benefit. *Okay. But make it before they reach Trakis Four. I want to see* The Endeavor *in action, and I want to see that piece of shit Hatcher blown to bits.*

*No problem. If you set your course to intercept, I'll tell him to expect you.*

*Good. You seem to have everything in hand. I'll see you soon.*

He closed off the link and sat on the edge of the bed, thinking for a minute. Then he closed his eyes. If he went to a certain place in his mind, he could sense the other members of the Collective. All of them were there. He just had to sift through the individual minds and find the one he wanted. He found Captain Harris easily, but didn't make contact. He needed to talk to Tannis first.

He found her in the galley with the rest of the crew. They all looked marginally better—he guessed that came from at least having a purpose. He grabbed a coffee and sat down next to Tannis, then leaned in and kissed her lips.

"I just found out that the Collective have sent *The Endeavor* to destroy the Church's headquarters on Trakis Four.

"*The Endeavor?* Wasn't that the prototype stealth ship we ran into after we picked you up?"

"That's the one. So we need to either find a way to stop it before it blows Alex to pieces. Or we need to find a way we can use it as a distraction to slip in and get her out. Though there is the danger with that option that we'll all get blown to pieces in the cross fire."

"No," Tannis said. "We don't need to do either of those things."

"We don't?" Callum looked into her face. She was fizzing with the old energy and purpose.

"No. What we need to do is steal her."

# CHAPTER 22

Tannis decided to wait until Devlin arrived before they discussed the plan in any more detail. He expected to intersect within a couple of hours.

Daisy was doing her best to watch for anyone coming after them and also gather whatever intel they could find on Trakis Four, but they missed Janey's expertise.

Jon was not doing well, but Tannis was sure that once they had a decent plan, he would pull himself together. Callum was confident he could take the ship, and she trusted him. Besides, she had the worst goddamn headache of her life. She had a feeling that time was running out and just hoped she would hang on until what was left of her crew was safe. After that, anything would be a bonus.

She took herself to the medical center—at least she could treat the symptoms. After dosing herself on the strongest painkillers she could find, she followed with a couple of antinausea pills because she felt sick, and she never reacted well to drugs, so chances were she was going to feel sicker any moment.

Lying down on the high cot, she closed her eyes and waited for everything to work. She supposed things could be worse. If she'd gone ahead with the treatment on Trakis Seven, her whole crew would probably be dead, and she'd face an eternity of guilt instead of what she was beginning to realize was days, rather than months or years. She could almost sense the poison in her system eating away at her. It was moving too fast. At the back of her mind, she'd had this hope that they would rescue Alex and there would be time. Time enough . . . She cut off the thought; it was unlikely now. She was dying.

Her headache faded, and she must have dozed off, because when her lids flickered open, she found Callum perched on the edge of the cot beside her.

"I didn't want to wake you, but Devlin's just boarding, and I thought you'd want to know."

She sat up and ran a hand through her hair—at least the headache was gone. "Hey," she said, "there's time enough to sleep when you're dead."

Pain flashed across his face, and she wished she could bite back the words. Callum was trying hard to get over his bout of self-pity, and she should be helping, not making wiseass comments about dying. But in a second, the expression was gone. He appeared to have regained his composure, and she was glad. He needed to be strong and focused right now.

She swung her legs over the side of the cot, stood, and swayed, so she had to balance herself. Callum put out a hand to help her, but she shrugged it off and straightened.

"Are you feeling worse?" he asked.

"No, actually I feel better. I'm just drugged up to the eyeballs. Go see if you can get me a stimulant. They should be in that drawer over there."

"Are you sure you should take more drugs?"

She just looked at him, and he went to get her drugs. It was a real pity they didn't have more time—if only she had him around longer, she might have gotten him trained.

"Pills or needle."

Tannis shuddered. She hated needles—they reminded her too much of her childhood and all the tests and experiments, but she needed this to work fast. "Needle," she said.

Callum handed her a syringe. Without allowing herself to think, she jabbed the needle into the muscle of her upper thigh. The effect was almost instantaneous, and she closed her eyes as energy flooded her body.

She crossed over to the small sink and ran the water, splashing her face, then patting it dry. For a second she stared at herself in the mirror, but she looked the same, and she turned away.

"Come on. Let's go save the day, one last time."

Devlin was already in the meeting room when they entered, sitting beside Skylar, his head leaning in close, talking to her in a low voice. He glanced up as Tannis entered with Callum close behind, then rose to his feet. A small frown played across his face as he stepped toward her. Tannis studied him; he appeared no different until she looked closely. Then the signs of grief were obvious—his eyes shadowed, the scar a vivid slash down his cheek, lines bracketing his grim mouth.

"I'm sorry," she said, as he came to a halt in front of her.

"Not your fault."

Well, that wasn't exactly the truth. She glanced behind him at Skylar, who gave a small shake of her head. Tannis presumed that meant Devlin was unaware of Tannis's part in the Trog's death. "What have they told you?"

"Not much, just that he was shot trying to save Janey." He considered her, his head cocked to one side. "Snakelady, did you know you look like shit?"

"She's fine," Callum said, resting a hand on her shoulder and drawing her back against him. She thought about pulling away, but the solid strength of him behind her felt too good.

"No, she's not. So are you going to tell me what it is I don't know?"

Tannis sighed. She really didn't want to go into this right now, but maybe Devlin deserved to know. If it weren't for her, his brother would, in all likelihood, still be alive. She just hoped that by the end of this conversation, he still wanted revenge on the Church more than he wanted revenge on her. She wouldn't blame him for hating her.

"Let's sit down." She gestured to the chair he'd just vacated and followed him across, sinking into the seat opposite with the low table between them. Staring over his shoulder for a minute, she considered what to say.

"So?" Devlin prompted.

She spoke quickly, confessing everything, then waited for the condemnation to come. Instead, his eyes filled with pity, and she clenched her teeth.

"So that's what's the matter with you—you have the Meridian poisoning?"

"Yes."

Devlin pinched the bridge of his nose, his expression bleak. "You know, we used to talk about it, Tris and me, about how with the lives we lived, there was never much hope we'd die in our beds. Tris was never cut out for this life, but at least he died for someone he cared about. I don't blame you, and I have no intention of killing you, but that bastard, Hatcher, is going to die."

Daisy appeared at that moment, waving a bottle in her hand. They all looked at her and some of the tension seeped from the atmosphere. "I got this from Rico's cabin. It's almost the last." She placed it on the table, then leaned across and kissed Devlin on the cheek. "I'm sorry about the Trog. He was really brave."

"Thank you."

She nodded, then went to fetch glasses from the cabinet at the edge of the room. After pouring the drinks, she perched on the seat on the other side of Skylar, twirling a strand of long green hair. Her skin was a pale, sickly green. She was taking this hard, but then she had hero-worshipped Rico.

"Where's Jon?" Tannis asked.

"Still in his cabin."

"No, I'm not." Jon stood in the doorway. He didn't look good, but at least he was still human, and the feral glint had gone from his eyes. He lowered himself into the seat next to Callum, stretched his long legs in front of him, and reached across for a glass. He swallowed the amber liquid in one gulp. "So how are we going to do this?"

Tannis turned to Callum. "Why don't you explain?"

Callum nodded. "Right now, *The Endeavor* is on her way to Trakis Four—"

*"The Endeavor*?" Devlin cut in.

"She's the Collective's new flagship. Top-of-the-range stealth technology. Anyway she's on her way to destroy the Church's headquarters, and we plan to steal her."

Tannis relaxed, sipped her drink, and let the rich tones of his voice wash through her. He had a beautiful voice and a way of talking that made everyone pay attention and sit forward in their seats. He was a born leader, that was obvious, and she couldn't help but wonder what he would do after . . . after she was gone. And after he had fulfilled his promise to see her crew right. Would he go back and rule the Collective? He'd said he'd come to hate the job, but maybe he'd just needed a break so he could see things clearly.

"How do we steal her?" Devlin asked. "I'm presuming she must have firepower far superior to anything we can put together."

"I'll sort that out," Callum said.

"Will you?" Devlin frowned. "Why would you go against your own people?"

"He will," Tannis said. "Trust me."

Devlin gave him a long look but then nodded.

A brief smile flickered across Callum's face. "Okay, so we board her and between us we'll work out how to fly her. Then we take her in to Trakis Four using the stealth technology. Meanwhile, Devlin can create a diversion with *El Cazador* and any of his people who can get there on time."

"No."

Callum turned to Devlin and raised an eyebrow. "No?"

"I want to be in the landing party. I want a chance at Hatcher. Tris was my brother."

"He's right." Skylar spoke for the first time. "Besides, we'll need him. The captain's not up for this." She glanced at Tannis as if expecting her to argue. Tannis opened her mouth, then snapped it shut again. Skylar was right, and it would be another day before they made it to the planet. Who knew what state she'd be in by then? Skylar continued, "We'll need Devlin. That will make three of us, me, Jon and Devlin. Jon will shift—he'll be able to find Alex better that way, but he'll need us to watch his back and probably fight our way out of there."

"I'm going in," Callum said.

Everyone turned to look at him.

"I hope this isn't some guilt-fueled suicide mission," Devlin said.

"Hardly—I'm not that easy to kill. But I think I can be of some help. I've been to the Church's headquarters before on diplomatic missions. I know my way around the place better than any of you."

"He's right," Jon said and Tannis glanced at him in surprise. She'd thought he still hated Callum, just for being part of the Collective. But he nodded to Callum, instead.

"Thank you. I know the only reason we're doing this is to get Alex."

"Not the only reason," Devlin growled.

"Yes, but we could wait for a better time for revenge, whereas we need to get Alex now. I can feel her, and she's hurting."

"She's a member of the crew," Tannis said. "So we go after her; it's a simple as that."

They started discussing details, and Tannis let the conversation wash over her. It felt odd to think of them going on a mission without her. She didn't think she'd ever been left behind before. If she wasn't careful, she was in danger of becoming sad and pathetic.

She almost jumped when Callum reached across and rested his hand on her thigh. He squeezed gently. The touch was in no way sexual. She knew it was meant to comfort her, and the thought made her want to cry. She concentrated on keeping herself together. Finally, it was over.

"That's it then—all we can do is wait until we intercept *The Endeavor*. And hope that we don't just fly straight past her."

Callum wanted nothing more than to just take Tannis to bed and hold her. She was being so brave, but occasionally he saw flashes of fear in her yellow eyes. He peered at her sideways, but she caught the look and scowled.

"I'm fine," she said. "Just concentrate on what you need to do."

What he needed to do was work with Daisy to set up the search frequencies so they wouldn't miss *The Endeavor* when she got within distance. He wanted to leave contacting Captain Harris until the last moment. While he presumed the Council had told Harris he was to pick Callum up, he also suspected they would have given him instructions to destroy *El Cazador*. The ship had been a pain in the Council's butt for too long now. It was unlikely they'd let her sail happily on her way when they had a chance to blow her to pieces. So he'd prefer to take *The Endeavor* and her captain by surprise. Not easy with a virtually invisible ship.

Two hours later, the bridge was empty except for Tannis and him. Everyone else had gone to try and get some sleep. She was flopped in a chair, yawning.

"You want to go to bed?" he asked.

"Hell no, there's—"

"Time enough to sleep when you're dead. I know."

He was trying hard not to think about the whole dying thing, because if he did, he wouldn't be able to function. There were times over the past few centuries when he'd regretted his immortality. He hadn't wanted to die exactly, but living had seemed more of a chore than a good thing. Strangely though, even now he didn't want to die. If Tannis died, the future was going to be bleak for a long time to come, but all the same, he wanted to live. He had to save Alex for her, then look after the crew, then maybe even go back and put the whole world to rights.

"What are you thinking?"

He glanced across at Tannis who, head cocked to one side, watched him.

"That you've taught me so much," he said. "Given me a purpose in life again—thank you."

She smiled. "Good, now finish your work."

He turned to the console and did a scan, but there was nothing showing up, and he adjusted the sensors—still nothing. The trouble was *The Endeavor* was good. When he looked again, Tannis's eyes were closed. He pressed his comm unit and got Daisy.

"Yes," she said sleepily.

"Are you okay to come up and watch the scanners for a while?"

"Of course. I'll be right there.

Five minutes later, she appeared in the doorway. As she glanced at Tannis, a frown flickered across her face. "Is she all right?" she whispered.

"Just sleeping."

Callum picked Tannis up in his arms. She didn't wake but snuggled close to him. Her skin was blue white with a fine sheen of sweat, and her lashes were dark against her pale cheeks. He hated to see her so vulnerable when she'd always been fiery and vibrantly alive.

"Shower," she murmured as he lowered her to the bed.

He slowly peeled off her clothes, kissing her bare skin. He needed her, but was afraid she was too ill, and he should leave her alone. But as he cupped her breast, she moaned low in her throat.

"Don't stop." Covering his hand with hers, she held it against her.

After a few seconds, he pulled free, finished undressing her, then picked her up and carried her into the small bathroom. He turned on the water to hot, then stepped into the shower. It was a close fit with his wings, but he could hold her in the spray with one arm around her waist as he soaped her body with the other. He stroked over the softness of her breasts, lingering on the tips as her nipples tightened under the attention. Then down the flat plane of her stomach, almost concave now, her ribs clearly visible under the translucent skin, to the silky curls at the base. She opened her legs as his fingers drifted through the curls, sliding between the folds of her sex to find her warm and wet.

He was already hard, but he held himself in check and stroked her gently, caressing the small swollen nub until she pushed against his hand. He went still wondering how far to take this. He didn't want to hurt her, but if he could give her some pleasure, some respite from the pain, he desperately wanted to.

"Please," she said as he hesitated. "I won't break, and I need to feel you inside me."

Setting the shower to air, he held her in the warm blast. When they were both dry, he carried her through to the bedroom and lowered her to the mattress. He came down above her, locking his elbows so his weight didn't touch her. She parted her thighs and he slid inside, heard her whispered sigh of pleasure. He made love to her slowly, until he felt her fly apart beneath him, and then he lay beside her and slept.

He awoke to the sound of coughing. Tannis was sitting up in bed. When she turned to face him, he saw the tracks of crimson from her nostrils, and he knew their time together was running out. She touched her fingertips to her face and held them up before her eyes. Her lids fluttered closed for a brief moment, and when she opened them, her expression was pissed.

"Shit," she said. "Shit. Fuck. Crap."

Yeah, that about covered it.

Callum rolled out of bed and hurried into the bathroom. Keeping his mind blank, he grabbed a towel and moistened it in the small sink, then went back to her and perched on the edge of the bed. Gently, he wiped the blood from her face, leaned in, and kissed her.

"You have to go," she said. "I just got a comm from Daisy—we're coming up on *The Endeavor*."

This was it then. His gut tightened with the almost forgotten mixture of anticipation and fear he'd always felt before he went into action as a pilot. However many missions he flew, it had always been the same. Once in the air, the sensation dissipated and he'd reached a cool, calm place where his brain and body functioned with a precision he never experienced on the ground. He just hoped the same would happen here, but he doubted it. Back then, there hadn't been so much at stake. If Tannis were to die, he had to make sure she went, knowing what was left of her crew were safe and those dead were avenged.

"I want you on board *The Endeavor*," he said. Whatever time she had left, he wanted her close.

"Just try and leave me behind."

# CHAPTER 23

Tannis watched through the scanner as they drew away from *El Cazador*. The ship had been her home for the last fifteen years. Now she was filled with the knowledge that she would never see her again, and a wave of sadness washed through her.

Four of Devlin's men had taken over *El Cazador*—she would be used as a distraction while they slipped onto Trakis Four on *The Endeavor*. At least that was the plan.

Rico would hate it that she was leaving his ship in the hands of strangers. At the thought, she blinked back tears and then quickly wiped her face with the cloth she held. No way did she want the others to see how bad she was; they needed to focus, not worry about her.

The small shuttle was crowded with the six of them. Whenever they'd gone on a mission before there had always been the buzz of excitement. Today, the atmosphere was subdued. It was good to know they were sad at her dying, but maybe she should say something cheery like—*hey, get over it, everyone has to go sometime*. But that wouldn't even be true in the present company.

She cast a sideways glance at Callum. He stood beside

her, his hand resting on her shoulder. He appeared composed and actually managed a small smile when he caught her gaze. He was trying so hard.

Beside him, Skylar stood, her expression distant as she, too, watched *El Cazador* disappear from the scanner. No doubt, she was thinking about Rico. But that would pass. She had time, after all.

The one she was really concerned about was Jon. He'd already shifted and lay on the floor of the shuttle, taking up most of the space. His head rested on his paws, but his amber eyes were open and watchful. If they failed . . .

She shut down the thought. They wouldn't fail.

"There she is," Skylar said.

The ship appeared out of nowhere on the scanner. One second they were staring at the vastness of space, the next the viewer was filled entirely with the matte black hull of *The Endeavor*.

"We're inside the shielding," Callum said.

The ship was huge—ten times the size of *El Cazador* and beautiful, all sleek, graceful lines. "So tell me again—how many crew?"

Callum cast her a wry look. Yeah, so she'd already asked, but she needed to take her mind off the coming separation.

"I told you—I don't know. She can carry up to one hundred men comfortably, but she can be flown by one person so long as they're Collective. I can sense five Collective members, but there could be others."

"Can she really hear your thoughts?" Daisy asked, her tone full of awe. Obviously, to Daisy's mind, telepathic people were nothing special, but a telepathic ship was way cool.

"Yes. We identified the frequencies of the telepathic brain waves and tuned her in."

"Can't you 'talk to her' from here?" Tannis asked.

"No. In case of attack I didn't want anyone to be able to remote control her. But if I can get close enough to the biometric reader, I can take over. She's my ship. I can override anything."

"Okay, I'm taking her in," Daisy said.

Directly in front of them, a split formed in the giant hull, revealing the docking bay beyond. Daisy flew them in and touched down gently beside a line of shining new shuttles that made Tannis's mouth water. In fact, everything was shining and new.

She was inspecting the docking bay through the monitor when Callum leaned down and scooped her up. Her mouth opened to protest that she was strong enough to walk but then snapped closed again—she was by no means sure it was true and besides, she liked being held in his arms.

He carried her down the ramp. A man waited for them at the bottom, his violet eyes showing he was one of the Collective. He was dressed in the black uniform of the Corps and drew to attention when he saw Callum.

"Sir, I'm to take you to the bridge. The captain will meet you there."

Tannis gazed around her as they walked along the wide silver corridors, then rode up to the next level in some sort of ultramodern elevator, just a wide shaft that swept them upward as if they were flying and opened directly onto the bridge. She quickly took in her surroundings, assessing what could be used to their advantage. Three men occupied the area, all dressed in the same black uniforms. All drew to attention as Callum entered.

He ignored them and carried her across to a chair situated in front of the main console.

"This place is huge," she said.

Compared to *El Cazador* it was. The ceilings were high, the corridors and rooms wide with little in the way of furniture.

"She was designed with certain physical attributes in mind," Callum said. Standing in front of her, he spread his wings.

"Very impressive," she murmured.

"I wasn't told anyone else would be boarding." The captain's voice took her attention from Callum. She studied the man. He appeared somewhere in his midthirties, but of course that meant nothing with the Collective. He could be anything up to four hundred years old, and when she looked closely, she could see the age and experience reflected in his eyes. He also sounded suspicious.

Callum gave her a small smile and then turned to face him. His posture changed; he appeared to grow, become more commanding. "I didn't think it was any of your business, Captain."

Tannis almost smiled at the tone—he sounded so like the old Callum—the Leader of the Universe who didn't have to answer to anyone.

The captain must have recognized it as well. He nodded. "I'll have someone show you to your quarters. We should be arriving at Trakis Four within a few hours and then we'll head home."

"I don't think so. I'd like you to gather your men together, Captain."

"Why? I'm afraid we don't have the time right now. We have a problem with the ship that I need to see to before we reach Trakis Four."

Callum swore softly. "Don't tell me—the reactor units?"

"Yes. How did you—"

"Because she failed the initial test runs on the reactor units. They broke down under pressure. That's why she was back in the dockyards. I gather they failed to tell you."

The captain remained silent.

"Idiots." Callum paced the deck for a few minutes, then turned to the captain. "I'll deal with it. You get your men together and gather in the docking bay." As he spoke, he strolled toward the bank of consoles. The captain frowned; he stepped forward, but it was too late. Callum reached out and pressed his palm to the reader on the console.

He flinched as the blood sample was taken, and then he smiled. "I'm taking over control of my ship, Captain. You can stand down."

"That's not in my orders, sir."

"Fuck your orders." Callum closed his eyes briefly and the captain swayed, his hand going to his head, his eyes widening. "That was only an example. Get your men to the docking bay. And if you feel bad about this, then remember—I'm still head of the Council."

The captain nodded and left the bridge, the other Collective members following.

"So did it work?" Tannis asked. She wanted reassurance that things were going to plan. Exhaustion tugged at her mind, and her body felt lethargic and heavy. The need to give in, to lie down, close her eyes, and just drift away was almost overwhelming. The painkillers were still working, but she was taking too many and could no longer counteract the effects, at least not without going completely wired.

"Yes—I have control."

At his words, she relaxed and allowed herself a huge yawn. Callum reached down and picked her up. "Come on, I'll get you settled, and then I need to make sure that the captain and crew leave quietly."

"You know, you're pretty sexy when you go all Lord of the Universe." Tannis spoke the words into his neck, her soft breath tickling his skin.

He glanced down and forced a smile. "Hold that thought."

The master cabin had been designed with wings in mind. It was huge and decorated in scarlet and black. Holding her with one arm, he stripped the coverlet and placed her in the center of the mattress, then removed her boots and pulled the sheet up to cover her. Sinking down beside her, he took her hand.

"Go to sleep," he said. "When you wake up, I'll be back."

Her eyes drifted closed, and her breathing evened out.

Would she wake up? Or would she be one of the lucky ones and die a relatively peaceful death in her sleep? Part of him hoped so; the other part wanted her to live as long as possible. That little hope niggled at his mind again and he leaned in close.

"Hold on," he whispered. "Don't leave me."

He sat and waited until he was sure she was asleep. Black rings surrounded her eyes. She looked small and tired in the enormous bed, propped up on the pillows so she wouldn't choke on her own blood. He wanted to stay, but he needed to spend some time with Daisy, make sure she could handle *The Endeavor* in case they were all captured or killed, and she had to take the ship up on her own. Still, he waited until the ragged sound of Tannis's breathing had smoothed, and then he gently tugged free of her hand and rose to his feet.

Would he ever see her again? He hoped so.

He kissed her forehead, then turned and left without looking back.

# CHAPTER 24

*The Endeavor* set down on a landing pad just outside the Church's main headquarters. Callum had considered taking her inside, but she'd have been seen as soon as they got close, and they'd lose the element of surprise. They could go for a quick extraction, but as they had no clue where Alex was being kept that was unlikely to succeed. The place was a warren, expanding over the years as the Church grew.

In the distance, the sound of guns rumbled. Darkness had fallen, and up in the sky to the north, he could see the flashes of the ongoing firefight, hopefully drawing the Church's attention away from *The Endeavor's* approach.

The plan was to find Alex first and then go after Hatcher.

Jon growled and pawed at the door, impatient to be off. Callum hoped he would be sufficiently in control not to be too conspicuous and give them all away. He knew little about werewolves, but he suspected control wasn't one of their stronger points. Rico would have known.

*The Endeavor* was equipped with her own speeders, and they took one for the short distance to Church Headquarters, pulling up at the rear entrance. There was a single guard on the small gate. Skylar took him out easily and they slipped through and found themselves in a deserted courtyard. Callum presumed that everyone was concentrating on the full-frontal attack by *El Cazador*. No doubt they would have recognized the ship.

Jon padded out to the center of the courtyard and sat on his haunches, his eyes closed, his nose raised to the air.

"Can he scent her from here?" Callum asked.

"I don't think so," Skylar replied. "But they have an almost telepathic bond, not like we do, more sensory, so if she's anywhere close, he'll feel it."

Jon's eyes opened, glowing amber. He peered over his shoulders and nodded his huge, shaggy head.

"We're on," Skylar said.

They followed the wolf to a door set in the far wall. He stood to the side as Skylar pressed her palm to the wood. The door didn't budge, and she stepped back and kicked out. The lock splintered, the door swung open, and Jon pushed past her. Skylar went after him, Callum squeezed through behind her, and Devlin followed.

It took a moment for his eyes to adjust to the dim light. They were in a narrow corridor with walls of bare stone, and a rock floor, which slanted downward. He guessed they were heading toward the dungeons. Obviously, they'd decided their little priestess wasn't to be trusted.

Metal doors lined the corridor, each with a small grill in the front. Callum peered into a few of the cells, but they were empty. Then Jon gave a small yip of excitement and he was off, still heading downward, deeper underground.

Up ahead, he came to an abrupt halt outside one of the doors. The fur along his spine stood on end. His ears were pricked, his hind legs trembling. He released a low whine and then frantically scratched at the metal.

Callum caught up, pushed past the wolf, and peered through the grill. Alex huddled on a small cot, but she stared toward the door, her eyes wide. Beside him, Jon let out a low, impatient growl.

Callum studied the door. A palm panel was built into the wall to the side—no way would they kick this one open—so it looked like they were going to have to blow the door in.

Skylar must have come to the same conclusion. "Stand back," she said.

The wolf peered up at her, then at the door, and finally he stalked a little distance away and turned to watch. Callum and Devlin moved to stand beside him as Skylar aimed her laser at the locking device.

The air filled with the acrid scent of burning metal, and above their heads, the high-pitched pulse of an alarm sounded. Callum cursed—they didn't have long—someone would be sure to investigate.

Skylar pressed her fingers to the door and pushed it open as Jon leaped forward and was through the door before anyone else could move.

"Stay here and keep watch," Callum told Devlin, and the other man nodded.

By the time Callum stepped into the small cell, Jon was on the cot. Alex sat with her arms around his neck, her face burrowed in his thick fur.

"We have to move," Callum said.

She raised her head, her huge gray eyes brimming with tears. "Thank you."

"Our pleasure. Now let's go."

Alex lifted her arm, to reveal the cuff around her right wrist. It was attached to a metal loop built into the stone wall.

"We'll have to shoot it off," Skylar said. "Stand as far away from the cot as you can."

Alex extricated herself from the wolf's embrace with difficulty. When she finally managed to stand, she kept one hand on the shaggy head, her fingers digging into his fur. She moved until her arm was outstretched, then closed her eyes against the glare of the laser. The chain gave in seconds, and she fell to her knees and hugged Jon. The cuff was still attached to her wrist, but she was free.

"We need to be out of here," Callum said.

Alex raised her head and nodded. She got to her feet and looked past him as though searching for someone.

"Have you got Rico?"

"Rico's dead." Skylar tone was harsh.

Alex's gaze flew to her face, her brows drawing together. "No, he isn't. Skylar, really he isn't. He's alive."

"What are you talking about? Hatcher told us he'd been executed, his body burned."

"If he told you that, he lied. That's what they plan to do, but they're going to have a public execution. I know because they want me to light the pyre as proof that I'm loyal. I told them to go to hell, which is why I'm down in the dungeons."

Skylar stepped up close to her. "Where is he?"

"Here somewhere. There's nowhere else secure enough to keep him. He has to be close."

Skylar was shaking. She chewed on her lower lip and Callum could see her consciously pulling herself together. "Jon, can you find him?"

The wolf lowered his head.

"I'll shift as well," Alex said. "Just give me a second."

"Quickly, then."

Callum turned away as she stripped off her clothes. When he looked back two wolves stood side by side. The smaller lifted one foot and the cuff slid off easily. Then she headed for the door.

He followed them out and watched as they crisscrossed the corridor, noses to the ground as they tried to pick up the scent. He was hardly daring to hope. Could Rico still be alive? And why had Hatcher lied? It had to be some effort to preempt a rescue mission. He didn't care. All he cared about was there was a chance.

He prayed Tannis was still clinging to life. She was tenacious; she wouldn't give in until she knew Alex was safe. Should he call her? But he didn't want to raise her hopes if this came to nothing. And would Rico be able to change her? Would he agree?

The alarm had stopped. Devlin was at the corner watching. He glanced at Callum and shook his head. Nothing yet.

Alex gave out a low yip, and then she was loping down the corridor. Skylar raced after her with Callum close behind. The red wolf skidded to a halt in front of one of the cells and went up on her hind legs so she could see through the small window. She turned to Skylar and yipped again, then dropped down to all fours and backed away.

This time Skylar didn't hesitate. She blasted the door, kicked it down in seconds, and rushed inside. For a moment, Callum hovered outside, unwilling to let his hope die so soon. Then he stepped into the cell.

Rico was chained with both arms fastened to loops in the wall. Skylar had stopped just inside the door and was staring at him as though she couldn't convince herself he was real.

"About fucking time," Rico said, but he was grinning.

Skylar dove toward him, wrapped her arms around his middle, and held on tight.

"Oh, God. Oh, God." Then she raised her head. "I thought you were goddamned dead," she snarled.

"Why the hell would you think that?"

"Because that bastard Hatcher told us he'd executed you."

"Well, he was a little premature, but I'm sure he would have gotten around to it, given time."

Rico looked a mess. He was naked from the waist up, his chest a mass of bruises, burns, and cuts. Callum knew he healed quickly, so the wounds must be recent.

Rico met his gaze. "Where's Tannis?"

"She's dying. Of the Meridian poisoning."

Shock flared on the vampire's face. "What? You were on planet. Why didn't she get the treatment?"

"We aborted when they killed Janey." Callum was almost scared to ask, but he pushed the question out. "Can you save her?"

Rico stared at him for long moments. Then he nodded. "But I won't do it unless she asks. I've offered in the past and she didn't want it."

"She'll want it." Callum prayed he was telling the truth.

"And I need to feed. I'm too weak right now."

"Let's get out of here first. You can feed in the speeder on the way back to the ship."

"*El Cazador* is here?"

"Not exactly. We'll explain on the way."

Devlin peered in through the open cell door. He glanced at Rico. "Nice to see you back from the dead, but we have to move. We'll have company any second now."

Skylar raised her pistol, aimed it at the shackles that held Rico to the wall. "This might sting a little."

"Darling, I don't really care. Do it."

Skylar blasted the chains close to the wall, even so, Rico winced, and the stench of scorched flesh filled the room.

"Sorry," she muttered.

"Don't be." Rico grabbed her around the waist and kissed her hard. "Let's get the fuck out of this shithole. Hey, have I mentioned how much I hate the Church?"

"Not recently. But feel free. I don't think anyone here will argue with you."

They left the cell and headed back the way they had come, the two wolves stalking at the front, Skylar and Rico in the middle, Callum and Devlin at the rear. They were almost to the door into the rear courtyard when a noise behind them made Callum whirl around.

A small group of men appeared around the corner, weapons in their hands. Callum heard a growl behind him and the two wolves burst past them, leaping at the first two guards before they had a chance to pull their triggers. The first died quickly, the huge black wolf ripping out the throat. The second was messier. He reckoned it was Alex's first kill as a wolf, but she got there in the end. Callum and Devlin took out the second two and he stood staring at the bodies. He couldn't dispel the notion that time was running out for Tannis. They needed out of there. Now.

A second group appeared but backed away when they saw the carnage.

"That was Hatcher," Devlin said.

He made to follow, but Callum stopped him with a hand on his arm. "Devlin, we have to get back."

"No, we have to get the murdering bastard who killed Tris."

"Tannis is dying. Rico can save her, but every second might make a difference."

Devlin's gaze shifted from Callum to the vampire. "You're going to change her?"

Rico nodded.

Devlin stared after Hatcher, and then he gritted his teeth and nodded. "Let's go."

"Thank you. And I promise you, we will return, and one day he will pay for Janey and for Tris."

The faint vibration of the ship's engines roused Tannis from a light sleep. They must be back. Either that or something had gone badly wrong and they were leaving without them. She rubbed her forehead, the headache had dulled to a throb, but she felt spaced out and not with it.

She had to hold on. She wanted to know they'd succeeded, and she wanted to see Callum one last time.

But when the door opened, it wasn't Callum standing there. For a second, she couldn't make her head process what she was seeing. Was she hallucinating? No, she couldn't be. If she had conjured up an image, then she was sure Rico wouldn't have looked quite so bad. His bare chest was crisscrossed with multiple cuts and burns.

Which meant he was real.

She swallowed and blinked. No way was she going to break down like some idiot. But, oh God, he was alive.

"You look like shit," she said.

Rico grinned. "Yeah, and you look *so* much better."

Tannis ignored the sarcasm. "I missed you."

"Of course you did. That's why you're lying in bed instead of out there rescuing me."

"I thought you were dead."

"I've been dead for a long time, sweetheart." He moved into the room and stood looking down at her. "You made a right crappy mess of this, didn't you?"

"Yeah."

Callum appeared and strode across the room, relief lighting his face as he saw her. He perched on the edge of the bed and grabbed her hand.

"You want this?" He glanced from Rico to her.

She followed his gaze and knew what he was asking. She studied the vampire, knowing he could save her and she would live forever.

But this would be the easy way out.

And she had never followed the easy way. Otherwise, she wouldn't have fallen in love with a man like Callum.

She wanted her dream.

The hope she'd hidden deep in her mind since they'd left Trakis Seven rose to the surface and crystallized into something hard and tangible.

Taking a deep breath, she looked back at Callum and shook her head. "No."

For a second, shock flashed across his face, then understanding. And she knew that he'd harbored the same hope.

"I want my dream," she said.

He stroked her hand, then raised it to his lips and kissed her palm. "We don't know how long you can last or how long it will take or even if we'll get through alive. I—"

She put a finger to his lips to stop the words. "I trust you."

"You're sure?"

"More sure than anything in my whole life. I don't want to die. But more than that, I want to be part of you, in your life and in your mind. All my life I've been a loner. Now, I don't want to be alone anymore."

His expression cleared, relief flooding his eyes, and the tension seeped from him. He leaned in close and kissed her. "Good. I'd hoped, but I didn't want to . . ." He rose to his feet. "We need to get moving."

Rico had been watching in silence. Now he frowned. "Does someone want to tell me what the fuck is going on?"

"No disrespect, Rico. You're my best friend, but I still don't want to be a sex-crazed monster. I want to be one of the angels."

He rolled his eyes. "Not much chance of that, sweetheart. So? Still in the dark here."

Callum grinned. "Ever wanted to know what's on the other side of a black hole?"

"Maybe." He sounded cautious.

"Well, you're about to get the opportunity to find out."

It had been three days.

Callum was doing his best not to hover over Tannis. He knew it irritated her. She was weakening, but holding on with a tenacity he would have expected from her.

Callum spent his time irritating Devlin instead, while he tried to get *The Endeavor* moving a little faster.

They were limping along and trying to get the stealth cloaking device working, but so far—no go. Which was a goddamned shame, because it appeared that half the universe was on their tail, and the other half was coming at them from the sides.

But they were almost there now. If they could just evade their pursuers a little while longer.

"How far away are they?" he asked Daisy who was attempting to track the ships following them. Her fingers moved slowly over the console, a frown forming on her face.

"I don't know."

"Well, how about how many?"

"I don't know that either." She glared at him. "I'm not Janey, and this stupid machine is not cooperating. But a lot, I think. Maybe all of them. But the good news is, were coming up on Trakis One now." She leaned across and flicked the monitor over to show a wider area. On their left, he caught his first glimpse of Trakis One. He'd never been there before. The planet housed the Collective's maximum-security prison and there was no reason to visit if you had a choice in the matter. The place was a shithole, totally inhospitable, including radiation levels that would burn through the hull of an ordinary ship in minutes.

And just beyond lay their destination.

The black hole.

He swallowed. Was he really planning to take them into that well of darkness?

Oh, yeah.

Time to wake Tannis up. If they were about to crash and burn, he wanted her at his side when it happened.

\* \* \*

As Callum carried her onto the bridge, her eyes were drawn to the black hole that filled the screen. It was mesmerizing, a vision of shimmering gases spiraling around a gaping maw. Callum's hands tightened around her, and she peered up at him.

"You really want to do this?" she asked.

She could be taking them all to their deaths. Though with the Church fast approaching from the rear, *The Endeavor* dying beneath them, and no doubt the Collective not far behind, they didn't stand much of a chance either way. And there was something strangely compelling about that yawning pit of night. Almost as though it called to them.

At least it took her mind off how crappy she felt. Though in truth, she was so drugged up that while the pain was there, it was distant, as though it belonged to someone else.

"Well, we're approaching the event horizon," Rico said. "So if you're going to change your mind, you'd better make it quick."

Rico was in the pilot's seat. Tannis reckoned he'd fallen in love with the ship, and was already planning a major refit. And she was to be renamed *The Blood Hunter Two*. Well, if they survived this and actually found something on the other side.

Callum had been staring at the monitor as if mesmerized, but at the words, he shook himself and looked away. He lowered her gently into a seat. "What do you think?" he asked.

Tannis started at the question. He knew what she thought. Then she realized he wasn't asking her. He was asking Rico.

"We're going," Callum continued, indicated the two of them. "But there's still time for the rest of you to get off. You can take one of the shuttles and probably slip away from our friends behind us while everyone concentrates on us." He nodded to the other monitor, which showed the fleet of ships at their back, then glanced around the room.

"Nah. We're in—wouldn't miss it for the world," Rico said. Beside him, Skylar nodded her agreement.

"Daisy?" Callum asked.

"Hell, yes." Daisy grinned—she was fizzing with excitement.

"Devlin?"

"I'm in."

To the left of the black hole, Tannis could see Trakis One, dark ocher encircled by spiraling radiation rings of palest yellow to blood crimson. A single moon revolved lazily around the planet. They'd researched it when they were planning to break Jon out of the prison, and she knew that the orbit and size of the planet kept it from the pull of the black hole. But anything approaching had no chance. Except for the brief period when that moon passed between them. Denser than the planet, despite being smaller, it provided sufficient cover for a ship to reach the planet's surface. But this time, they weren't aiming for the planet; they were aiming for the hole itself.

They were insane.

Jon and Alex appeared in the doorway, hand in hand, and hurried over to where she sat.

"Captain?" Jon said, shifting from foot to foot.

"What is it?"

"We're not coming. We'd like to but . . ."

"Er, running out of time here," Rico said behind them.

"Alex is pregnant."

Tannis's gaze dropped to her stomach—it looked as flat as ever. "That's . . . fabulous." Actually, she wasn't sure, since she'd never thought much about babies, but Alex looked pleased.

She tugged free of Jon, leaned down and hugged Tannis. "Take care," she whispered. "And come back."

"I will." She hoped.

"Aw, puppies," Rico murmured. "How cute."

Jon grinned. "Piss off."

"So where are you going?" Rico asked.

"We've talked about it," Jon said, "and we're going to try and slip away, head over to Trakis Two and hole up until the birth."

"Take one of the bigger shuttles," Callum said. "They've got the range, and they're fitted with the stealth control."

"Thanks." Jon came forward, wrapped his arms around her ever so carefully. She wanted to snap that she wouldn't break, but she wasn't sure it was true.

"Thanks for everything, and we'll see you when you get back." He straightened then turned to Callum. "Look after her."

"I will."

Tannis collapsed in her seat and watched as Alex hugged everybody, and then the two of them disappeared from the bridge. Would she ever see them again? She doubted it.

Callum came to stand beside her and rubbed her shoulder. "You will."

"Are you a mind reader?"

"Yes."

"That's the shuttle clear," Rico said a minute later. "Let's do this. And you might want to strap yourselves in. I'm thinking it's going to get a little bumpy."

Crouching down in front of her, Callum fastened the harness. When she was all strapped in, he sat back on his heels.

She forced her mind to concentrate. She needed to tell him something. "I just want you to know—whatever happens—this was worth every moment."

"I know. Me, too."

He kissed her quickly, then took the seat beside her.

They were in the grip of the gravitational pull now,

dragging the ship closer. She glanced sideways at Callum. He leaned forward in his seat, his hands clamped around the arms, his violet eyes glowing. Catching her gaze, he reached across and gripped her hand. "I love you," he said.

She squeezed his fingers. "I know."

A deafening roar filled her ears. Their speed increased abruptly, forcing her into her seat, and she lost her grip on his hand. Tannis wrapped her fingers around the armrests and held on.

"That's it." Rico's voice sounded as though from a distance. "We've lost control, and we're going in."

On the monitor, the black hole loomed closer as though all the brightness was being sucked from the world. The ship's lights flashed on, then off and she caught brief glimpses of Callum. Then they went out, leaving them in darkness.

The pressure built until the air was squeezed from her lungs. She was losing control of her senses, everything closing in, until she was aware of nothing but the emptiness ahead.

She tried to keep her eyes open, but it didn't matter as the ship dove headfirst into the very center of the hole. Everything went black, and her last thought was that yeah, just possibly, this whole job might have been a huge mistake.

But still she couldn't regret it.

# CHAPTER 25

Tannis sat in the darkness and realized she was alive.

That was unexpected.

The lights flashed back to life, and she blinked and looked around her. The bridge seemed in good shape, and the others were all awake and unharmed. Callum was already out of his seat and at the monitors. He turned and grinned, his eyes gleaming with barely suppressed excitement.

"Stay there."

Yeah, like she was going to get up and start leaping about. She settled back and watched.

The main monitor showed the black hole they had just come through. From this side, it appeared harmless, golden like a sun. On a second monitor, a huge ship floated on the screen. *Really huge*.

"Fuck me, that's *Trakis One*," Rico said from behind her.

"I know." Callum didn't do anything obvious, but the monitor zoomed in, and she read the words clearly on the side of the ship. *Trakis One*.

"Do you know who's on board *Trakis One*?" Rico asked her.

"Actually, no."

"Only Max Beauchamp, the last President of the Federation of Nations. And the first family." He prodded Callum in the arm. "Hey, didn't you have a thing with Max's daughter. What was she called, Tracey, Theresa . . . ?"

"Tamara," Callum said. He cast Rico a sour glance. "And thanks for bringing that up."

"A *thing*?" Tannis asked, her eyes narrowing. Callum shifted.

"Yeah, a *thing*." Rico grinned. "Made the front pages— romance of the decade. And didn't she go and dump you for some sailor?"

"We mutually agreed to part." Callum studied the monitor. "Do you think they're alive after all this time?"

"I'm picking up life-forms," Daisy said. "Lots of them. But no movement."

"Maybe the cryotubes are still functioning."

"Could be," Rico said. "We'll board her later and find out, but first we need to give the ship a once-over and find Callum's alien friends." He turned to Devlin who was flicking through the console, carrying out a systems check. "How's she looking?"

"Not too bad. I'm going to pop down, check on the engines."

Tannis sighed. The drugs were wearing off, and she felt like shit. She studied Callum to take her mind off it.

He was leaning in close to Daisy, talking to her, but he must have sensed her stare, because he straightened and came toward her. Her gaze dropped down over his body. He was beautiful, long and lean, the wings folded neatly against his back. "I can sense them," he said.

She shook her head, trying to make sense of his words. "What?"

"They're here, somewhere. We have to follow the voices in my head. Just hold on. All right?"

She nodded, tried to feel something, but the world seemed distant. The hope was still there but buried beneath the weight of pain and weakness. She had to hold on for a little while longer, but her vision was fading.

"Tannis!" His voice was filled with panic.

She opened her eyes as wide as she could and gave him a smile. "Still here."

"Stay with me."

"I will."

And she tried, concentrating as hard as she could, but the darkness was creeping up on her. Occasionally, she was aware of Callum talking to her, encouraging her, and some part of her nodded and smiled, but even those moments faded to nothing, and the world blurred into one endless background buzz of pain.

Finally, she sensed something different.

She was in Callum's arms, and she pried her heavy eyes open.

"Soon," he murmured against her skin.

She clung to him as he laid her on the ground. This was the end. She couldn't hold on any longer. Something touched her arm, tentatively at first, then twining around her wrist, tightening. Then the background pain vanished in a blaze of agony so vivid, she jolted upright.

Fire flowed through her blood. It grew, consuming her, until the blessed relief of darkness.

She came to, lying on a sandy floor. She blinked a couple of times and stared up at the ceiling. She was in some sort of cave. The light glowed violet.

*Are you all right?*

It took her a moment to realize the voice was Callum's, and it was inside her head. She turned so she could see him.

He sat close to her, leaning against the rough stone wall of the cave. His eyes were shadowed. He looked like he'd aged a hundred years, but as she stared at him his worried expression cleared and he smiled.

"I'm good." In fact, her whole body tingled with energy. A smile tugged at the corners of her mouth, as she looked inward. The pain had gone, vanished as though it had never existed. Beside her lay a shriveled tentacle-like structure. She prodded it with her finger, but it remained lifeless.

She rolled onto all fours, then crawled across the floor. Callum met her halfway, opened his arms, and she didn't stop until she was held tight against him. "Thank you," she murmured against his chest.

He twisted her in his arms so she was under him, the sand silky soft against her back.

"Say thank you properly," he growled, pressing his body against her. She didn't think to stop him; life pulsed through her veins, a wild exhilaration waking inside her. His hands moved over her body. He didn't try to undress her, just ripped her shirt down the front to bare her breasts.

"I thought I'd lost you."

Tannis heard the desperation in his voice as his mouth trailed down her throat, to kiss and nip her breasts. Her spine arched beneath him. His teeth raked over one peak, then he bit down, and pleasure shot down through her body as wet heat flooded her sex. He moved to the other breast, and she could feel the barely leashed power in his touch. He lowered his hips so the hard length of his erection pressed into her, and her hips rose up to meet him.

His hand moved to her waist, and he tore open the fastener of her pants, pushed them almost roughly down over her hips. She had to kick off her boots to allow him to drag them down over her legs. And finally, she was naked beneath him, while he was fully dressed. He stared down at her, his gaze like fire as it trailed over her body.

They were both breathing hard now.

His hand moved between their bodies, and he swore softly as he fumbled with the fastener of his own pants. Then he was free and for a second she felt him hot and hard against her belly.

Then he was inside her. Inside her body and inside her head.

*I love you.*

The words echoed through her mind.

Tentatively, she reached out with her own thoughts. And she could sense his feelings, exultation, happiness, need . . . love.

*I love you.*

He smiled down at her, and she knew he'd heard her words. Then he started moving inside her and all thoughts fled her mind as she gave herself up to him.

Afterward, they dressed. Callum took her hand and led her out of the cave. She'd been too out of it to notice her surroundings when they'd arrived. Now she looked around her.

All her senses were more acute, the air soft against her skin and filled with a sweet scent like flowers. Off to the east a crimson sun was setting over a rocky landscape. As she watched, winged creatures rose from the rocks, silhouetted against the glowing sky. They swooped and swirled in an intricate dance, graceful and so beautiful her heart ached.

She turned to Callum. "Are they . . . ?"

He nodded. "Can you hear them?"

Closing her eyes, she opened her mind and a wordless song filled her head. Callum squeezed her hand and they stood together as the music washed through them.

She'd come so close to death, stared it in the face, and finally, defied it.

"You know," Callum said, "my people told me I was

making a big mistake." His thumb rubbed over her palm, sending prickles of sensation down her nerve endings.

"Funny, so did mine."

He leaned in close and kissed the corner of her mouth. "And what do you think now?"

"Biggest mistake I ever made." Sliding her arms around his waist, she pulled him close. "And you know the best thing about it?" She kissed the pulse point at his throat. "Now I get to live with my mistake—forever."

# ACKNOWLEDGMENTS

When I wrote *Break Out*, book one in my Dark Desires series, I had little hope of finding a publisher. But it was a book I wanted to write, a book for me, with all the things I love the most, science fiction, vampires, pirates, romance . . .

Then I saw that a new publisher, Entangled, was looking for space operas. All the information on them looked great and I decided to give them a try and sent off *Break Out*. I received a reply within the day:

*"Is this a series? Please say yes."*

That was from Liz, soon-to-be my fabulous editor! Three years later, I'm writing book six in the series. So, I'd like to say a huge thank you to Liz for all her support, encouragement, and boundless enthusiasm. Thank you!

And also a huge thank you to my long-suffering husband, Rob, who has to put up with me regularly zoning out of the real world and playing around in worlds of my own making. He even manages to listen to my plots and refrain from telling me: it's not real, you know (at least after the first time!).

# CRASH LANDING

*500 years ago*

"We've lost contact, Captain. The signal is dead and there's been nothing from them in over three hours."

"Shit." Callum sat back in his chair, and studied the monitors while he considered his options.

He'd been captain for ten years now, ever since he'd been woken from cryo, and in all that time he'd never had to make a decision. He was out of practice. The ship virtually flew herself, the crew had trained together for years before they left Earth, and everything worked like a well-oiled machine. Or had done until *Trakis One* vanished off the scanners.

Five hundred years they'd survived in the vastness of space.

Now, they'd finally reached a system which appeared—at least at first sight—to be able to sustain life. Then, just as things were looking up for mankind and the long trip was finally over, disaster struck.

*Trakis One* was their lead ship and carried the president of the Federation of Nations as well as his daughter, Tamara. He'd been engaged to Tamara for a while back on Earth until he'd realized what a bitch she was. Hard to believe that was over five hundred years ago. If he and Tamara hadn't parted company, then in all likelihood, he would have been aboard *Trakis One* as well. And now he'd be . . . he didn't know . . . wherever *Trakis One* was. Maybe they'd never know what had become of the ship.

But the real problem was that the captain of *Trakis One* was also the man who made the final decisions for the fleet. Now the rest of them were wandering around like headless fucking chickens. About time someone stepped up to the mark.

He leaned forward and pressed the comm unit that would connect him to the other ships. "This is Captain Callum Meridian of *Trakis Seven*. I say—let's do this." Then sat back and waited.

Tasha, his second in command, entered the bridge and came to stand behind him, resting a hand on his shoulder and watching the monitor.

"Hi, sweetheart," he murmured. Tasha was an excellent officer; she'd also been sharing his bed for the last five years—pretty much since she'd been woken, and he'd decided he'd had enough of celibacy.

"What's happening?" she asked.

"Just waiting to see if anyone out there has the balls to see this through. Or whether we're just going to sit here for another five hundred years."

There were nine ships in all, well, eight now that

*Trakis One* had vanished. Twenty-four had set off from Earth, named imaginatively, *Trakis One* to *Twenty-four*. Each ship had carried ten trained crews, nine of which were placed in cryo as they set off on the long journey, to be woken as they were needed. Callum was the tenth captain of *Trakis Seven*, and the last. In addition, each ship carried ten thousand "Chosen Ones." The future of humanity.

Twelve of the ships had gone their separate ways long before Callum had been woken from cryo. They'd had no contact from them in over three hundred years. Another three had been destroyed in unexplained explosions. He supposed that was good going—none of the technology had really been tested before they left Earth. There hadn't been time.

Finally, when he'd decided they must have all gone to sleep, the comm unit crackled. Everything was getting old; it was only a matter of time before bits started to fall off—another reason to get off their asses and get moving.

"You'll take point?" Captain Crane of *Trakis Three* asked.

Obviously everyone was a little nervous after what had happened to *Trakis One*, and no one wanted to be first to follow wherever they had gone. But it was time to grow some goddamn balls. Adrenaline spiked in his system at the thought of some action at last. Back on Earth, he'd been a fighter pilot, a whole different ballgame than captain of a space cruiser. No amount of training had prepared him for the boredom.

Callum grinned and squeezed Tasha's hand. "Yeah, I'll take point."

One by one the other captains gave their agreement. When the vote was in, it was unanimous. "Looks like we're on," Callum said. "Set a course through the system."

"Are you sure that's a good idea, sir?" That was his third in command, Aiden Ross. He cast the man a glance. What stroke of bad luck had given him Aiden-No-Balls-Ross as his third? "Hell, yes. I want off this ship. Don't worry, we have the last co-ordinates of *Trakis One*—just make sure we steer clear of that spot."

It would be a while before anything happened. Before *Trakis One* had inconveniently disappeared, each ship had been allocated a planet. They were to approach, do an initial survey of conditions, and if they met certain pre-set criteria, then they were to land and investigate further. This system had two suns and thirteen major planets circling those suns in various orbits, plus a number of outer planets at the edges. Callum's planet was one of the thirteen, but on the far side of the system. He settled back into his seat, rested his booted feet on the console in front of him, and lapsed into an almost hypnotic state, staring at the monitors, until something jolted him awake.

"Shit," Aiden muttered from beside him.

"Too right." They were passing the first planet at the edge of the system, keeping a safe distance as these were the last known co-ordinates of *Trakis One*. Callum stared at the image filling the screen and got an inkling of what must have happened to the ship.

The planet itself was dark ochre encircled by spiraling radiation rings of palest yellow to blood crimson. But it wasn't the planet that drew his attention. Beyond that was a gaping pit of blackness—as though all the light had been sucked out of the world. The planet was orbiting a black hole. He'd never seen a black hole before and a shiver ran through him. Had that somehow sucked in *Trakis One*? Poor bastards wouldn't have stood a chance if they'd inadvertently crossed over the event horizon.

"Let's hope the rest of the system is a little more hospitable," he muttered.

Through the next days they had confirmation that *Trakis Four* and *Five* had landed safely and their planets were habitable. It looked like mankind had found a new home at last.

It took them a while longer to reach their designated planet. By the time they were in orbit, Callum was itching to get on solid ground. Unfortunately, the preliminary checks didn't look hopeful. While there was an atmosphere that could sustain life, the oxygen levels were lower than optimal, the nitrogen higher, and there didn't appear to be any water. Anywhere.

Plus, the view out of the scanner hardly appeared welcoming. A barren surface of grey-green rock, the landscape pitted with mountains interspersed with vast flat plains. No vegetation to be seen or at least nothing they recognized.

But he could see no reason not to continue the investigation. Even if the planet turned out to be uninhabitable, there might be valuable resources. He set

*Trakis Seven* on course for one of the flat plains which should prove a safe landing site for the huge ship.

Within minutes of setting the new course, they were in trouble. It was as though a huge fist had closed around them and was dragging them in. No longer heading for the flat plain, they were on a collision course for a rocky outcrop. And they were speeding up.

His pulse raced and he gritted his teeth as he fought to wrest back control, but the ship was unresponsive. *Shit.* No way had he survived five hundred years wandering the vastness of fucking space just to crash now.

After five totally unproductive minutes, he turned to the rest of the crew. "Strap yourselves in. We're going down."

He threw himself into the captain's chair and buckled the harness. A waste of time. At this speed a crash would shatter the ship, smash her into a thousand pieces with no chance of survivors. He'd faced death a hundred times as a fighter pilot back on Earth, but this was different. He wasn't so much scared of dying as pissed off with the sense of powerlessness. "Goddamn it."

Then the ship slowed as though caught in a net, maybe some sort of gravitational field. They were still travelling too fast, but if he could get back the steering, there was a chance.

At the last minute, she came back to him. Huge and unwieldy, she was slow to respond. He only had seconds but managed to turn her slightly from her course. The scream of tearing metal sounded loud on the bridge as they grazed the rocky outcrop, then bounced along the ground. Callum was flung across the bridge as his seat broke loose and he landed with a crash. The lights flashed off, leaving them in darkness. Then the emergency systems kicked in and a dim, orange glow lighted the bridge.

Finally, they skidded to a halt. He lay staring at the ceiling for a minute. When he was sure they had actually stopped, he unstrapped his harness and pushed himself to his feet. A groan escaped his throat, but really, apart from bruises, he was fine. He glanced around. Tasha's seat had held and now she unstrapped her harness and staggered to her feet. She rubbed her ass. "Great landing, Captain."

"Yeah. You okay?" he asked.

"A bit sore, but otherwise undamaged."

"I'll kiss it better later," he promised and turned to survey the chaos. "Everyone else okay?"

"Dex is down. Broken neck."

Shit, Dex had been a good guy. Callum headed to the spot where his seat should have been and opened up the diagnostic screens on the console in front of him. The ship didn't look in too bad a shape and could no doubt be repaired sufficiently to get them off this piece of shit planet and onto one of the more hospitable ones. But the repairs would take time and he might as well find out what he could about the place.

He turned on the external monitors. As the prelims had shown, the air was thin but breathable, the temperature within viable ranges. "Wake the environmental team from cryo," he told Aiden. "They can do some tests while we go take a look around."

An hour later, the engineers were hard at work fixing the ship, and the environmental team was coming around from their five-hundred-year sleep. There was nothing else he could do back here so Callum took a team of five men and headed down to the docking bay. For the first time since he'd woken, he strapped on a weapon at his waist. Who knew what they might find here. Aliens? Little green men? Excitement filled him—there was a whole new world out there.

"You're in charge," he said to Tasha. "Keep them working. I want out of here ASAP."

As he opened the outer doors, the sense of wrongness hit him. He couldn't think of another way to describe it. There was nothing tangible, just everything felt fucked-up. He stared out across the flat plain trying to analyze what was making him want to turn around and lock the doors tight behind him. The suns had only just gone down and a dull crimson glow still bled over the edges of the horizon.

"Are we sure this is a good idea?" Aiden asked from beside him. "Maybe we should wait in the ship."

That decided him. "Shut the fuck up, Aiden. Where's your sense of adventure?"

Aiden stiffened but didn't say anything. Actually, Callum was having second thoughts about how good an idea this was. And third thoughts. The sense of wrongness increased as he strode down the ramp. Everything seemed fine. The air was a little thin but breathable, and he could smell nothing "off" in the atmosphere. His handheld monitor wasn't beeping or flashing, but walking felt like pushing through fog. Tendrils curled around his mind and nausea roiled in his stomach.

"I don't like this place," Tyler said from behind him. "It's a shit hole."

"Yeah. All the same, let's go see what sort of shit hole it is."

He stood at the bottom of the ramp, orienting himself. The rocky outcrop loomed to his left, and to the front and right stretched the vast gray plain. Far in the distance a mountain range was silhouetted against the dim light. He closed his eyes and breathed deeply, but the sense of wrongness didn't ease.

Something flickered at the edges of his mind, tugging at his consciousness, and he gazed toward the outcrop. The dark rocks were cut by fresh scars where *Trakis Seven* had scraped down their side. Lower down, he could make out the darker shadow of some sort of fissure cut through the rock. It was somewhere to start. "This way."

They were all breathing heavily by the time they reached the opening in the rocks, and Callum's heart was beating double time trying to get enough oxygen to his starved lungs. The gap was too narrow to take his shoulders straight on and he turned sideways so he could enter. He half expected complaints from his men—he wasn't sure this was a good idea himself— but they followed him in silence. Maybe they too felt the strange compulsion to go forward.

The tunnel widened, but they were headed underground now, and the last of the suns' rays vanished quickly. He flicked on the light from his monitor and kept moving.

Up ahead a dull violet glow lit the passage, drawing him forward, until finally it opened into a huge cavern, pulsing with purple light.

"What the fuck . . . ?" Aiden said from beside him.

Callum stepped forward slowly, and a ripple ran through the place as though the rocks were alive. He caught a movement out of the corner of his eye and whirled around. As his sight adjusted, he could make out snake-like structures growing out from the walls. Some sort of rock formations? But they moved as though with a life of their own. "What are those things?" Tyler asked in a hushed voice.

Part of Callum knew this was a really bad idea and they should get the fuck out of there as fast as they could run. But his feet didn't want to move. Not in a sensible direction anyway. Instead they took him closer to the wall with its mass of writhing tentacles. He slowly reached out a hand and stroked his fingertips along the growth, and it shivered beneath his touch. The blind head slithered across the skin of his hand. Then, faster than thought, it wrapped around his arm. Red-hot daggers of pain jolted through him as it tightened.

He collapsed to his knees, lava pouring through his blood, scorching up his spine, melting his brain. Smashing to the ground, his back arched as he tried to tear the thing free. The pain built and built until his mind could take no more and he crashed into darkness.

He wasn't dead.

That was his first thought as he came awake. The second was that the pain had vanished as though it had never been. He lay on his back, the sand soft beneath him, unwilling to move in case something bad happened. But in fact he felt good. Way better than he had since he'd stepped onto this godforsaken planet. Actually, if he was truthful, better than since he had first woken on *Trakis Seven* ten years ago.

He lifted his arm, but the thing was gone, and though his shirt was burned away below the elbow, there was no mark on his skin. As he rolled his head to the side, he spotted shriveled remains lying on the ground beside him like a snake that had shed its skin. The rest of his men lay unconscious or dead on the ground, a withered tentacle by each of them.

All around him, Callum could hear the murmur of the tentacle-like structures as they waved languidly from the walls. Finally, he pushed himself to his feet and stretched. There was no damage that he could discern though he felt odd, somehow changed in ways he couldn't identify. And his body buzzed with energy.

He crossed the space between them and crouched down beside Tyler, feeling for a pulse. It was strong and Tyler's skin was warm to the touch but not seriously so.

A groan filled his mind, and he glanced up, searching the chamber for the source.

*What the fuck . . . ?*

He heard the words inside his head, but couldn't see where they had come from. Then Tyler rolled over, his eyes blinked open, and Callum reared back in shock. The eyes staring up at him glowed a deep, inhuman violet.

*What the fuck just happened?*

Again, the words echoed in Callum's head, but Tyler's lips hadn't moved. Holy shit. Had he just heard Tyler's thoughts? Or was he crazy? Tyler gazed up at him as if waiting for an answer. What the hell, it was worth a try.

*Something really fucking weird,* Callum replied.